Never Smile Again

Never Smile Again

Tim Kent

For my mom and my wife—
the two most important women in my life.

Published by:
Bluewater Publications, LLC
1812 CR 111
Killen, Alabama 35645
www.BluewaterPublications.com

"The South never smiled again after Shiloh."

George Washington Cable

Introduction

This is my third book on a battle of the Civil War. Many people that have read my first book feel that the actual battle tends to be confusing. There is an important reason for this. The first few battles of the Civil War were indeed confusing. Not only were the soldiers new to warfare, but the commanders, regardless of where they earned their education, were learning to command large groups of troops for the first time. Shiloh was one of those battles. Most of the Confederate troops and many of the Federal troops were seeing their first action.

With this book, as with all my books, I've attempted to keep everything as accurate as possible. During the second day's events, I chose to follow the action of General Hardee and his men on the right flank. I could have followed Polk and Bragg's commands in the center and on the left, but it would have proven repetitious. The same thing was occurring across the field.

I also want to talk about one thing that has troubled me concerning my previous book. There have been a few complaints about the language used by some of the characters. While I don't condone the language, I would like to give the reader a true understanding of the personalities of these men. If Forrest were somehow prevented from cursing, his vocabulary would have been cut in half. Grant, on the other hand, never cursed. That has been the rule I've followed. My publisher is extremely religious, and she said she could deal with the language because I'm attempting to make the book as accurate as possible. I explained to her that I would never use the "f-word" in my book. Her reply was, "Please don't; just say the guy broke wind."

I have lots of people to thank for assistance: Angela Broyles, who owns Bluewater Publications, for believing in me; Terri Treloar for the excellent job of editing that she always does; and Lanny Perry for the use of his collection of Shiloh material. I also have to thank my wife and parents for the usual support. I would never sell a book without Stacie, who works tirelessly to arrange speaking engagements and keeps my website up to date. When I'm forced to work on the computer, I immediately grab the hammer! Our oldest children, Chase and Carlee, have also worked hard selling books for "their old man." My buddies Jerry Smith, Todd Richardson, and Lance Underwood have continued to encourage me to write. Jerry's great-great-grandfather was Charles Warren, who fought under Bedford Forrest, and you will encounter him in the chapters dealing with the famed "Wizard of the Saddle."

Prelude

Fort Donelson, Tennessee
February 16, 1862
CSA

It was after midnight. Nathan Bedford Forrest rode toward the Dover Hotel. General Floyd, the commander of Fort Donelson, had called a council of war among his top leaders. Forrest was exhausted. He took a deep breath and exhaled, the breath turning to vapor in the cold air.

It had been a long day. They'd been fighting since sunrise. Forrest had two horses killed beneath him and fifteen bullet holes in his frock coat to show for it. The plan had been to push the Federal right wing back so the trapped Confederates could escape to Nashville. The plan had worked perfectly, and the road out was clear. He'd fought his cavalry dismounted as infantry and lost a lot of good men accomplishing that goal.

It was at the moment of success that General Pillow had inexplicably ordered the men back into the fortifications. Forrest remembered a story he'd heard about Gideon Pillow in the Mexican War. The man ordered his men to dig breastworks with the firing step on the wrong side. Everyone had made fun of Pillow for that incident. It may have been funny then, but Forrest wasn't laughing at the predicament Pillow had gotten the army into now.

Major Kelly, one of Forrest's aides, rode at his side in silence. The man had been a preacher before the war, but that didn't affect Forrest's behavior at all. Forrest still cursed and lost his temper as he always had. He thought about what he'd said to Major Kelly when the Federal gunboats attacked the fort. They'd come four abreast, banging away with their heavy artillery as they approached. Forrest had turned to Kelly and said, "Parson! For God's sake, pray. Nothing but God almighty can save that fort!"

Forrest had been wrong. As formidable as the enemy fleet had appeared, the Confederate artillery had disabled every ship. Everything had worked out as planned for the Southern army— everything except the decisions made by the commanding generals.

Forrest and Kelly approached the hotel and noticed a lot of horses tied outside. Two sentries armed with rifles stood at each side of the door. Forrest stepped onto the porch and began to stomp the snow from his boots. The two sentries noticed the stars on Forrest's collar and saluted. Kelly said, "Sir, I'll just wait out here."

Forrest ignored the sentries and stepped inside. There in the lobby sat Generals Floyd, Pillow, and Buckner. The conversation between Pillow and Buckner was heated. The two men despised each other and had for years.

Buckner looked like an officer. With light hair and a dark mustache that extended well beyond his mouth, he looked and acted like a gentleman. Buckner

2

stopped in midsentence, as if he realized he couldn't talk with Pillow, and turned to General Floyd.

He said, "The way was wide open. All we had to do was march out of this trap. Pillow ordered our forces back to their original positions, and only God knows why."

Pillow, who was scratching at his thick, gray goatee, brought his fist down hard on the table. Forrest noticed that he wore black leather gloves.

Pillow shouted, "Our men were exhausted. I brought them back for rest. Besides, they needed to get their blankets and coats before leaving. We'd lose half of them to hypothermia marching in this weather at night."

Forrest couldn't help but notice his air of superiority. Pillow truly believed he was the greatest military commander in the Confederacy.

Floyd began to shake his head. He held up one hand in an attempt to stop the bickering and with the other hand began to rub his temples. The man's head was like a stump. The thick, gray beard he was growing did nothing to help that appearance.

He said, "Regardless, what has happened cannot be changed now. It is my belief that we must still try and cut our way out."

"We'll have to push the enemy back again in the morning," Pillow said. The man leaned far back in his chair and stared down his nose at Floyd. If one didn't know better, he would believe that Pillow ranked Floyd.

Pillow paused for effect and then continued, "I've sent two scouts out, and they report enemy campfires all the way back around our left, almost to the river. That can only mean one thing—we're surrounded again."

Forrest cleared his throat, and the three officers looked in his direction. Forrest said, "There are fires over there alright, but there ain't no enemy to be found. I've rode all over that place. The wind has just stirred their fires up from this morning. We can still get out."

Floyd looked at Forrest through his sad, drooping eyes. His large cheekbones drew more attention to his face than anything.

Floyd said, "I have reports that dogs are barking out there. They've got to be barking at Federal troops returning to the area."

"They're probably barking at me and my men," Forrest replied with disdain. He was growing weary of the sound of hopelessness in his commanding officers' voices. "We been out on the field picking up abandoned Federal rifles and our wounded. I've been as far as two miles out the Forge Road. The only Yankees we've seen are dead and wounded."

Floyd perked up a little. He asked, "Colonel Forrest, can we get the men across Lick Creek?"

"We can get across," Forrest replied. "The men will be forced to wade water almost knee deep, but the route to Nashville is open."

Floyd began to shake his head. "My medical director says that only a fourth of the men will survive a march to Nashville in this weather. Not a man will survive if they're forced to wade a creek. He reports that many of our men are suffering from frostbite now. I can't order those men to wade freezing water."

Pillow was nodding in agreement. Buckner said, "It would be cruelty to expose the men to anymore suffering."

Floyd looked at his two subordinates and asked, "Well, gentlemen, what is our best course of action here?"

Pillow shook his head and said, "I can't bear the thought of surrender. If Buckner can hold his position, I still believe we can fight our way out of here."

"My position can't be held," Buckner replied. His voice betrayed his agitation with Pillow.

Pillow slammed the table with his fist again. "I believe you can, sir."

"I believe I understand my position better than you, General Pillow," Buckner refused to even look at the man as he spoke. "Besides, you haven't even viewed my lines."

Pillow said, "I know what…"

"The route was open before you ordered us back," Buckner interrupted. "The responsibility for the mess we're in here belongs on your shoulders."

Pillow was shaking his head in disagreement. His voice almost became a shout as he began to argue his point. "The agreement before we began the battle this morning was for us to return to camp and gather as much of our equipment as possible and then escape under cover of night."

Forrest was growing angrier by the minute. If that had indeed been the plan all along, he wondered why they weren't escaping at this very moment.

Buckner turned to Floyd and said, "The only way out is by boat. We've already ruled out fording the creek. Grant is getting reinforcements as we speak. We don't have enough boats to escape before morning. There are rumors that Grant is pushing his artillery around to cover our escape route and will shell our retreating men along Forge Road. We have no choice now except for surrender."

Forrest could feel his face becoming more flushed than before. He couldn't believe what he was hearing here.

Floyd began to squirm in his chair. He rubbed his temples and said, "I can't surrender. As you gentlemen are aware, I was Secretary of War under President Buchanan. The United States Congress has charged me with treason. If I surrender, I will probably be hanged without a trial. The Federals would love nothing more than to get their hands on me. Therefore, I must pass command to General Pillow."

"I accept the command," Pillow nodded his head. He sat up as if he were actually going to accomplish something now that he had command. "I'm the best field commander in the Confederacy, and our nation won't be able to win this war if I'm in a Federal prison. Now, I'm obliged for my country's sake to pass the command to General Buckner."

"I accept it," Buckner said as he turned to one of his staff officers seated against the wall. "Bring me pen and paper so I can write General Grant for terms."

Nathan Bedford Forrest had remained quiet for as long as he could. He said, "I will not surrender my men to a northern prison in mid winter. That would be far worse than marching them across a damned crick tonight."

The three senior officers looked shocked at Forrest's outburst. They watched as he stepped forward toward the table and pointed his long, bony index finger in their direction. He continued his rant. "I, by God, did not come here to surrender."

4

Buckner didn't know Forrest very well. He thought it might settle the man down if he just agreed to allow him to take his men and leave. He said, "Colonel, take your men out of the fort if you can, but you must leave before I begin my negotiations with Grant."

"I'll leave now," Forrest was almost shouting. His already shrill voice became almost a scream. "I'll take as many men who want out of this foolishness with me when I go!"

Buckner couldn't help but notice that Forrest wasn't asking for permission to leave but was informing him that he'd be leaving. Under other circumstances, he would have believed the man to have been insubordinate. Just now, however, Buckner was happy to see the hot-tempered officer leave.

Forrest stomped out of the hotel, his heavy riding boots making the windows rattle. He slammed the door behind him.

Major Kelly looked surprised. He asked, "What's happening?"

"We're surrendering," Forrest said as he stomped past the sentries toward his horse.

"Surrendering?" Kelly repeated. "Everyone?"

"All fifteen thousand men," Forrest said as he climbed into the saddle. "All except my men. We're gonna escape if we have to cut through the whole damned Yankee nation and it costs me every man."

****

Part I

"An army marches on its stomach."

Napoleon Bonaparte

April 2, 1863

CSA

The quaint little cottage General Pierre Beauregard was using for his headquarters was called the Fish Pond House. He could never cease to be amazed at the prospect of someone lining the roof with a copper-lined basin and placing goldfish on top of their house. He wondered how the fish survived the summer heat.

He stared at the stack of papers on the desk in front of him. He'd been hard at work ever since his arrival here in Corinth. It seemed the work would never be done. He was taxed with the difficult task of organizing the army, assigning commands, and also the never-ending task of trying to keep the army supplied.

Beauregard realized he should have gone to bed hours ago. Doctor Choppin, his staff surgeon, had diagnosed him with a nervous affection of the throat as a result of the surgery he'd had a month ago. He had no idea what a nervous affection of the throat was, but with the monumental task he'd been assigned, he was lucky that only his throat was nervous.

He'd arrived in this small Mississippi town feeling like a drowning man grasping for a straw. He had been so weak he could hardly climb out of bed. Doctor Choppin had ordered him to get some rest. He'd explained to Beauregard that any more undue stress could cause him to have a nervous breakdown. That was just a week ago. *So much for getting any rest, the general thought.*

He took a break from the mountains of paperwork and looked at the flowers on his desk. There were vases filled with beautiful flowers scattered all around the room. So many admiring southern belles had sent flowers to him that they'd run out of places to put them. Every room in the house smelled like fresh flowers.

Beauregard reached up and pulled at the tuft of hair just below his lip and thought about his current predicament. After Sidney Johnston's army had been pushed from Kentucky and Tennessee, President Davis had ordered him west to save the Confederacy. At least that was what he'd been led to believe initially. If a man wanted to save his country, it only made sense to send his best general. It was a position he'd been pleased to accept. Before leaving Richmond, Secretary of State Judah Benjamin had promised Beauregard that he had seventy thousand troops waiting for him here. After his arrival, to his mortification, he'd found less than thirty thousand poorly-equipped troops. If that wasn't enough of a shock, he found the army completely disorganized, and that's the reason he was up at such a late hour now.

Beauregard exhaled and turned and watched Colonel Thomas Jordan working at the table behind him. He shook his head and spoke in a raspy voice, "So, this is my punishment for quarreling with the President?"

"That's the rumor," Jordan glanced up from his stack of papers. The man was loyal to Beauregard and was always willing to help inflate his idol's ego. "I know it's hard to believe, sir, but the government is against you now. They have told everyone you have a vast army here. Now if you fail, they will heap all the blame on your head."

"Yes," Beauregard paused and lowered his head. "They have given me the helm when the ship is already on the breakers and beyond saving."

Jordan said nothing. Beauregard picked up the list of generals in the Army of Mississippi and studied it carefully. "Have we received word about the officers I've requested from Virginia?"

"Denied," Jordan said flatly. "He claims the officers we have here are fully capable."

Beauregard began to shake his head. *Davis would truly rather lose the war than see me succeed, he thought.* He said aloud to no one in particular, "Davis is a fool."

Jordan burst into laughter behind him. It didn't matter how many times Beauregard called the president a fool; Jordan always thought it was funny.

Beauregard began to scan over the names on the list. He paused at one name and said, "Daniel Ruggles. That grouchy old man couldn't lead a horse, much less a division. How old is he anyway?"

Jordan scratched his head and said, "Early fifties I believe, but the old cuss looks almost seventy to me."

"I've heard his health is not well." Beauregard thought about what he'd just said. He had little room at the moment to condemn a man because of his health. He thought about gray-haired Daniel Ruggles, with the long gray beard that ended at a point just above his belt. "I don't know a soul who likes the man. Why wouldn't someone like that just resign? There's really no shame in it."

Jordan laughed at how naïve General Beauregard seemed. "You know why, sir. Every man in the South thinks he's the next Napoleon."

Beauregard lowered his head. Jordan was right of course. It truly was a problem in the South. Every man believed himself a great general, and so far, Beauregard hadn't found a decent general among them. He had studied under Napoleon's lieutenants in prep school, and he was the only one in this country that had the potential to be the next Napoleon.

Maybe President Davis doesn't like me, Beauregard thought, but at least Sidney Johnston is intelligent enough to seek my council. He thought about how disorganized Johnston had allowed the army to become after the fall of Forts Henry and Donelson. *Hell, I had to convince the man to concentrate the army here in Corinth. I convinced him to strike Grant at Pittsburg Landing before Buell arrives with his forces. So far the man has agreed with every suggestion I've made.*

Beauregard turned back toward Jordan. "I have one concern about the coming campaign, Colonel. If we succeed, Davis will make sure Johnston gets all the credit. If we fail, the government will make me the scapegoat."

There was a knock at the door. Lieutenant Chisholm opened the door and stepped inside. "General, sorry to disturb you, but we have just received a message from General Polk. It's marked important."

Beauregard nodded. Chisholm brought him the message, saluted, and left the room. Beauregard unfolded the paper and began to read. Jordan watched him; his expression betrayed his impatience.

Beauregard finished the message and rose to his feet. He held onto his desk to steady himself. "Colonel, it's time. Grant has detached one of his divisions. We must hit him while he's divided. Take this down for General Johnston."

Jordan grabbed a clean sheet of paper and waited. Beauregard rubbed his eyes and forehead as he dictated the message. "General, as you know, the Federal army is foolishly camped on our side of the Tennessee River. They have a creek on both of their flanks and the river to their backs. We have them trapped in a box with nowhere to go. I have just received information that he has detached about five thousand men at Crump's Landing. Now is the time to strike. Grant's camp being but twenty miles away, we have just enough time to destroy his army before General Buell arrives to reinforce him. We can then cross the river, destroy Buell's army, and march up the Mississippi River to take St. Louis. What say you to this grand plan?"

Jordan was used to Beauregard's theatrics. When he finished writing, he said, "Sir, it's brilliant. Johnston would be a fool to not agree."

Johnston is no fool, Beauregard thought. But still, there was no need in taking any chances. He said, "You hand deliver the message, Colonel. Make certain he understands that this is the time to strike."

"Right, sir," Jordan answered. He stood, put on his frock coat, and left the room. This wasn't the first time Beauregard had sent him on such a mission. He enjoyed the fact that Beauregard counted on him more than any other members of his staff. Jordan had always been successful, except when dealing with Jefferson Davis. No one could change that man's mind. He reminded Jordan of the most stubborn army mule in the country.

After he'd gone, Beauregard thought about how lucky he was to have Jordan. He was glad that William Mackall had been sent to Island Number Ten. That had opened the door for Jordan to become the army's adjutant. Mackall had been a dry, unimaginative man who always tried to find faults with Beauregard's brilliant plans. *Jordan will see that things work out the way I intend, he thought.*

Jordan left the Fish Pond House and walked seven blocks to the Rose Cottage. The home was owned by William Inge and had been General Sidney Johnston's headquarters since his arrival. To Jordan's relief, there were still lights on inside. When Jordan knocked on the door, Lieutenant George Baylor greeted him and welcomed him inside. Augusta Inge had retired for the night. Her husband, William, was colonel of the 10th Mississippi Cavalry and was away scouting Federal troop positions, but Johnston was still awake. Jordan entered the parlor with Baylor and asked to see the general. They entered Johnston's bedroom, and Jordan saluted and handed him the message. He tried to study the expression on Johnston's face as he read the note, but the man's expression portrayed nothing.

Johnston finished reading and placed the note in his pocket. He lowered his head in thought and began to pace. He paused a moment to light his pipe and continued pacing. *He thought, I've lost Kentucky and Tennessee; but the worst part was losing Nashville, with all its industry and military supplies. Something must be done to reverse these misfortunes.*

He stopped pacing and turned to Jordan. "Beauregard is right. We will fall on Grant like a hurricane and overwhelm him. After we force him to surrender, we'll cross the river and deal with Buell. If this campaign is a success, it'll make up for all of our past failures."

"Those are my feelings also, sir," Jordan nodded his head in agreement.

"Come on," Johnston motioned toward the door. "Let's go see General Bragg."

They crossed the street to the Veranda House, Bragg's headquarters. The house was small, but built to be as elegant as any large plantation home. It earned its name from the porch that wrapped all the way around the house.

Jordan understood why they were going to see Bragg. He was the army's new chief of staff. Beauregard had suggested giving Bragg the position so he could command Leonidas Polk, who actually outranked Bragg. Jordan shook his head as he thought about Polk. The man had been the Episcopal Bishop of Louisiana when the war began, but because of his friendship with President Davis, he was made a major general and given a command. Beauregard detested the man.

They were greeted at the door by Captain Hypolite Oladowski, Bragg's Chief of Ordnance. The man was from Poland and only spoke broken English. He said, "De sheneral is in bed. Muss you wake him?"

They waited just outside Bragg's bedroom while Oladowski woke him and lit a lamp. When they were allowed inside, they found Bragg sitting up in bed still in his night clothes. Johnston handed him the message from Beauregard and waited as Bragg read. Bragg was a haggard-looking man with one bushy eyebrow that went all the way across his forehead.

Bragg finished reading and said, "I have to agree with General Beauregard. It's now or never."

Johnston thought about the condition of his army. He decided to play the devil's advocate for a moment to gauge how Bragg reacted. Johnston said, "General, the troops are nowhere near ready."

Bragg started to speak, but Jordan interrupted. "Sir, this is our only chance. The only way we're gonna get any stronger is to wait for Van Dorn's army to arrive from Arkansas. He's probably still several weeks away. If we wait any longer, Buell will reinforce Grant and then the opportunity will have passed."

Johnston paused in thought. *Just yesterday I gave an order for the army to be prepared to move at a moment's notice. Ready or not, this is the only opportunity we have to fight on equal terms. What other choice do we have?* He began to pace again. Suddenly, he spun around, "Colonel Jordan, would you write out an order for me?"

"I'd be honored, sir," Jordan sat at a table General Bragg had been using for a desk.

Johnston walked over and peered over Jordan's shoulder. "Please write an order to Generals Bragg, Hardee, and Polk. Tell them to have their troops ready to march at first light. That is all."

After Jordan finished writing, Johnston reached over his shoulder and took the message. He said, "Thank you, Colonel."

Bragg said, "I'll have my aide make copies for you, Colonel Jordan. I know you have more pressing matters to attend to. I'll see they get delivered if that's alright with General Johnston."

Johnston nodded. Jordan thanked Bragg. Together the two officers excused themselves. Jordan watched Johnston walking back across the street to the Rose Cottage. He heard the man say to himself, "The coming campaign will silence all my critics." He watched Johnston pause in the street a moment and add, "And it will restore my tarnished reputation."

April 3, 1862

CSA

The five generals were gathered around the dining room table, where Misses Neely had just served them plates heaping with eggs, bacon, and biscuits. Beauregard's throat was still sore, and he didn't have much of an appetite, but he was too much of a gentleman to offend his hostess.

Johnston took a bite of bacon and said, "I've ordered five hundred coffins built. I'm hoping that'll be sufficient."

"If my plans succeed the way I'm expecting," Beauregard swallowed hard, the look of pain evident on his face, "we'll have to send the dead back here for the coffins. This army will be marching north and taking the battle to the northern states."

The ever-grouchy Bragg looked up and shook his head. He wasn't nearly as confident as Beauregard. "I don't put a great deal of faith in the soldiers we have here. I doubt most of these men have performed a day's work in their lives."

General Polk nodded his head in agreement. "One of my artillery batteries has never heard their cannons fire because of the lack of powder. That's not the way I'd like to begin a campaign."

"Gentleman," Beauregard spoke with confidence, "we must at least try something, even if we die in the attempt. If we sit here and do nothing, all will be lost. We're not gonna get any stronger until Van Dorn arrives with his fifteen thousand men. That could be weeks away. Meanwhile, Buell will join Grant, and they will advance together against us here. Together they will outnumber us more than two to one."

Colonel Jordan walked into the room. His hair waved wildly, and his eyes were bloodshot. Misses Neely handed him a plate. He bowed gracefully and sat next to his commander.

Beauregard gave Jordan a gentle pat on the shoulder. "After breakfast, I need you to write the battle plans for me."

"Yes, sir," Jordan took a sip of coffee. It was just what the overworked man needed this morning.

Beauregard began to explain the marching orders to the others. Jordan continued eating, trying to come awake. Beauregard's plan called for the army to take two parallel roads to Shiloh. There were points along the route where divisions would halt to wait for the passage of other units. It sounded rather complicated to Jordan. If one unit fell behind schedule, the entire army would be behind schedule.

When Beauregard finished with his complicated marching plan, Johnston said, "When we get there, I want Polk on the left, Hardee in the center, and Bragg on the right. Breckinridge will be the reserve behind Bragg. That will place our strongest corps on the right so we can push Grant away from the landing and into the swamps to the northwest. Once we scatter his army in the swamps, we'll have the high ground, and he'll have no choice but to surrender."

"We should be able to plunder his stores at that point," Beauregard added. He turned to General Hardee and said, "General, your corps will lead the advance. Because everything has been thrown together at the last minute, I've changed the departure time to noon."

"Right," Hardee nodded.

The generals finished their breakfasts. Beauregard said, "If there are no further questions, you may return to your commands. Make sure all your men are prepared for battle and each man carries three days' rations in his haversack."

The generals began to excuse themselves. Each thanked Misses Neely for breakfast. Johnston left with his corps commanders, saying he needed to send a telegram to President Davis.

After they had gone, Beauregard turned to Jordan and said, "I'm not feeling well this morning, Thomas. I think I'll return to bed for a while. I'm leaving you in charge of the battle plan."

Jordan was taken aback. He felt honored that Beauregard trusted him that much. He asked, "Do you have anything in mind, sir?"

Beauregard swallowed hard. He was having difficulty with his speech. "You will have to use your own discretion. After you finish, I'll read it and give the final approval."

Jordan nodded and continued with his breakfast. Beauregard rose unsteadily from the table and made his way toward his bedroom. *I have just the thing to make him feel better, Jordan thought. The man's hero is Napoleon, so that's the battle plan he will get.*

Jordan spent all morning working on the Confederate plan of battle. Beauregard arose before eleven. He walked out to the kitchen and washed his face in a basin of water. Back inside the house, he found Jordan at his desk, hard at work. He asked, "What do you have for me?"

Jordan was startled. He was so caught up in his work that he hadn't even noticed Beauregard behind him. He looked up to see the general peering over his shoulder. "I'm almost finished, sir."

Beauregard noticed a copy of Napoleon's plans for the Battle of Waterloo lying on the desk. He picked it up and asked, "What's this?"

"Sir," Jordan smiled. "I know how much you admire Napoleon. I just happened to have a copy of his battle plans in my trunk. So I wrote our attack plan the same as his."

Beauregard began to smile and then shook his head. "Thomas, why the Battle of Waterloo?"

12

"It's the only battle plan I have of Napoleon's, sir." Jordan had a sheepish expression on his face.

Beauregard laughed. "You're aware Napoleon lost that battle?"

"Yes, sir," Jordan began to sound nervous. He'd been working hard all morning. If Beauregard didn't approve of the plan, all that work would be for nothing. He added, "I still believe his theory was sound."

"Relax," Beauregard patted him on the back. "You've sold me. Three lines of infantry should hit the Federal army like three giant tidal waves. Good thinking, Colonel."

Jordan breathed a sigh of relief and asked, "Do you still plan on attacking in the morning at first light?"

"We've gotten a late start." Beauregard laid Napoleon's battle plans back on the desk. He walked over and peered out the window. "It's only a twenty-mile march. We should be in position to attack by noon tomorrow at the very latest."

"I guess I should get these orders to General Johnston for approval." Jordan rose from the chair and began to organize the papers on his desk. "I've called them Special Orders Number Eight."

"Don't worry about getting approval, Thomas." Beauregard turned away from the window. "I'll take care of Johnston."

CSA

It was half past noon, and the march still hadn't gotten under way. The roads were clogged with soldiers, cannons, and wagons, but no one was moving. It was one huge traffic jam. General Hardee sat on his horse watching the mess. He'd sent Lieutenant Hunt ahead to find the cause for the delay.

He could feel the frustration building inside by the minute. This was not the way he had hoped the campaign would begin. This was getting off to an inauspicious start.

General Hardee stared across the mass of men in the road. On the other side was a red-haired general from Arkansas. He nudged his horse and began inching that way through the crowd of men. There was something about him that Hardee liked. The man had been born in Ireland and immigrated to America about a decade ago. He'd gotten a job clerking in a drug store in Helena, Arkansas. Through hard work, he'd earned a law degree and become one of the town's most prominent citizens. When he was placed under Hardee's command, the two men had become fast friends.

When Hardee cleared the mob, Cleburne saluted and asked, "What exactly is going on here?"

Hardee had been amazed that Cleburne was born and raised in Ireland, yet he had learned to speak without a hint of an accent. The man had worked hard to blend in with the people of Helena. Hardee replied, "Damned if I know. I've sent ahead to find out. This campaign's not getting off to a very good start."

Cleburne nodded. He reached up and wiped sweat from his forehead. "Sure is hot for April. Feels more like August."

Hardee gazed back across the mass of men in the street. Very few of them were dressed alike. Most were barely equipped. He jerked a thumb in their direction. "What regiment is this, Pat?"

"Sixth Mississippi," Cleburne replied. "About four hundred twenty-five men. They don't look like much, but I've drilled 'em pretty hard."

"Come on," Hardee said. "Let's ride forward and see what's the matter."

It was a struggle for the two generals to ride through the crowded street. They'd gone about a hundred yards when they met Colonel William Bate, commander of the Second Tennessee Infantry. That regiment also belonged to Patrick Cleburne's brigade.

"What a mess," Bate said as he saluted his superiors.

"Any idea what's going on?" Hardee asked. He began scratching at his scraggly gray goatee.

"Beauregard passed by earlier," Bate began to shake his head, "The little Frenchman is pretty pissed. He was raving about General Polk running his trains out in front of everyone."

Cleburne looked over Bate's regiment. The majority of the Second Tennessee was between the ages of sixteen and eighteen. They were mostly just young, eager boys, but they were Cleburne's favorite regiment.

Hardee looked over at Cleburne and said, "If Beauregard's up there, he'll straighten this mess out. There's no need in us worrying through this crowd."

The two men made their way to the side of the street and found a shady spot to wait. Hardee dismounted, stretched out in the shade, and was soon asleep. Cleburne pulled his chess board from his bag and began a game with Major William Doak, Colonel Bate's second in command.

The mass of men finally began to move at about three. It was painfully obvious they wouldn't be marching very far today. It really couldn't be called a march. The pace would be fast one moment and at a complete standstill the next. Ladies lined the sides of the streets waving. Hardee, who was known for his fondness for girls half his age, was attempting to look his best. He held his head high, his chest stuck out. Cleburne thought he looked like a king leading his soldiers.

Hardee looked over the small town. It wasn't big enough to be called a city. The homes were small but majestic. Some had fancy names just like the big plantation homes back in Georgia. He looked back over his shoulder toward the Tishomingo Hotel. It was named for a famed Chickasaw Indian chief. The hotel was the only place in town that served iced tea. As he rode past the post office, he couldn't help but wonder whose idea it was to paint the building pink. Other than the Corona Female College on the west side of town, there wasn't much else here.

This is not a planters' town, Hardee thought. It's a railroad town. If not for the crossing of the Mobile and Ohio Railroad and the Memphis and Charleston Railroad, we wouldn't even be here now. The Memphis and Charleston line must be protected at all costs, he thought. After all, it's not called the "Backbone of the Confederacy" for nothing.

14

As they came near the Rose Cottage, Hardee could see General Johnston standing in the yard surrounded by his staff. He motioned to Cleburne, and the two officers made their way to the other side of the street.

Johnston saw Hardee approaching and walked to the edge of the road. The two officers reined up in front of him and saluted. Johnston said, "I'm giving battle flags to all the units that haven't gotten one yet."

"We're not off to a very good start," Hardee said for the fifth time since noon.

"Just do the best you can. It's only a twenty-mile march. We may still get there in time to attack tomorrow." Johnston extended his hand. After shaking Hardee and Cleburne's hands, he watched them ride north with their troops.

Outside of town, the marching didn't improve very much. The frequent halts had pretty much stopped, but the going was still slow. The rain had turned the roads to mud, and there were deep ruts cut into the road by the wagons and cannons. The men couldn't walk along the edge of the narrow road because of the vast wilderness on each side. Men were slipping and falling in the muck. At first, everyone burst into laughter when a man fell; but it hadn't taken long before it had grown weary to them. Especially since most of them had fallen at least once. Now when a man fell, the only reaction was cursing. The road wound around ridges and up and down hill after hill. It was extremely rough for men not used to long marches.

Hardee continued to ride beside Pat Cleburne. For a while, they didn't say much. They rode along listening to bayonets and canteens clanking together. The hooves of their horses made sucking sounds with each step in the mud.

Cleburne bowed his head in an attempt to avoid a low-hanging limb. The branch grazed his kepi, knocking it off his head. He just managed to catch the hat before it tumbled into the mud. He shook his head as he placed it back on.

Hardee smiled. Cleburne didn't seem to think it was funny. Hardee said, "Pat, I've got to be honest with you. I'm pretty apprehensive about the upcoming campaign."

Cleburne was taken aback. He asked, "Why so?"

"How should I say this?" Hardee lowered his head, choosing his words carefully. When he spoke, it was almost a whisper. "Johnston is not what you'd call a forceful leader."

Cleburne's eyes narrowed. It went against everything he'd read in the papers about Sidney Johnston. The man looked like a leader. He was a tall man, broad shouldered with a solid build. He could think of no one that looked more like a general. He said, "I would have never guessed looking at the man."

"He's a gentleman," Hardee spoke quickly. He glanced around to make sure no one else could hear their conversation. "Very modest and likable. He's too nice for command, if you understand what I mean…" Hardee looked over at Cleburne and saw the look of bewilderment on his face. "No? He doesn't have the traits that true commanders have for seizing authority, knocking stubborn subordinates around and forcing them to do his will."

"I'd read that he was a great commander of Texas forces in the Mexican War." Cleburne remembered all the southern journals praising Johnston when he first took command. They were calling Johnston the greatest general who ever lived. Of course, they had also turned against him after the loss of Kentucky and Tennessee. Cleburne was surprised that Hardee was in agreement with them now.

"Yes," Hardee nodded, "but he saw very limited action there. The man is overrated. He received his commission because of his friendship with President Davis. He was a few years ahead of Davis at West Point. Everyone there liked Johnston. Like I said, he's a very likable man. He sort of became Jefferson Davis's personal hero at the Point, mostly because everyone liked Johnston and few people liked Davis. The president thinks that Johnston can do no wrong."

"I see," Cleburne was shaking his head. The beginning of a major campaign was a hell of a time to be learning about all of this.

"It's not just me," Hardee held up a hand. He wanted to make sure that Cleburne understood that he didn't feel this way about Johnston because of petty jealousy. "Generals Polk and Bragg feel the same way. Members of Johnston's own staff feel the man is in over his head. Do you know Colonel Gilmer, his chief engineer?"

Hardee watched Cleburne shake his head and said, "No? Well, he told me that there wasn't a hint of a Napoleon in Johnston or Beauregard either one."

"I thought things were different in this country." Cleburne was shaking his head again. "I thought in this country a man's position was based on merit, not who you are or who you know."

"Not quite, no," Hardee smiled at the innocence of Pat Cleburne. The man truly believed that if he did what was right, the world would always be fair to him. "You've heard the story about General Polk being the Episcopal Bishop of Louisiana?"

Cleburne nodded.

"He's another of Davis's friends from the Academy." Hardee nudged his horse forward to keep pace. "He resigned from the army as soon as he graduated. He's commanding a corps, and he's never led troops in peace time, much less into combat. He's another problem for Johnston. He's been a church leader so long that he's forgotten how to follow orders. He's the type of subordinate that must be forced to obey orders, and Johnston's not the type of commander to bowl over a recalcitrant subordinate."

Cleburne's horse slipped in the mud. He tugged at the reins. The animal regained its balance and continued on. Cleburne asked, "Is he the reason we lost Kentucky and Tennessee?"

"The blame always falls on the man in charge, regardless of who is at fault. It's just the nature of the game."

Hardee had written a book on tactics before the war. He loved discussing military affairs. He'd found Cleburne to be like a sponge, soaking up everything Hardee taught him.

"General Crittenden is responsible for the loss of Eastern Kentucky because of drunkenness. He gained his commission because his family is close friends with Jefferson Davis. Generals Floyd and Pillow lost Fort Donelson. Both were political generals. The loss of Fort Donelson hurt our cause worst of all. When the fort fell, we surrendered fifteen thousand fighting men. Johnston, of course, was blamed by the papers, but Davis has said that if Sidney Johnston is not a general, the South has no general."

"In your opinion, the entire loss of Kentucky and Tennessee is the fault of Johnston's subordinates?" Cleburne asked.

"Johnston is to blame also." Hardee hadn't gotten his point across yet. "Not once did Johnston leave his headquarters at Bowling Green, Kentucky, to see if his orders were being followed. He left everything up to those bumbling idiots."

Cleburne was learning things about his country that he'd had no idea existed. He began to feel uneasy. He said, "I heard a rumor that Breckinridge replaced Crittenden after the drinking episode because of his political standing."

"Pat, now you're beginning to understand what I'm saying." Hardee raised his hand in the air and brought it down with force. "We keep repeating the same mistakes time and time again. Common sense would have dictated giving Crittenden's corps to General Bowen. The man has been in the army for years and understands how to lead troops. Johnston gave Breckinridge the command because he is the former vice president of the United States."

Cleburne was beginning to question all his superiors. He asked, "How did Bragg receive his commission?"

"Bragg actually returned from the Mexican War a hero." Hardee laughed. "The man is a disciplinarian. Though, I must admit, his troops are the best drilled and disciplined in the entire army. The only problem with him is his inability to get along with others. He is arrogant and stubborn. His own men hate him. Some of his men tried to kill him in the Mexican War by lighting a cannonball and rolling it under his cot while he slept. It's only a matter of time before he learns that he can bully over Johnston also."

Cleburne rode on in silence for a few moments. *There's nothing I can do about this mess, he thought. All I can do is continue serving my country.*

Hardee continued, "Johnston was a descent commander in the old army, where the routine was slow and everything was laid back. I'm just not sure he'll ever adapt to the way things need to be done in wartime. He places too much confidence in his subordinates, believing that they'll do the right thing when the time comes."

"Let's hope, for the country's sake, that he's learning," Cleburne said. He couldn't bear the thought of sacrificing his men for a lost cause.

April 4, 1862

USA

He made the trip almost daily. It was nine miles from his headquarters in Savannah to where the army was camped at Pittsburg Landing. Grant's steamer, the *Tigress,* had been forced to wait fifteen minutes before it could reach the landing. There was only room enough for two steamers to dock at a time.

Grant stood alone on the bow of the boat, smoking a cigar as he waited. He could see men on shore busy unloading supplies. As soon as the bow eased forward, two sailors ran out the gang plank. He walked down the plank and into the muck. The entire landing from the river to the top of the hill had been worn clean of vegetation. The spring rains had turned the hillside into a sea of mud. Most of the men unloading the boats were covered in mud from head to foot from falling.

"What a mess," John Rawlins said. The man was Grant's adjutant who shadowed him everywhere he went. He considered himself Grant's guardian angel. Like Grant, Rawlins's father had been an alcoholic. The man drank his family into poverty. He considered it part of his duty to make sure Grant didn't do the same.

Grant said nothing. He carefully made his way to the top of the hill, where the horses waited. He'd made his headquarters at the Cherry home in Savannah to await the arrival of Buell. The place was right on the river; therefore, he'd left his horse here at the landing.

At the top of the hill, Grant turned and surveyed the river one hundred feet below. There were steamers waiting to unload at shore, while others steamed back north for another load of supplies. Rawlins thought about saying something about the view, but decided not to interrupt Grant's moment.

The two men turned and walked toward the small cabin and open area where the horses were. The rest of the ridge was covered with wilderness, steep hills, and deep ravines. An occasional field was carved out of the forest by small farmers.

They mounted their horses and rode west along the ridge and onto the open plateau beyond. They turned south and followed the Corinth-Pittsburg Landing Road. Because of the scattered fields and lack of camping areas, the army was spread over a three-mile area.

They were forced off the narrow road to avoid the teams that were pulling wagons of supplies through the mud. No one paid attention to Grant. No one seemed to know who he was, and that's the way he liked it. Even growing up he'd never been much of a people-person. He'd always preferred the company of horses.

He caught the strong smell of a latrine. Diarrhea had been running rampant among the troops. The men all referred to diarrhea as the "Tennessee Quickstep."

Grant listened to the sound of axes pounding away in the forest, mules braying along the road, drums beating in the camps, and the occasional shout of men horse-playing. Each field looked like a sea of tents. The Sibley tents, where the soldiers slept, resembled giant teepees. One tent slept sixteen men. He noticed a few men playing horseshoes, while others sat around gambling with either cards or dice.

Who can blame them, Grant thought, there's absolutely nothing else to do while we wait for Buell to arrive. It was times like these when Grant was most tempted to drink. Sitting around with nothing to do, he often became homesick, and that made him miss the bottle.

Grant said, "Well, Rawlins, they may be bored, but they seem to be in good spirits."

Rawlins was startled that Grant had spoken. The man could go for hours without saying a word to anyone. He began to nod, the ostrich plume in his hat dancing wildly in the air. He didn't quite know what to say. He pointed toward the trees and said, "My favorite time of year."

"Umm," Grant said.

"The trees are turning green, and the dogwoods are blooming." Rawlins took a deep breath of spring air. "It's not too hot. Still getting a bit cool at night though."

Grant's mind wasn't on the weather just now. He tugged at the horse's reins and turned into the field where Will Wallace had his headquarters.

Wallace was standing in front of his tent talking to one of his staff officers. He pointed toward the south with his long bony index finger. There was something about him that Grant liked. He wasn't a professional soldier, but a lawyer. Yet his men loved him. That told Grant all he needed to know about the man.

Wallace turned, saw Grant, and gave a crisp salute. There was nothing striking about him. He was actually very unattractive. Grant pulled the cigar from his mouth and stared at Wallace's long, clean-shaven face. His nose was long also. There was nothing about the man's appearance that would betray why his men loved him so.

"I'm riding down to see Sherman," Grant said. "Care to join me?"

"I'd be honored," Wallace replied. "Allow me to get my horse."

Grant watched him walk to the horse. He was tall and had a loose-jointed gait that looked quite comical. He reminded Grant of a man named Ichabod Crane, from a book he'd read once called *The Legend of Sleepy Hollow*.

Once Wallace was mounted, the three men rode south. Riding behind the two generals, Rawlins couldn't help but notice how odd they looked together. Grant was short, about five-seven, and barely weighed a hundred and thirty pounds. Wallace was a tall man who looked awkward riding a horse. He thought it was strange that Wallace never wore a hat. The man's hair was receding, and he had a large clump of hair in the center of his head that he kept combed into a neat little curl.

Wallace smiled at Grant and said, "My wife wants to come here and care for me."

Grant suddenly remembered that Wallace had a severe cold that he hadn't been able to shake. He'd gotten the infection back in February while fighting in the snow at Fort Donelson.

"What did you tell her?" Grant asked.

"As bad as I'd like to see her, I told her we probably will have advanced to Corinth before she could arrive here." He nudged his horse to keep pace with Grant's. "Besides, they won't allow citizens aboard the transports."

Grant thought about his wife, Julia. She wasn't considered to be a pretty woman, but she was beautiful in his eyes. Unlike other people, he didn't seem to notice that her eyes were slightly crossed.

He said, "That's the most difficult part of war for me. As long as there's action, I make it all right. When we're enduring the boredom of camp life is when I miss my family."

Wallace was nodding his head in agreement. "I just hope Ann listens to me. She's a very strong-willed young lady."

Up ahead, Grant could see Shiloh Church. It didn't look like much. It was made of rough-hewn logs with a clapboard roof. He could see men moving among the tents that were scattered around the churchyard. Finally, Sherman's wall tent came into view just behind the church. The three men rode that way.

As the three men dismounted, Generals Sherman and Prentiss stepped out of the tent. Sherman nodded, while Prentiss gave a sloppy salute. Sherman motioned the three men toward some camp chairs beneath a large cedar tree.

"How are you, Cump?" Grant asked as he shook Sherman's hand. Sherman's middle name was Tecumseh, after the famous war chief, but he'd always been called 'Cump.'

"I'm tolerable," Sherman pointed at a chair. "Prentiss and I have just been discussing all the skirmishing along our front."

Grant sat down and lit another cigar. He said between puffs, "Johnston's not fool enough to fight us here. We'll have to lay siege to Corinth. I'm sure he's got his troops dug in like a big fat tick by now."

"See there," Sherman reached over and slapped Prentiss on the knee. "Like I said, there's nothing out there but some rebel cavalry trying to feel us out and see when we're going to advance."

Prentiss didn't look very convinced. He asked, "What's the latest from 'Old Brains'?"

'Old Brains' was the nickname for Henry Wager Halleck, Grant's boss in St. Louis.

Grant said, "He's received word that Beauregard brought fifteen infantry regiments with him from Virginia to make up for the Confederate losses at Fort Donelson."

Sherman leapt from his chair and almost shouted. "The son-of-a-bitch is gonna need 'em!"

Prentiss gave Grant a solemn look. "I've got four thousand men in my division, but there's not a one of them that's seen combat yet."

"I'm not worried about Beauregard or his reinforcements," Grant mumbled. "I only wish Halleck had let us move on Johnston without Buell. We've given him time to concentrate his scattered army and entrench."

Sherman ran his hand through his thinning red hair as he paraded among the chairs. "The man's cautious. He's not like our General Grant here. The only thing Grant knows is hit 'em and hit 'em hard. He doesn't care for tactics a damned bit. He reminds me of a bulldog—get a hold on 'em and don't let go. He believes in getting his enemy off balance with some hard knocks and then destroying him."

Grant loved to watch Sherman when he was all worked up. He was extremely high-strung and talked without knowing what he was saying at times. They had become fast friends when the war began. *It's true what they say about opposites attracting, Grant thought.*

Grant lowered his head as he thought about General Halleck's preferred mode of warfare. *The man likes for every little detail to be in place before advancing. Then he wants to lay siege to the enemy because it's safer.* Grant preferred to throw caution to the wind.

He said, "If Halleck would have allowed us, Johnston's army would have been destroyed by now, and we would have been deep into Mississippi already."

Sherman and Wallace were nodding in agreement, but Prentiss still had the same solemn expression on his face. *This man is a different matter altogether, Grant thought.* He and Grant had argued over seniority when the war first began. With a little help from Congressman Washburn, Grant had won that battle. Prentiss had been cordial ever since, but Grant believed he still harbored ill feelings toward him.

"I guess I'm just overreacting," Prentiss scratched at his neatly-trimmed beard. His upper lip was clean-shaven just like President Lincoln's. "It would have been prudent to have waited for Buell at Savannah on the other side of the river and out of reach of the Confederate army."

"Prentiss," Sherman said as he walked back to his chair and plopped down. "You know damned well I picked this position. This is the best campsite around and a hell of a lot closer to Corinth than Savannah. I want to be ready to move when Buell arrives. Will you just relax a little?"

Prentiss took a deep breath and let it go. *Perhaps they're right, he thought.*

Grant puffed on his cigar and said, "You fellows need to stop worrying about what the rebels will do to us and start thinking about what we'll do to them."

"That, right there, is the difference between Grant and me," Sherman jumped from the chair again. "What the enemy is doing out of his sight doesn't bother him a damned bit, but it scares the hell out of me."

Wallace laughed. He was the junior officer here and felt uncomfortable speaking unless asked for his opinion.

Grant smiled and asked, "Have I told you about my first engagement as a commander?"

"Not that I recollect," Sherman replied.

"When the war began," Grant pulled the cigar from his mouth and watched the smoke rising, "I was just a colonel commanding a regiment. We were sent into Missouri to fight this particular Colonel Harris, who was causing a lot of trouble for the union people in the area. The man was supposed to be a fearless and aggressive commander. We found where his men were camped, and I was ordered to go there and defeat him. The closer I got, the more it seemed my heart would rise up into my throat. As we were marching up the hill where he was camped, I thought I would actually cough my heart up. I would have given anything at that point to be back home, but I didn't have the courage to let the men know I was afraid. So we kept advancing."

Sherman was shaking his head and hanging on Grant's every word. He could understand what Grant had gone through. He'd just recovered from a nervous breakdown himself—a condition caused by Johnston and all his bluffing during the winter. The Rebel general had made false advances here and there, and all the while he didn't have enough men to even hold his position.

Grant continued his story. "Upon reaching the top, we found that Colonel Harris and his men had fled. That's when I realized that the enemy was just as much afraid of me as I had been of him. That's the reason I don't fear what the enemy is doing."

Prentiss began to nod. He understood what Grant was saying. *Perhaps I am overreacting, he thought.* He said, "I was inspecting my men yesterday when a private asked me where we would fight if attacked here. I explained to him that we would fight

21

right here in the woods. He looked at me as if I were insane. He said that every painting he'd ever seen showed battles in open fields."

Wallace laughed. Sherman nodded his head and said, "They've got a lot to learn."

Grant wasn't thinking about fighting here. He turned to Rawlins and asked, "Exactly how many men do we have here?"

"Forty-two thousand," Rawlins replied without a moment's hesitation. The man kept information available in his mind. He was like a human encyclopedia with useful information on the army.

"And how many of those are combat-ready?" Grant asked.

"About thirty-four thousand, sir," Rawlins replied. If the man was one thing, it was thorough. "The rest are teamsters, cooks, hospital staff, that sort of thing. At last count, we had one hundred and two cannons and a small scattering of cavalry."

"One other thing, gentlemen," Grant turned his attention back to his generals. "Halleck has given strict orders that we are to avoid a battle at all costs until Buell arrives."

"Shouldn't be a problem," Sherman began to pace around the chairs again. "I'm 'bout ready to move. I don't like this sitting around while the enemy reinforces and strengthens his position. Any idea when Buell will arrive?"

"Any day now," Grant puffed on the cigar. "As soon as he gets here, we will lead the advance. So have your men prepared to march on short notice."

"I'll have McClernand and Hurlburt notified," Rawlins spoke up.

"That shouldn't be a problem, Rawlins," Sherman laughed. "Hurlburt will be in his tent passed out drunk or working on some shady land deal. McClernand will be in his tent writing campaign speeches."

"The president has passed out a lot of commissions to political friends," Grant took the cigar out of his mouth. "I suppose that's the price one pays for getting elected. I'm just proud to say that I obtained my position through hard work, not favoritism."

Prentiss looked up. *He thought, Grant will never admit that he got his position through the offices of Congressman Washburne. Besides that, Grant has done the same thing with his own staff. Every one of them is a politician from Grant's hometown.*

Sherman walked back to his chair and sat down. "I'll never forget the first time I met Lincoln. You all know my younger brother John is a congressman. Anyway, he took me to meet the president to secure me a commission. When John explained to Lincoln that I was an old soldier, the president said, 'I suppose you want a general's commission; that's what everyone else wants.' I wish you could have seen the look on his face when I told him to make me a colonel and that I would work my way up to general if I earn the position."

Prentiss rose from his chair. He shook Sherman's hand and said, "I guess I'll be returning to my command."

Sherman pumped Prentiss's hand vigorously. "Prentiss, just relax over there. We're in no danger here."

"Right," Prentiss nodded. He turned and gave Grant a sloppy salute and then excused himself.

Wallace rose from his seat, turned to Grant, and asked, "Sir, how is General Smith?"

Grant took the cigar from his mouth. "He's still in bed. The leg looks bad. I hate the thought of him losing a leg from such a trivial accident."

"Please tell him I'm praying for his recovery," Wallace's voice was solemn. "To have him back, I'd gladly give up division command and return to my brigade. He's a good soldier."

"He is a good soldier and a good man," Grant reached out and took Wallace's hand. "You're also a good soldier and a good man. Your men love you. I can't think of anyone other than you I would prefer in his place."

"Thank you, sir," Wallace said. "I'd best be getting back."

After he'd gone, Sherman said, "He's a good man. There is absolutely nothing about his looks that would convince you he would make a good commander."

Grant smiled. He was glad the others had left. Now he would get Sherman's honest opinion on the current situation. Ever since the nervous breakdown, Sherman rarely told others what he really thought for fear of being called crazy again. Grant thought about how Sherman hated reporters. When he'd said it would take two hundred thousand men just to conquer the Mississippi Valley alone, they had written that Sherman was insane.

"So how are things, Cump?"

"Come to my tent," Sherman jerked a thumb over his shoulder. "I'll have the boys cook us a steak."

Grant followed the feisty redhead inside and sat down. Rawlins waited outside with Sherman's staff. Sherman sat at his camp desk and opened a large, dark bottle. Grant was aware that Sherman used opiates for his headaches.

"Laudanum?" Grant asked.

"Yeah," Sherman replied as he took a swallow. "Have to take it every day for these damned headaches."

"I get headaches occasionally," Grant lit another cigar. "Doctors say it's migraines. They're pretty bad, but luckily I only get one every now and then."

"Try having one every damned day," Sherman sat back in the chair and tried to relax. Doctor's had said that Sherman suffered from headaches because he was so high strung. He realized he needed to relax, but for a man like him it was easier said than done.

"So Cump, are we in danger here?" Grant asked.

"Well, their cavalry has gotten a lot saucier lately. I'm sure that's all it is, just cavalry. They're watching us to let Johnston know the second we advance."

"Halleck is worried about us." Grant puffed on the cigar. "The man doesn't entirely trust me. He's afraid I'll do something rash and embarrass him. You're aware of my reputation."

Sherman thought about Grant's reputation as an alcoholic. All of Washington had been made aware of his fondness for the bottle.

"Don't worry about it," he said. "Buell will be here in a few days, and we'll finish this war in short order. You know as well as I that the Rebs have no fight left in them."

Grant took a long draw on the cigar, let his head back, and blew smoke toward the top of the tent. He thought about what his father had told him a few months back. *"You're a general," the old man had said. "It's a good job; don't mess it up."*

"Damned shame about Smith," Sherman said.

"What a way to get knocked out of action," Grant was shaking his head at the thought. "Climbing from a steamer into a rowboat and falling. Peeled the skin all the way from his ankle to his knee. Went right down to the bone. I hate to see the old man in such pain. As if that weren't enough, now it's become infected."

"He's better qualified than anyone here for command," Sherman lowered his head in thought. He could feel the laudanum already beginning to work.

"You know he was the commandant of cadets while I was just a student at West Point." Grant swatted at a mosquito. "He may be the best we have. I talked to him about how awkward it was for me to give him orders, but being the way he is, he said he wouldn't have it any other way."

"Sounds just like him," Sherman jumped from the seat and opened the tent flap. "Let me get the cook on those steaks."

Grant stayed until well after dark. He had a large meal and was enjoying Sherman's company immensely. Before there was any indication, it began to rain again. He and Rawlins huddled in Sherman's tent waiting for the weather to ease up. It soon began to thunder. Lightning was crashing among the trees.

"I'm afraid it's set in for the night," Rawlins said as he peered out the tent flap into the darkness.

"You fellows are welcome to bunk here for the night," Sherman offered. "There's plenty of room."

"I've got to be getting back," Grant mumbled. "Halleck will be expecting a wire tonight. You know what happened at Donelson."

Sherman thought about Fort Donelson. Grant had taken the fort and become a hero overnight. Halleck had become jealous of his lieutenant, and because Grant hadn't sent telegrams daily, Halleck had relieved him of his command. The only reason he was back in command now was because President Lincoln had demanded to know why his most successful general was sitting out the war."

"I'll visit again tomorrow, Cump," Grant said. He and Rawlins were buttoning their coats and trying to prepare themselves for the long, wet ride back to the landing.

The two men rode north, but the going was slow. It was the darkest night Grant had ever seen. The only way they could tell if they were still on the road was by the lightning flashes. It took about an hour to reach the landing, just three miles away. As they approached the little cabin that overlooked Pittsburg Landing, Grant shouted at Rawlins, "Let's just take the horses with us."

Grant led the way down the steep hill. The horse was having trouble negotiating in the dark. Suddenly, the horse slipped, tried to regain its balance, then fell hard on its side. Everything had happened so fast, Grant didn't have time to get clear of the falling animal. Pain shot through his ankle. The horse rose quickly to its feet, but Grant was in too much pain to move.

Rawlins dismounted and saw the look of agony on his commander's face in the lightning flashes. He yelled, "I'll get help. Lie still."

24

He felt dumb for saying the last part. Of course the man would lie still—his leg was probably broken. He found several men to help him carry the general down to the waiting steamer. He tried to make Grant as comfortable as possible during the trip back downstream.

When they reached the landing at the Cherry Mansion, they were forced to carry the general up three terraced stairways to reach the house. Inside, Grant's surgeon, Doctor Hewitt, was forced to cut the boot off because his foot had swollen so much.

After a thorough examination, Hewitt said, "You were lucky this time, sir."

"I don't feel very lucky," Grant mumbled.

Hewitt nodded. "You should take a shot of whiskey for the pain."

Grant glanced at Rawlins. Rawlins could tell the general was in severe pain. He said, "It'll be alright this time, sir—but just one shot."

The doctor continued with his diagnosis. "The mud saved you from a broken leg. It's just a bad sprain. You'll be on crutches for a few days."

Misses Cherry, who was hovering in the background, said, "I suppose we could just stick him in bed upstairs with General Smith."

Grant actually smiled at the thought. "War's rough on us old men," he said.

April 4, 1862

CSA

Albert Sidney Johnston awoke just before dawn. Augusta Inge, wife of William Inge, was extremely happy to have the second highest ranking officer in the Confederacy using her home as a headquarters. She went out of her way to make sure he was happy. He ate every bite she prepared him for breakfast.

"Can I fix you a lunch for later?" Augusta Inge asked.

"No thank you, ma'am," he replied, "we soldiers travel light."

She slipped into the foyer and placed two sandwiches and a piece of cake into his coat pocket without his knowledge. Augusta Inge watched him move to the front door and take his coat. She couldn't help but notice there was a gleam in his eye this morning. He thanked her for the use of her home and pulled on his frock coat as he stepped onto the veranda. His staff was already climbing on their horses, waiting for their commander. Johnston seemed lost in the moment. He stared at the ground just beyond the porch and finally announced, "I believe I have overlooked nothing."

He mounted his horse and rode north out of town through an occasional rain shower. His staff trailed along behind. Johnston hadn't said a word since leaving Corinth. His mind seemed far away at the moment. It was as if he were a great warrior riding toward his destiny.

Tennessee Governor Isham Harris spurred up beside Johnston and said, "The morale of the men seems to have improved with this forward advance."

Johnston thought about the poor governor, driven from his own state. There seemed to be something sad about a governor with no place to govern. *The man is willing to do anything to recover Tennessee, going so far as to serve as a volunteer aide on my staff for the coming battle. If we can only succeed, he thought.*

Johnston said aloud, "Morale is nothing more than faith in the man at the top."

"Right," Harris was nodding his head. The forty-two-year-old politician looked far older with his bald head and thick gray mustache. He'd been the governor of Tennessee since 1857.

"Relax," Johnston smiled at Harris, "I've always done my duty. I will do everything in my power to win this battle. Always remember; they may annihilate us, but they can never conquer us."

Harris nodded. He didn't know quite how to respond. The man was a politician. He didn't care for fancy military rhetoric; he wanted to hear the man say he would recover Tennessee and place him back in his rightful place. And that place was Nashville, Tennessee.

Still, Harris couldn't be very disappointed at the moment. He had the two best commanders the Confederacy had to offer. Beauregard and Johnston were possibly the two best living generals in the entire world.

"So you met President Davis at West Point?" Harris asked, changing the subject.

"Not exactly, no," Johnston spun his head toward Harris. "We actually met at Transylvania College in Kentucky before going to West Point. Well, he says we met, but I don't remember seeing him there. He's younger than me."

"Really," Harris shook his head in disbelief. "So you were thinking about becoming a lawyer?"

Johnston shook his head. "Not really. It was just one of those points in my life where I wasn't sure what I wanted."

Both men laughed at the comment. Harris quickly added, "You wouldn't make a very good lawyer or politician. You're way too honest."

Johnston smiled at the comment. Harris asked, "If I'm bothering you, sir...I mean, if you'd prefer to be alone in your thoughts...."

"Not at all," Johnston was shaking his head. "I need a distraction. I keep going over the same things in my head. You know, afraid I've forgotten something. We must win the coming battle."

"President Davis certainly has faith in you," Harris hoped Johnston wasn't taking this the wrong way. "I mean, he sort of made you his personal hero, didn't he?"

"I'm not really sure why." Johnston listened to the sucking sounds his horse's hooves were making in the muck. Since forty thousand men had passed this way, including the army's cannons and wagons, the road was a mess. "I've always been told I'm a likable person. Personally, my friendship with Jeff Davis has helped me quite a lot in life."

Harris looked confused. Johnston continued, "Well, Governor, my life has been full of twists and turns. Just when things begin to look bright for me, it seems I'm faced with another tragedy. Just when it seems to me that my life is over, Jeff is always there to pull me back up."

"I was never aware of this," Harris looked surprised.

"I was forced to resign from the army when Henrietta came down with tuberculosis," Johnston lowered his head as he remembered that sad period of his life twenty-eight years ago. "She died soon after, and there I was, raising our son alone—making a living farming—something that I hated. I was born to be a soldier, Governor."

Harris was nodding. He jerked a thumb over his shoulder in the direction of the trailing staff officers and asked, "Was she the brother of Colonel William Preston?"

"That's right," Johnston nodded. "I named my son after him, William Preston Johnston. He's serving on the president's staff. The Mexican War got me back in the military. After it ended, by a chance of fate, Jeff became Secretary of War. He formed two elite cavalry regiments and gave me the 2nd United States Cavalry. That was a great outfit. Lots of good men there—Lewis Armistead of Virginia and his close friend William Scott Hancock of Pennsylvania, and of course you've heard of the Garnetts of Virginia."

Harris nodded. He enjoyed watching Johnston's mood improve as he reminisced about the good times.

"Richard Garnett was with me there," Johnston lowered his head. "That was when the war came. Secession was a difficult thing. At first I wasn't sure what to do. I finally went with my heart. Little did I know that Jeff would make me the ranking field general in the Confederate army, but here I am."

"Yep, here you are."

They rode on through an occasional rain shower, following in the wake of the advancing army. Johnston lost himself in thought. He worried about what would become of Eliza and his five children if something were to happen to him. *This campaign must be a success. Davis can't keep saving me.*

Johnston looked up and saw a courier approaching. The young man rode up and saluted. "Sir, I'm Lieutenant Thomas Hunt," he said. "General Hardee begs to report, sir."

Johnston nodded and waited.

Thomas Hunt looked no more than eighteen. He cleared his throat and looked down as he tried to remember everything he'd been told to say.

"Sir, the general says that yesterday's march has turned into a nightmare. During the night, Hardee bivouacked his corps along the side of the road, and for some unknown reason, General Bragg kept advancing right past him. He blocked the road, and it's taken all morning to sort everything out. General Ruggles never read the date on his orders and therefore left a day late. Now he's behind the entire army. Breckinridge's artillery is stuck in the mud just outside of Farmington."

"Tell General Hardee that everything will be fine," Johnston didn't get upset with the news. He could see the look of relief on Lieutenant Hunt's face. "Buell's army is headed toward Decatur. We've got plenty of time to deal with Mister Grant."

"Right, sir," Hunt saluted. "Will that be all, General?" he asked.

Johnston shook his head. "How far are we from Mickey's?"

"'Bout five miles, sir," Hunt thought for a moment. "You'll be running into the troops bringing up the rear in a couple of miles. General Ruggles's men, like I said, are behind everyone."

"Thank you," Johnston saluted the young man. "Send my compliments to General Hardee."

Johnston watched the lieutenant spin the horse and attempt to gallop back up the road. The mud was so deep and the roads so messy that the horse struggled to make much speed.

They rode northward, Johnston appearing to be in deep thought again. Suddenly, he spun his head toward Harris and said, "Governor, Davis hasn't been as supportive of me as I expected."

Harris was taken aback. All he had ever heard was how much Davis worshiped Sidney Johnston. He wondered how Johnston could feel unsupported by the president.

"Why do you say that?" he asked.

"Before I lost Tennessee, there was a shipment of thirty thousand Enfield rifles that arrived in Savannah, Georgia, from England." Johnston looked down and began to shake his head. "My men are so poorly armed that I requested the majority of those weapons be sent to this army. Jeff said those guns were reserved for the troops in Virginia. My men only received a thousand of those guns. Do you know what he told me?"

Harris shook his head.

"He said that I could arm my men with shotguns, old flintlocks, or even pikes if they were needed." Johnston let it all go with a sigh. He looked toward Harris and said, "It's as if he is only concerned with Virginia. I mean, Joe Johnston has ninety thousand men there defending a line of about a hundred and fifty miles. Whereas, I'm forced to defend a line over four hundred miles long with forty thousand men."

Harris tried to cheer the general. "Might I also add that you did a superb job of holding that line until two months ago?"

Johnston laughed. "Do you know why?"

Harris shook his head.

"I was forced to resort to bluff, that's why." Johnston nudged the horse with his spurs. "It was the only thing I could do under the circumstances. I figured if I could keep the Federal army on the defensive waiting for an attack, I could buy time to convince Davis to send more arms and men."

Harris smiled. "Well, sir, it kept them on the defensive for six months at least."

"And it gave Cump Sherman a nervous breakdown, if nothing else." Johnston smiled to himself. "There's a problem with using a ruse, though. I was forced to mislead my own people. I had it printed in every newspaper that I had plenty of men and was only getting ready to use them in an invasion of the northern states. It all came crashing down in the end. It lulled the southern people into a false sense of security. My reputation suffered from that. The people believed me and now assume I must be a horrible general if I lost Kentucky and Tennessee with such a vast army."

Harris reached up and began to rub his chin. "Davis remained unmovable throughout I suppose."

"Exactly," Johnston was letting it all out. He'd been keeping this to himself, and he needed to get it all off his chest now. "I sent my adjutant general, Colonel Mackall, to Richmond to see Jeff. I thought sending him there in person might help Jeff see the seriousness of the situation. I wasn't aware the two men disliked each other.

28

Mackall found Davis in a sour mood. Before he could explain the problem, Davis cut him off. He asked Mackall where he was to get more troops, but I had coached the man well before he left. Mackall told him exactly what I wanted and that was to bring the troops sitting idle on the east coast to the west. I mean, there was no threat there. We have thousands of men sitting around idly defending the coast when we've lost two states here."

Harris was shaking his head. This was all news to him. He began to have some serious doubts about the president of the Confederate States.

Johnston continued. "He told Mackall that I have plenty of men here. He wants me to arm them with shotguns, old obsolete flintlocks, or even pikes if necessary. Can you imagine that? Men marching into battle against rifles and carrying nothing but pikes?"

Harris shook his head. He didn't quite know what to say. He looked up and noticed they were approaching the tail end of the army. Men were standing in the road ahead. No one was moving. The army had ground to a halt.

Lieutenant White Jetton, a young aide on Johnston's staff, rode forward and began to shout for the men to clear the road for the commanding general. Normally, Johnston wouldn't force the weary men from the road, but in this thick forest, it was impossible to ride around them. Men could be heard grumbling as they moved into the briars.

Johnston and his staff followed behind Jetton, the young man still screaming for the men ahead to clear the road. Some of the men saluted, but there was no cheering. It didn't take a genius to realize these men had lost faith in Johnston. If Beauregard came riding past, there would be lots of cheering.

Johnston began to worry about the coming battle. *If the Confederate army won this fight and regained Tennessee, he wondered, who would the people give credit to for the victory?* He put the thought out of his mind. All he wanted was a victory to clear his name.

They arrived at the crossroads at Mickey's, and to Johnston's surprise, there was nothing there but a farmhouse. It amazed him how a place could be marked on a map when it really wasn't a place at all. A small clapboard farmhouse sat beside the road. There was a cluster of horses gathered in the front yard.

Beyond the horses stood Beauregard, Bragg, and what appeared to be a Federal officer. Johnston dismounted and began to rub his legs. He'd been in the saddle since he'd left Corinth, and his body was stiff. He walked toward the three men.

Bragg saw him coming first and saluted. Beauregard turned and gave a slight nod. Johnston watched the Federal officer straighten himself as erect as possible and give a crisp salute.

Beauregard said, "Sir, we've captured this…"

"Major Leroy Crockett, Seventy-Second Ohio Infantry, at your service, sir," the Federal interrupted. "You have a fine set of fellows with you. I would have mistaken them for my boys if they were in blue. Fine set of fellows, I tell ya."

Johnston didn't quite know how to take the man. He extended his hand, ever the gentleman, and said, "Sidney Johnston. Glad to make your acquaintance. Though I wish it were under different circumstances."

Beauregard said, "Sir, he reports that the Federal army doesn't have a clue…"

"They don't," Leroy Crockett interrupted again. "Not a clue. I tell you, sir, nobody back there has any idea you're this close. I'll tell ya what happened. We had some pickets missing, and I took a handful of boys from the Fifth Ohio Cavalry to see if I could find them. Well, I found them. Trouble was they was with you fellows. Now you got me too. Fellow by the name of Clanton from Montgomery. Nice enough fellow, but I wouldn't want to cross him."

The way the man talked and kept interrupting General Beauregard forced Johnston to suppress a smile. He said, "I'm sure General Beauregard will see that you are well taken care of."

Beauregard motioned for a cavalryman to take the major away. Johnston glanced around at the crowd that had gathered trying to listen. He pointed toward the back of the house. "Gentlemen, let's move around back and discuss a few things."

They began to walk away, when they heard a horse galloping through the mud. It was General Breckinridge up from Farmington. He quickly dismounted and joined the group. Mud covered the man from head to foot from racing his horse up the miry roads.

Reaching the back of the house, Beauregard slumped on a stump. The man didn't look well. His voice was raspier than before. Bragg looked more haggard than usual. Johnston wondered what the men had on their minds.

Aside from the mud-covered uniform, Breckinridge looked as striking as always. His bright blue eyes seemed to pierce a man's soul.

"Sir, my corps is bogged down just this side of Farmington," he said. "I'm not sure how long it'll take to get them up here. My artillery may not make it at all."

Johnston said nothing. He noticed the army's adjutant, Thomas Jordan, approaching. Jordan nodded as he reached the group.

"We have a problem," he said. "General Hardee's line isn't long enough to extend across the entire front."

Beauregard shrugged. "General Bragg, what have you got in the second line that you can send forward to extend Hardee's line?"

"I'll order Gladden's brigade forward," Bragg replied brusquely. "They're on my right. The bigger problem seems to be that my corps is not yet on line. Polk is behind me and then Breckinridge."

Johnston took out his watch and noted the time. "Two hours until dark; we'll never get in position in time to attack today."

The three generals nodded in agreement.

"Major Munford," Johnston turned toward his staff. The young aide stepped forward. Johnston said, "Ride to General Polk and tell him to get his corps on line. We will attack at eight in the morning."

He watched the man move away. Johnston removed his hat and ran his hand through his hair. "Gentlemen, please do everything in your power to be on line by first light. That'll be all."

The group broke up, each man moving to his own area of operations.

April 5

CSA

The storm had hit about two this morning. Johnston had laid a blanket roll on a tree root as a pillow, but the storm prevented him from getting enough rest. It was with great difficulty that a fire was started.

Johnston stood beside the fire and pulled out his pocket watch. It was nearly five. He began sipping at a cup of weak coffee when the rider arrived. The freckle-faced young man climbed from the horse and made his way to the general's side and saluted. He had on a large slouch hat that reminded Johnston of a sombrero. Johnston fought to stifle a smile and waited.

"Sir, General Bragg sends his compliments," the man paused to see if Johnston had anything to say and then continued. "The general says he can't move as scheduled. It's just too damned dark, begging your pardon, sir. The roads are flooded from the rain, and I thought my horse would sink up to the ears just getting here."

"Tell General Bragg to just do the best he can," Johnston replied. There wasn't much he could say anyway. He knew if Bragg couldn't follow orders and move there was no one else in this army who could.

The courier turned to leave but paused, remembering something he had forgotten. "Sir, he did say he would begin moving at first light."

"Thank you," Johnston turned back to the fire. There was nothing left to do but wait for sunrise. He still had every intention of attacking Grant by noon.

Just after seven, the freckle-faced courier returned to report that Bragg's men were on the road now. Johnston thanked the man and continued to wait. There wasn't much else he could do at the moment. The waiting was beginning to grate on his nerves. At least the army was beginning to move into position.

They'd finally gotten the fire going enough to provide sufficient heat, and Johnston pulled a camp stool close to the fire. He stared into the fire and reminisced about the Mexican War. There was nothing in his life that suggested to him that he'd be leading an army of over forty thousand men into battle—nothing except his friendship with Jefferson Davis. He felt strange being the Confederate president's personal hero and wondered how he had warranted the attention.

Johnston heard the sound of horse hooves sucking in the muck and looked up to see a perturbed-looking General Leonidas Polk. Polk dismounted and splashed ahead through the muck to the campfire.

"This is a mess, General Johnston," said the former bishop, never bothering to salute. "I can't bring my corps on line with Bragg's corps stalled in the road ahead."

Johnston stood and extended his hand. Polk was taken aback. He realized he'd allowed his emotions to take control of him. He said, "I must apologize, sir."

Johnston held up a hand. "No apologies are necessary, Leonidas. Please sit."

Polk's large frame sat heavily on a camp stool and waited. Johnston offered him some coffee, but Polk declined. Johnston said, "Bragg has been delayed by the storm. It couldn't be helped. It was extremely dark last night, and he couldn't see to march his men up until the sun rose. Everything will be fine. We'll be in position to hit Grant by noon. I'm sure of it."

Polk sighed and calmed down. He wanted to be in position on schedule, but he also didn't want to receive the blame if they failed to begin the attack on time. He said, "Right, Sidney. Again, I apologize for entering your camp in such a state of distress."

"Not at all," Johnston smiled.

Polk couldn't help but admire the man. Johnston just seemed like a natural leader—a man that commanded respect. Now he understood what Davis loved about him.

A courier approached from the north. The boy practically leaped from his horse. He saluted the two general officers and said to Johnston, "Sir, General Hardee begs to report. He is still on line and awaiting word to advance. Sir, we can actually hear drums in the Federal camp. He is afraid if we wait much longer the enemy will be prepared for us."

Johnston smiled. "Give General Hardee my compliments, sir. Tell him we will all be on line shortly, and he will be ordered forward. Tell him the rain has things backed up a bit."

"Right, sir," the man was nodding. "He also wanted me to point out a problem we have."

"Problem?" Johnston asked.

"Yes, sir," the man rubbed his temple as he thought. "Let's see, what was the man's name? Ah, yes. General Gladden has been ordered to extend our line. General Bragg sent word that Gladden's brigade is in the rear of his corps, which means he will be the last to arrive."

Johnston began to shake his head. He looked at Polk and said, "Leonidas, why would General Bragg volunteer to give a brigade to Hardee that is in the rear of his entire corps?"

"Your guess is as good as mine, Sidney." Polk shook his head. He didn't like Bragg. There were very few people who did like the man. Polk was also harboring ill feelings for Bragg because he outranked him, and Beauregard had made Bragg the army's chief of staff so he could give orders to Polk. Leonidas Polk would never state this publicly of course.

"Young man," Johnston turned back to the courier, "please inform General Hardee that I will do everything in my power to get the rest of the army on line. Tell General Hardee I hope to give the order to advance by noon."

The courier was dismissed and had sense enough to know it. Polk watched Johnston as he stared into the fire, his head shaking.

Suddenly, Johnston brought his fist down into his open hand. The army was supposed to attack yesterday, and as of now, they were still not in position. He'd postponed the attack until this morning, and it was growing painfully clear that it still wasn't going to happen.

Johnston stood from the stool and said, "Excuse me, but I must ride back and see what is taking so long."

Polk watched the heavyset man and his staff climb on their horses and ride toward the south. He couldn't help but admire the man. There were many in the army who didn't think Johnston was capable of commanding an army, but at this moment, he had proven to Polk that he was the right man for the job.

Johnston rode south a few hundred yards and found Bragg sitting beneath a tree, surrounded by his staff. Protocol would have been for Johnston to dismount before talking to his subordinate. In the South, it wasn't proper for a gentleman to talk down to another gentleman. Johnston didn't have time for protocol. He had steadily grown frustrated with all the delays.

"General Bragg, why aren't your troops moving?" He asked.

"Sir," Bragg rose to his feet and pointed toward the road, "I'm waiting for the sun to dry the roads a bit. I can't possibly march my men through this quagmire."

"General Bragg," Johnston sounded more forceful than Bragg had ever heard him. "You will move your troops up at once. The entire army is stalled because of your command."

"Right," Bragg spun and began shouting at his staff officers. Johnston spun his horse and moved back toward the north. He returned to his temporary headquarters and waited the arrival of Bragg's corps. It wasn't long before they began to trudge by. Every man in the corps had a coat of mud up to their knees. Johnston took out his watch. They should be in position by noon, and with a little luck, Polk's corps would be on line soon after.

It was just after noon when the rear of Bragg's corps passed by. A few of Polk's men began to trickle past. An officer approached from the north and dismounted. It was Lieutenant David Urquhart, an aide to Louisiana Governor Thomas Overton Moore. The man had received a lieutenant's commission when he offered to serve as a volunteer aide to General Bragg.

Urquhart said, "General Bragg has a problem, sir."

"What's that?" Johnston asked. His voice betrayed his mood. He wondered what could possibly be wrong now.

"Sir, Ruggles's division is missing," Urquhart said. "That means we have six thousand misplaced men."

Johnston shook his head and said, "I thought Bragg's entire corps was on line."

"Everything but Ruggles's division," Urquhart shrugged. "General Bragg has sent couriers back searching for them."

"Hell, they've got to be close," Johnston was growing exasperated with the situation. He added, "How do you misplace six thousand men?"

"Not sure, sir," Urquhart replied. He felt uncomfortable standing here before the commanding general of the army and attempting to explain how a subordinate had lost an entire division.

"Have Bragg inform me the moment he finds them," Johnston nodded. "Polk should be showing up any moment now."

Johnston watched the lieutenant salute, climb back in the saddle, and ride northward. The day was turning into a nightmare, and the mental strain of trying to get something done was wearing on Johnston. He looked up and saw Captain Henry Brewster adjusting the saddle on his horse.

Johnston called out, "Captain Brewster, a word please."

Brewster spun around in surprise and hurried to his commander's side. He loved being a staff officer under the ranking field general in the Confederate army.

"Yes, sir?" he said.

Johnston began to rub at his temples. "Captain, I need you to send a telegram to President Davis. Tell him the rains have slowed our march, but I fully intend to attack Grant about four this afternoon."

Brewster glanced at his pocket watch. It was nearly one already, and Polk's corps was not on line yet. He started to say something, but Johnston interrupted. It was as if he read the captain's mind.

"I know it's late, Henry," Johnston shook his head. "As soon as Polk is on line, we're gonna hit Grant without waiting for Breckinridge's reserve corps."

"Right, sir," Brewster pulled a pencil from his pocket and began to scribble furiously in his journal.

Johnston suddenly realized that he'd had nothing to eat since this morning. He asked the camp cook to fix him something, and it didn't matter what that something was at the moment.

Eating seemed to give Johnston his second wind. He mounted his horse and eased out next to the road, where he offered encouragement to the passing troops. They were exhausted. Most weren't used to marching, and trudging through the mud made things more tiring.

Johnston turned to his staff and said, "Major Munford, please find General Bragg and ask him if he has found his missing division yet."

"Yes, sir," William Munford spurred the horse toward the north.

The man was back within ten minutes. He saluted and said, "Sir, Bragg says he has sent a courier to the rear, but he hasn't received any information on his missing division."

Johnston shook his head and asked, "What exactly is Mister Bragg doing at the moment?"

"Sitting under a tree waiting, sir," Munford almost laughed at how strange that sounded.

"Let me get this straight," Johnston paused and rubbed his temple. "He has six thousand men missing from his corps and he is just sitting at the front waiting while he sends couriers to locate them."

"That's about the gist of it," Munford nodded. "He did say that he would forward information to you as he receives it."

"Hell, I'll know before he does. I'm right here on the road." Johnston looked toward the sun, wishing he could stop it in the sky the way Joshua had done in the Old Testament. He took out his pocket watch and noted the time. The noble commander spun in the saddle, looked at Colonel Preston of his staff, and almost yelled.

"This is perfectly ridiculous! This is not war! Let's ride back and see if we can find them."

Colonel Preston glanced at Munford as they turned their horses toward the south. It was rare for Johnston to show emotion, but it was even more unusual for the man to lose his temper.

The general rode southward, followed by his staff, past Polk's men marching northward. Behind the marching men were some of Polk's supply wagons sitting idly in the road. Johnston spotted General Ruggles sitting on his horse beside a field full of men. Johnston spurred that way.

Johnston rode up to the fifty-two year old division commander and asked, "General Ruggles, why haven't you moved your men to the front with the rest of Bragg's Corps?"

Ruggles raised himself high in the saddle and exhaled slowly. He had an air of superiority about him that made him disagreeable. Johnston understood that Ruggles was a strict disciplinarian, perhaps more so than Braxton Bragg. It explained why Ruggles's men despised him so. Johnston thought about the story he'd heard about Ruggles making one of his staff officers sleep at night with his head on his desk in case Ruggles needed to send an order.

"Sir, my division is blocked by Polk's supply train." Ruggles motioned toward the wagons with a nod. "I've sent some of my staff through the woods to see if there is a way I can cut a road to the front."

Johnston shook his head. He couldn't believe Ruggles was actually contemplating cutting a new route through the woods. It would take several days to cut a road a mile through this wilderness. He spun the horse back toward the wagons. Within five minutes, he had Polk's wagons clear of the road for Ruggles to move his division past.

Johnston turned to Major Munford and said, "Tell General Ruggles he has a clear path to the front. Tell him I don't want to have to repeat the order for him to move up immediately."

"Right, sir," Munford dreaded giving that order to the grouchy old man. He was sure there would be some sarcastic remark in reply.

Johnston rode north past his old headquarters to the main line. He waited there until Polk's Corps had come on line. He saw Ruggles's men arriving and beginning to file past Polk's men to join Bragg's main line. He took out his pocket watch and noted the time. It was after four. There was no way the attack could get under way this afternoon. He would have to delay the assault until daylight tomorrow morning.

Johnston lowered his head and rode back down the Corinth-Pittsburg Road to his temporary headquarters site. There he found Beauregard and Bragg in what appeared to be a heated discussion. Johnston shook his head and wondered what the two could possibly be arguing about.

He climbed from the saddle and watched Breckinridge's troops file past as they headed north. At least Breckinridge was attempting to get on line as soon as possible. Johnston was weary from the day's events. He stood beside the horse a moment before approaching his two subordinates.

Bragg appeared to be in a sour mood, his one long, bushy eyebrow took a dip just above his nose. His eyes were wrinkled at the corners. Johnston could hear him complaining about the long march.

Johnston passed his horse's reins to Major Munford and walked toward the two men. He nodded at Bragg and asked, "Are you alright, Braxton?"

35

"Got a migraine," Bragg continued to frown. "Sir, this campaign has become a disaster. We've had delays getting the troops on line. My men seem to be the only troops we have that are disciplined enough for combat. There has been a total disregard for secrecy. Hell, Hardee's men have been firing all day to make sure the rain didn't foul their powder."

Beauregard was nodding in agreement. He added, "I sent one of my staff officers to silence a drummer in our camp. Turns out, he was in the Federal camp. If we can hear them drumming, you know they can hear us firing."

Bragg continued his rant. "My men have eaten up all their rations. We were supposed to have already whipped Grant by now, and we should be eating his rations."

Johnston couldn't believe what he was hearing. He looked at Beauregard and asked, "What are you saying, General?"

Beauregard looked at the ground for a moment before he spoke. "I'm saying that if we attack them in the morning, they'll be entrenched up to their eyes."

"Gentlemen, this is no time to lose your nerves," Johnston was still in shock that two of his best subordinates had lost heart for the fight.

"It has nothing to do with nerves," Beauregard quickly added. "The game is up. There will be no surprise. They have to know we're here by now."

Bragg said, "We must fall back to Corinth and regroup."

"What in hell for?" Johnston asked louder than he meant to.

"For all the reasons we've given you," Bragg replied. He couldn't believe Johnston wasn't agreeing with them. The man had always shown a tendency to follow his subordinates' advice.

"What do we do then, Braxton?" Johnston needed more of an excuse to quit the fight than what they'd told him.

Bragg was at a loss for words. He paused in thought and then turned to Beauregard for help.

Johnston turned to Major Munford, who had just finished handing the horses off to a couple of sentries. "Major, ride north and find General Polk. Tell him to come to my headquarters for an impromptu council of war."

The sun had set by the time Polk arrived for the meeting. A fire had been built, and Beauregard sat on a camp stool, using a drum for his writing desk. Polk dismounted, walked to the fire, and shook Johnston's hand. Breckinridge had arrived ahead of Polk, reporting that his men were moving on line now. He lay on a blanket near the fire.

Seeing Polk, Beauregard rose and began to wave his arms wildly. He said, "General Polk, you are responsible for all the delays in getting our army here, and with you rests the responsibility for us having to cancel our attack and return to Corinth."

Polk's face grew red. He stepped toward Beauregard, his large frame looking down on the small Frenchman. He said, "I've been under orders to follow Bragg's Corps, which sat inactive most of the morning. I had to move my corps aside to allow one of his divisions to pass through. I haven't received orders allowing me to pass Bragg's Corps. I don't understand how you can place the blame on me?"

Johnston stood away from the fire, just at the edge of the light, and listened carefully. Beauregard wore a gray cape over his uniform. He threw the cape on the ground and continued his rant.

36

"We have been behind schedule most of this march because of your actions. You ran your trains out in front of Hardee at Corinth, and today you have been sitting idly in the rear."

"I sat idly because I couldn't move ahead." Polk wasn't about to take the blame for this fiasco. Besides, he wondered why Beauregard thought the attack was being called off. His men had been coming on line for the past couple hours. No one had notified him the attack was cancelled, and if it was, why was the entire Confederate army on line in front of the Federal camps.

He added, "Bragg's troops blocked the road, and I believe, according to your marching orders, I was required to follow his troops."

Johnston stepped from the darkness and asked, "General Breckinridge, are your men in position?"

Breckinridge sat up on the blanket and turned to the only aide he'd brought with him. "Will?"

Lieutenant William Stevenson cleared his throat. "Sir, the last brigade is coming on line now, if they're not in position already."

Breckinridge lay back on the blanket and relaxed. Johnston stepped back into the shadows, his manly form outlining the night sky behind him.

Beauregard was still excited. He waved his arms over his head. His voice was still hoarse from the throat surgery. "We must fall back. To attack now would bring on disaster. They'll be entrenched to the eyes."

The officers heard several horses approaching and turned to see General Hardee and a few of his staff officers. The gray-haired Hardee dismounted and approached the group. He said, "Sorry I'm late. I didn't get the message until a few minutes ago."

Leonidas Polk found a camp stool and sat down, staring into the fire. He was obviously still upset about Beauregard's attack on him for the delays.

Bragg ignored Hardee. He'd been waiting for the opportunity to give his advice. He said, "We must fall back. Besides the delays, this army has shown no discipline during the march here. An attack will result in slaughter. You see, General Johnston, it is difficult for a disciplined attack to succeed, but this rabble we command can never win. The state of this army requires that we fall back and go on the defensive until we acquire officers capable of forming them into an efficient fighting force."

Beauregard quickly added, "In the battle tomorrow, we will be facing men just like ours—western men who know how to fight. This would be a desperate struggle under normal circumstances. If we could push them back to the river, they'll make a determined stand there and slaughter our men by the thousands. I see no way we can accomplish anything by fighting here tomorrow."

Johnston was shocked that Beauregard and Bragg were still talking about retreating without a fight. He looked at General Polk, wondering what he was thinking. The man sat on the camp stool, elbows on his knees and chin on his fists, staring into the fire.

Beauregard continued dominating the council of war. "The enemy knows we're here. Men have been noisy, some firing their rifles. They have to be expecting us. If we go in there tomorrow, we'll find them entrenched, and we'll suffer a bloody repulse.

Besides, General Bragg's men have eaten all their rations. They've consumed five days rations in two days. Gentlemen, we must abandon the campaign."

Johnston stepped from the shadows and asked, "General Polk, what is your opinion?"

Polk looked up with a start. He'd been listening to the conversation but was surprised that Johnston wanted his opinion so soon. He thought they would want to hear from him last.

"Sir, my men are in good shape. My men are ready," he replied. "I think it would destroy the morale of this army to retreat without a fight. Half the army will probably lose confidence and desert. No, sir, the attack must proceed."

Johnston nodded and asked, "How are your men on food, General Breckinridge?"

Again Breckinridge sat up on the blanket. He turned to Johnston and said, "My men have plenty of food."

Polk added, "I can have my men share rations with General Bragg's men. We have more than enough for a day's fight."

Bragg smirked at Polk. He wondered if Polk was insinuating that Bragg's men weren't as disciplined after all since they'd eaten all their rations in two days.

Beauregard ignored Breckinridge and Polk. He said, "General Hardee's men have made the most noise, cheering and firing their rifles less than a mile from the Federal camps. Men have been beating drums and blowing bugles. I rode down the line today encouraging the men, and I jumped a deer. Some men cheered the deer and others took shots at it. I couldn't force those men to keep quiet. The enemy must know we're here. We must fall back now, if for no other reason than that."

Hardee stepped forward. The fire reflected off his forehead and almost-white hair. His eyes reminded Johnston of an elderly oriental man's eyes. They were narrow, and crow's feet spread from the corners. He resented Beauregard placing the blame on his men.

He said, "General Beauregard, I have captured a Federal surgeon today who reports that Grant has returned to his headquarters in Savannah. Now, if the commanding general were considering an attack tomorrow at daylight, why would he leave the field and travel ten miles upriver?"

Beauregard ignored him. He turned to the large man at the edge of the darkness. "General, please consider retreating. There is no possible way the attack can succeed now."

Johnston stepped into the light again. All his subordinates and their staff officers were looking to him awaiting a decision. He felt the weight of his responsibilities resting on his shoulders. He had the power to order men to their deaths or to retreat and save their lives. He'd been letting his subordinates push him around since he'd taken command, and that had accomplished nothing but failures. Johnston decided it was time to take command. He spoke with a firmness he'd never used before.

"Gentlemen, we will attack at first light tomorrow. I place my faith on the iron dice of battle. The enemy is just sitting there with their backs to a river, just begging to be attacked. I'm gonna oblige."

He watched Beauregard's chin drop on his chest. The meeting was over. Johnston felt good having finally stood up to his subordinates and making a decision he knew in his heart to be the correct one.

After the generals had all left to rejoin their commands, Johnston stood near the fire with his chin held high. He turned to Colonel Preston, and with his voice filled with emotion, he said, "I would fight them if they were a million. They can't possibly make a stronger front between those two creeks. The more men they crowd in there, the more targets we'll have. Our men won't be able to miss."

Preston said, "I was happy to see General Polk take your side."

Johnston nodded in agreement. "Leonidas is a true soldier and a great friend. I would have hit them this afternoon if I would have had another hour of daylight. We'll let the men rest tonight and deal with Mister Grant in the morning."

Major Munford had just returned from the front on a minor mission and approached Johnston. He asked, "What's the situation?"

"I've ordered an attack at daylight tomorrow," Johnston replied. "I intend to hammer 'em."

Munford was shocked to see Johnston so full of emotion. It wasn't in the man's nature. He'd never even heard him raise his voice before.

Johnston walked over and laid a gum blanket next to a large oak tree and lay down. He placed a wool blanket on a large root to use for a pillow and covered himself with another. His personal physician, Doctor Yandell, walked over and made a bed beside him.

Yandell lay down and stared through the tree limbs at the stars. He noticed Johnston was looking at the sky also. He asked, "Is everything alright, sir?"

"I'm thoroughly disappointed with General Beauregard," Johnston said in a quiet tone. "I've allowed him to pretty much run the army up to date, but now that we are on the brink of battle, the man seems to have lost heart."

Yandell pressed Johnston. "You don't put much stock in his opinion?"

"It's not Beauregard," Johnston replied. "He is still suffering from the effects of his surgery. Therefore, his opinion must be disregarded. I've come to an important decision tonight."

"What's that?" Yandell asked.

Johnston cleared his throat and whispered, "I'm having General Beauregard remain in the rear and forward troops to the front while I command on the field. We've had too many reverses for me to risk another. We must succeed tomorrow."

Johnston stared through the tree limbs at the sky. Sleep wouldn't come easily tonight. He'd allowed Beauregard to run the entire campaign up until now. The man had changed his plans to hit Grant's left flank, pushing him into the swamps to the northwest. Now the Confederate army would be forced to push Grant into the river because Beauregard had altered the alignment. Johnston had finally put his foot down with his subordinates. Beauregard was losing his nerve and had convinced most of the others the attack was destined to fail. Johnston would attack Grant tomorrow, and there was no way they'd talk him out of it.

Johnston said to Yandell, "There is no way we're turning back without a fight. The hopes of eight million people rest on this movement."

"I agree with you, sir," Yandell tried to change the subject, hoping he could get Johnston's mind off the battle so he could get some rest. "Tomorrow, you'll be fighting against the same men you commanded out west. The old army seems like a thousand years away now."

"Those were some of the most enjoyable times of my life," Johnston smiled to himself. "I miss the West Coast and that beautiful blue water of the Pacific Ocean. Have to wonder if I'll ever see it again."

Yandell laughed. "Well, if we win this war, you may return there as a foreign ambassador."

"I was torn when the war began," Johnston's voice began to betray emotion. "I wasn't sure which side to choose. I mean, I'd spent my entire adulthood in the army I'm battling against now. That's not an easy thing to rush into. Texas seceding pushed me a step closer to resigning, but you'll never guess what finalized my decision."

"Jeff Davis being president would be my guess." Yandell thought about how much Davis worshiped Johnston.

"I like Jeff; don't get me wrong," Johnston's voice became lower as he spoke. "The Federal government never gave me the benefit of the doubt. They automatically assumed I'd go with the South. They sent Edwin Sumner to relieve me under an assumed name. That really hurt that they'd be so deceitful. After all those years, and that's the way they thank someone."

"I wasn't aware of that," Yandell understood Johnston's sadness.

"At least in the South a man's honor and conduct as a gentleman has some meaning." Johnston shook his head. "I don't know what's happened with those people up north. They've allowed greed to overcome them. This entire war is about nothing but money."

"All wars are about money, sir." Yandell said. As a physician, Yandell had a hard time understanding why there were people like Johnston—people who could enjoy the army. There was nothing about killing and maiming other men that he found likable.

Johnston closed his eyes and reminisced about the farewell party back in California. It was at Captain Winfield Hancock's house, one of his subordinates. Hancock's best friend Lewis Armistead of Virginia was there. This war had forced the two men to face each other in battle. Richard Garnett was present. Everyone was extremely sad about the state of things. Friends were forced to part ways and fight each other for what they believed in. He'd never forget Armistead with tears running down his cheeks as he told Hancock and his wife, Elmira, goodbye. He'd actually said he wished God would strike him down if he was forced to raise a hand against his best friend. *There'll be a lot of good men struck down before this war is over, he thought.* Thinking about that night, Albert Sidney Johnston would finally fall asleep.

Johnston slept fairly well that night considering he was sleeping on the cold ground in the cool spring air. He was up well before dawn. He'd sent out orders that no fires were to be lit, but his headquarters was far enough in the rear to prevent the enemy from seeing it. He sat on a camp stool, patiently waiting for a cup of coffee.

An orderly handed him the hot cup and said, "Careful, sir; it's hotter than a tin roof in August."

Johnston thanked the man and began to blow the liquid inside. He attempted to take a sip, but it was still too hot. He was shivering from the cold. His poor men were out here without a fire or a cup of warm coffee. That pained him because they were his men.

He heard a commotion on the road and turned to see Beauregard and Bragg approaching, followed by their staffs. Bragg looked more haggard than usual. Both men approached Johnston and saluted. Always a gentleman, Johnston stood and extended his hand.

Both men took a camp stool and sat close to Johnston. Beauregard's voice was extremely raspy this morning from sleeping outdoors. The two commanders were quite a contrast sitting together. Johnston was tall and powerfully built. Beauregard was short, which didn't bother him at all because his hero Napoleon was only five feet five inches tall.

Bragg said, "I've been out all night looking for my missing ration train, but I've yet to find any sign of it. My men can't fight without rations, sir."

"Did General Polk not send you some rations?" Johnston asked.

Bragg smirked. "I doubt the man has enough rations for his own corps."

Johnston lowered his head, closed his eyes, and began to rub his prominent brow. "General Bragg, you'll just have to do the best you can."

Beauregard cleared his throat. "Sir, we must fall back. They'll be entrenched by now. They must know we're here. We haven't enough rations for the men. It can't be helped."

Johnston was shaking his head as he listened. He was growing tired of all this talk of retreat from his subordinates.

"We can fall back to Corinth and wait for Van Dorn's troops to arrive." Beauregard exhibited no signs of letting up his argument. "We can attempt to attack Grant when he moves south."

Johnston looked at the two generals and said, "Gentlemen, we are going into battle today. There is no point in further discussion."

"But…" Beauregard began to argue again but stopped when rifle fire suddenly broke out to the north. All three of the men's heads spun in that direction, but there was nothing to see in the darkness.

Johnston stood from the stool and said, "Gentlemen, the battle has begun. It's too late to change our dispositions now."

Johnston walked to his horse and climbed on. He looked back and said, "General Beauregard, I want you to stay in the rear today and forward all the reinforcements you can to the front."

Beauregard nodded.

Johnston looked north into the darkness and said, "I'll be at the front."

He nudged his horse, "Fire-eater," forward down the dark road toward his destiny. It wasn't long before he reached a line of Confederate troops. Their commander was also mounted and waiting in the road. Johnston asked, "What troops are these?"

"Thirteenth Louisiana Infantry," the officer called out. "I'm Colonel Randall Gibson commanding."

41

Johnston smiled into the darkness. Gibson was a good friend of Johnston's son. He reached out and patted Gibson on the shoulder. "You be careful today, Randall."

"Yes, sir," Randall replied. "It sounds like the ball has opened."

Johnston stared ahead into the darkness in thought. He spoke more to himself than to Gibson. "We must win a victory today."

He looked around at his staff and said, "Gentlemen, tonight we will water our horses in the Tennessee River."

Part II

"Attack him where he is unprepared, appear where you are not expected."

Sun Tzu

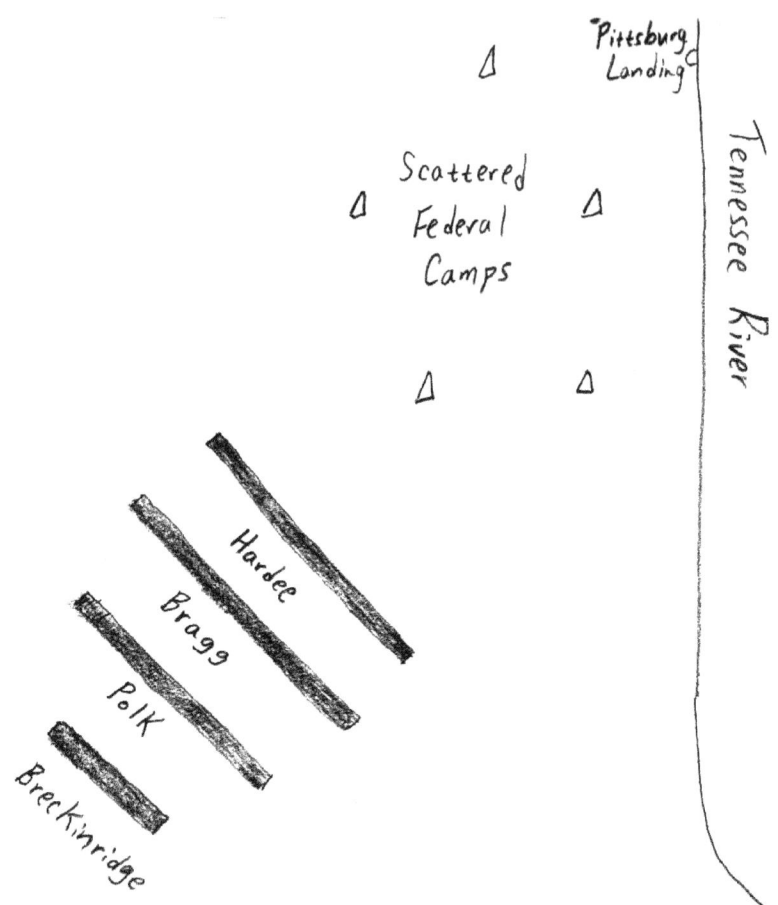

The alignment of the Confederate troops, each corps stacked behind the other was based on Napoleon's battle plan at Waterloo.

USA

Colonel Appler of the 53rd Ohio Infantry took out his watch and noted the time. It was just after six. Firing could be heard to the south of his position and appeared to be growing in intensity. He had been worried about an attack since yesterday. He pondered what he should do. He decided it would be better to be safe and bring the regiment on line.

As the men began to form for battle, Appler turned to Lieutenant Fulton and said, "Lieutenant, ride to Sherman's headquarters and tell him there is heavy firing just beyond my camp. Ask him what he thinks we should do."

Fulton saluted and climbed on his horse. He smiled to himself as he rode away. It was growing painfully clear that Appler was too nervous to command a regiment. The man didn't realize that his men were making fun of him behind his back.

Appler paced behind his battle line until Fulton returned. The firing to the south began to ebb, and Appler began to worry that he may have jumped the gun again. He looked up in time to see Fulton galloping back with a smile on his face.

Fulton didn't bother to wait until he got all the way back to Appler before he began to shout. "Colonel Appler, General Sherman says to take your damned regiment back to Ohio. There is no enemy nearer than Corinth."

The entire regiment burst into laughter and began breaking ranks without permission. Appler was embarrassed, but he was also still worried. He walked over to Lieutenant Dawes and asked, "What do you think?"

"I'm not sure, sir," Dawes replied. He felt sorry for Appler. The man meant well.

A horseman approached from the regiment's rear. It was Colonel Hildebrand, Appler's brigade commander. He quickly dismounted, ignored Dawes and Appler's, salutes, and asked, "What's the firing about, Jesse?"

"Not sure, sir," Appler shook his head. "I've notified General Sherman, and he says there are no enemy troops nearer than Corinth."

"I just left Sherman's headquarters," Hildebrand said as he rubbed his chin. Unlike most men in this army, he had no mustache or beard but wore a bummer with a large bugle sewn on the front. The man would be sixty-two years old next month. "He says he has received reports that there are only a couple regiments of Confederate cavalry and infantry between us and Corinth."

"Sounds like they are all within a mile of here," Appler shook his head. He reached up and scratched his nose. Hildebrand couldn't help but notice the man's hand was shaking. Appler continued, "That's a lot of firing."

"General Sherman is of the opinion that they are here watching us so they can report back to Corinth when we begin to advance," Hildebrand patted Appler on the arm.

Appler asked, "How does he know what's in our front?"

"Guess he has intelligence from somewhere. I don't believe he would just pull those numbers out of thin air." Hildebrand shrugged. "I'll send a reconnaissance force out in the morning and see what I can find out for myself."

"Right," Appler watched the old man struggle to climb back on his horse. He wasn't sure they would make it until tomorrow morning before the Confederates actually attacked.

He caught sight of movement in the tree line to the south. Small groups of Federal soldiers began to move across the field through his camp. Appler walked out to meet them. Some were limping, others holding an arm, and one man had a white handkerchief wrapped around his forehead. There appeared to be blood on the rag.

A young boy came past, holding his right arm across his stomach with his left hand. Lieutenant Dawes asked, "You fellas shooting at squirrels this morning?"

"Yeah," the boy said sarcastically, "squirrels with rifles. There are Rebs out there thicker than fleas on a dog's back. You'll see soon enough; they're coming this way."

Appler ordered the regiment back into line of battle. The men seemed more eager to form up since seeing the wounded passing by to the rear.

Appler stood just in front of his line with Lieutenant Dawes. Both men looked to the right and saw General Sherman and his staff entering the field from the tree line. Sherman stopped and raised his field glasses to his eyes. At that moment, a Confederate skirmish line emerged from the trees just a few yards south of Sherman.

Lieutenant Dawes yelled to Lieutenant Ball, who was on the right of the line near the general. "Ball, Sherman will be killed!"

Lieutenant Ball spun and saw the Confederate line. He began to race toward Sherman, yelling, "General, look to your right!"

Sherman saw the Confederate's bringing their rifles to their shoulders and dropped the field glasses. He yelled, "My God, we're being attacked!"

The general instinctively threw his hand up to protect himself at the same moment the gray line opened fire. His orderly, Sergeant Thomas Holliday, was struck in the head, dying instantly, and crashed to the ground with a thud. The Confederates were firing buck and ball, which consisted of a bullet and three small buckshot. One of the buckshot struck Sherman in his extended hand.

He quickly spun his horse and raced toward Appler. As he rode past, he yelled, "Appler, hold your position. I will support you!"

Appler watched Sherman continue riding past and toward the rear. It unnerved him to receive orders to hold his position from a man who was racing for the rear. Sherman had a look of panic on his face as he rode past, and Appler doubted he would see the man again.

Appler moved behind his line and stared hard through the trees. On the hill to the southwest, he could see Confederate cannons unlimbering as a long gray line advanced through the ravine toward his camp. It seemed as if thousands of enemy soldiers were swarming through the forest directly at his lone regiment. He spun around to see teamsters, cooks, and sutlers headed for the rear. He also noticed a good many of his soldiers going along with them. Appler decided at that moment that he had made a mistake coming here. He would have given anything to be back in Ohio just now.

CSA

Brigadier General Patrick Cleburne watched his men move through the white frost. The cool spring air made him shiver. Counting the artillery in his brigade, he commanded over 2,700 men. His men were advancing up the Corinth Road, but he was in the woods to the right of the line, attempting to stay connected with Wood's brigade.

The Confederate line topped a hill and began to move down into a ravine. Ahead, through the trees in a field, Cleburne could see a line of Federal soldiers behind their tents. He rode back to the road and found Captain Trigg.

"Bring one of your howitzers up here and see if you can wake the enemy up with a few shells," he said.

"Right, sir." Captain Trigg spun his horse toward the rear.

Cleburne rode back into the ravine toward his two right regiments. It was obvious there were nearly a thousand men on top of the hill in his front. He would have to send his men through bales of hay and Sibley tents to reach the Federal position.

He rode to his left and found that his brigade had split in two. His left four regiments had been forced to skirt a swamp at the bottom of the ravine and continue toward the north. This meant that Cleburne wasn't going to be attacking a thousand Federals on this hill with his full brigade but merely eight hundred men in these two regiments.

Pat Cleburne didn't have time to worry with that just now. He rode back to his right. He turned his horse into the stream to cross with his men. The horse slipped down the steep, muddy embankment. The animal attempted to regain its balance but reared and fell onto its rider. If the ground hadn't been so soft from the rain, it might have seriously injured Cleburne.

He struggled to his feet while one of his staff officers grabbed the horse by the reins. Cleburne's new gray uniform was covered in mud. He waded across the stream and up the steep bank. It was so steep that he had to grab onto roots in order to pull himself up. His men were there waiting for the order.

Cleburne looked across the field toward the Federal line on the hill. He was angry that he'd been ingloriously thrown in the mud by his horse. He shouted, "Fix bayonets!"

He loved the sound of eight hundred bayonets being thrown on rifle barrels. He waited a moment to rethink what he was about to do. It was obvious that the enemy rifles and cannons covered the field in his front. It would be a desperate fight, but what choice did he have at the present? His orders were to strike the enemy in his front, and that was what he decided to do. He yelled, "Charge!"

The line sprang up and began moving toward the clearing. They broke into a run as they cleared the thick woods. The Sixth Mississippi surged ahead on the left and the Twenty-Third Tennessee on the right. The lines became broken as they encountered the tents and hay bales. As they were about to clear the obstacles, the Federal line opened fire. Men began to fall all down the line. The Confederates stopped in mid-charge in shock. It was their first time under fire, and they spun and raced down the hill as fast as they had charged up.

Cleburne's aide had handed him his horse, and he rode forward to meet the panicked men. The Twenty-Third Tennessee raced right past him, ignoring his pleading for them to stop and reform. There was no sense in chasing them. He turned the horse and met the Sixth Mississippi. The trees in the ravine gave them a feeling of security. They stopped in the ravine and listened to Cleburne.

Cleburne rode among them and said, "Boys, don't be discouraged. That is not the first charge that was ever repulsed. We must give them the cold steel to move them. Now let's go back up there and take that hill. Forward! Charge!"

The Sixth Mississippi surged from the ravine again. They were alone, without any aide, and they had begun with just four-hundred and twenty-five men. There were still nearly a thousand men waiting on top of that hill. Cleburne followed behind them into the edge of the field. There was probably no way they would succeed, but still he had to try.

He watched the line race forward through the tents and hay bales again. Every one of them was screaming like a banshee. As they cleared the tents this time, Cleburne could actually hear the Federal Colonel, a man he would later learn was named Appler, yell, "Retreat, men, and save yourselves!"

The man then turned and demonstrated the best way to do just that. The regiment raced away from the hill. The charge was over, but there were still cannons and infantry on the next hill, and they were still putting a severe fire into the Sixth Mississippi. They soon gave up the hard-won hill and fell back to the ravine. Of the 425 men Cleburne had sent up the hill in the Sixth Mississippi, only 60 managed to return to the ravine. The hill was covered with their dead and wounded. Colonel Thornton and Major Lowry were both wounded. Cleburne was proud of the courage exhibited by this one regiment, but there was nothing else he could do with so few men. He ordered them to pull back and reform and spun his horse to the left to catch up with the rest of his brigade.

He arrived around the morass in time to see the Second Tennessee Infantry advancing from the forest into a field of dry grass. The Federals were positioned in the tree line across the way up a fairly steep grade. The sun was shining through the trees by now, and the bayonets and gun barrels glistened in the morning light. Clearing the undergrowth, the regiment opened fire and then charged through the battle smoke they had just created.

Halfway across the field, the Federal line returned fire. Cleburne saw both Major William Doak and his horse fall to the ground. The regiment was shattered by the fire and fell back to the tree line. Colonel Bate immediately reformed his men and led them back into the field against the Federals posted on the hill.

The regiment got almost as far this time as before. The Federals blasted away again, and this time Colonel Bate went down. Several men brought their major and colonel back to the shelter of the trees.

General Cleburne rode to where they lay and dismounted. William Bate lay against a tree with tears running down his cheeks and into his beard. Cleburne asked, "Are   you   seriously   wounded,   William?"

"It's a broken leg," Bate wiped at the tears on his cheek. "My brother was just killed by my side. He's lying back there in that damned field."

Cleburne patted Bate on the shoulder. "There's nothing more we can do now. Just relax, and we'll get you to the rear. Tennessee can never mourn a nobler band than you led here today, Colonel."

Bate nodded as he continued to wipe at the tears on his face.

Cleburne turned and asked one of the soldiers squatting beside Major Doak, "How bad is it?"

"Hit nine times, sir," the young man looked up at Cleburne. "I'm afraid he's a goner."

"Don't give up just yet," Cleburne patted the man on the shoulder. "I want you to get some men and get Doak and Bate to the rear. Find them a surgeon. Can you handle that?"

"Yes, sir," the man looked proud that Cleburne would entrust him with this much responsibility.

Cleburne rode on to where the Fifteenth Arkansas was attempting to reform. Federal artillery shells ripped through the trees above his head. He ignored the incoming rounds and falling limbs. He stopped in front of Lieutenant Colonel Archibald Patton and dismounted. He asked, "What's the situation, Arch?"

"It's damned bad, sir," Patton shook his head and looked at the ground. "I lost Major Harris. He advanced out in front of the entire regiment with his pistol, blazing away before they shot him dead. I've lost a lot of good men. I think I'm the only field officer that's still alive."

"Never mind that," Cleburne took Patton's hand. "You've done your duty, and that's all anyone can ask of you. Now finish reforming your men and wait until I get back."

Patton frowned and asked, "Where are you going, Pat?"

"I've got to find General Hardee and report my situation to him." Cleburne climbed back on his horse and rode south through the trees.

As Cleburne rode to the rear, he began to reflect on what he'd learned here today. He had assaulted the Federals as soon as he found them, and that hadn't worked out very well. He had been flanked by the enemy on both sides. If he ever led another assault against an enemy, he planned on flanking them from their position instead of wasting men in a massive frontal assault.

He found Hardee back down the road about a quarter of a mile. Hardee rode up to a tree where a Confederate soldier stood hiding. Cleburne rode that way in time to overhear part of the conversation.

Hardee was chastening the man. "From Texas?" he asked. "Why would a brave Texan be back here hiding in the rear?"

The man never missed a beat. He replied in a strong Texas drawl, "Well, you back here, ain't ya?"

There wasn't much Hardee could say to that. He began to shake his head when he saw Cleburne approaching. "How goes it, Pat?" he asked.

Cleburne saluted and shook his head. "It's damned bad. I hit the Federal line with everything I've got, but we were flanked on both sides. I have my brigade reforming now, but I'm not sure they're gonna be worth much. The Sixth Mississippi hasn't got sixty healthy men left. It's the same throughout my brigade."

"You had over twenty-five hundred men just thirty minutes ago, Pat," Hardee looked confused. "Surely, you got enough left to continue."

"Not at the moment," Cleburne said. "I doubt I have a thousand men left, and they're scattered and disorganized to hell and back."

"I see," Hardee shook his head. "Just round up all these stragglers you can find back here in the rear and then attach them to what you get reformed. Move back up when you got a good enough force to engage with again."

"Right," Cleburne saluted and began to ride past Hardee.

"One more thing," Hardee motioned for Cleburne to stop. "It's war, Pat. Men die; it's not your fault."

Cleburne nodded and rode on past Hardee.

USA

Ulysses Grant had just sat down at the table in the dining room of Misses Cherry's home. She was busy preparing breakfast for him and his staff officers. He sat with a civilian coat that contained no insignia, out of respect for her southern sympathies. Strange as it was, she respected this Federal commander. He was always polite, and regardless of the rumors she'd heard about him, he'd never drank in front of her. He'd even insisted on her introducing him to her mother and sisters.

Misses Cherry placed a cup of hot coffee down in front of Grant. He thanked her and raised it to his lips to blow on the hot liquid inside. The man was about to take a sip when he heard cannon fire coming from up the river. The cup froze an inch from his mouth. He quickly placed it back on the table and listened. There was more cannon fire. Grant looked around the table at his staff and said, "Gentlemen, the ball has opened. Get your things, and let's be off."

There was a mad scramble around the house as his staff went racing for their effects. Grant stood from the table, apologized to Misses Cherry, grabbed his crutches, and headed for the door. His staff helped him down the terraces to the river. The steamboat *Minnehaha* had just pulled alongside of Grant's boat. Grant watched his orderly, Private Edward Trembly, lead his horse onto the boat for him. Grant struggled along behind on his crutches. They helped him up to the second deck and found him a chair.

Rawlins pulled a chair up beside Grant and sat down. Grant said, "The Confederates may have attacked Crump's Landing. Lew Wallace is alone there with his one division."

"Sir, while we wait for the pressure to build," Rawlins nodded toward the stacks leading from the boilers, "should I write any orders for Nelson's division?"

"Right," Grant nodded as he pulled a cigar from his pocket. He reached for a lucifer and struck it. After a few puffs on the cigar, he said, "Tell General Nelson to begin marching his division down the east bank toward the sound of the battle. We'll ferry his division across to the battlefield when he gets there."

He watched Rawlins as he scribbled furiously. When he had finished, he began to rise.

"Wait," Grant said. "Send a message to General Buell and tell him I apologize for not being able to meet him here as planned. Tell him there seems to be a major battle going on upriver. That'll be all."

Rawlins wrote out the second message and delivered it to Private Trembly to deliver to a courier. He returned and sat beside Grant. If the man was nervous, he hid it well. Rawlins asked, "Sir, what do you think?"

Grant puffed on the cigar and eyed Rawlins a moment. "I'm not worried about Pittsburg Landing. Lew Wallace is the one that could be in trouble. The bulk of our army is at Pittsburg. We have a lot of provisions at Crump's Landing and few men to guard 'em."

Both men looked up in time to see a short woman coming up the stairs toward them. The lady was rather plain looking with dark hair tucked neatly in a bun at the back of her head. She seemed to be moving toward Grant.

She walked up to the general and asked, "Are you General Grant?"

"Yes, Ma'am," Grant replied.

"Excuse me for intruding," she said. "I'm Ann Wallace, wife of William Wallace. I was on board the *Minnehaha*. Would it be alright if I continue to Pittsburg Landing aboard your boat?"

"That'd be fine," Grant replied. Ann Wallace wasn't anything like he had pictured her in his mind. William had described her as beautiful. The young woman before him wasn't ugly; she just didn't fit the image Grant had in his mind. William was tall and lanky, and this woman was short and rather compact.

Ann Wallace began to fidget with the lace gloves covering her dainty hands. "My husband has been sick and, because of his sense of duty, would never allow me to come and tend to him. I found it to be my duty to come here. What I'm trying to say is I don't want you to punish my Will, because he has no idea that I came here."

"Not at all," Grant waved her off. "I've placed General Wallace in command of General Smith's division while he recuperates from a nasty fall. I'm proud to have your husband available at a time like this."

"Thank you, sir," Ann Wallace nodded.

Grant added, "I hope your trip here has been pleasant."

"Immensely enjoyable," Ann smiled. "All the soldiers on the *Minnehaha* found out I was a general's wife and picked flowers for me at every stop. I haven't received as much attention since Will was trying to win my hand in marriage."

Ann excused herself and took a seat a little ways away as the boat surged into motion. The small, twin-stacked steamboat struggled against the current. It was nearly eight when they reached Crump's Landing. Grant stood on the crutches and made his way to the railing around the second deck.

Brigadier General Lew Wallace was on a steamboat tied at the landing and waited on the second deck of that boat also. The *Tigress* pulled up alongside the other boat. Ropes were thrown from one boat to the other to steady them, and the steam engine shut off.

Grant leaned across the railing and said, "Have you heard firing?"

"Yes, sir, all morning long. It's been going on since daylight." Wallace scratched at his thick, black beard. His mustache and beard were so thick and dark that you could barely tell where the man's mouth was.

Grant stared into Wallace's dark eyes. "What do you make of it?"

Wallace pulled off his wide-brimmed hat and rubbed sweat from his forehead. He said, "It's got to be a major battle of some kind."

Grant looked at the small man with the tiny head and knife-like nose. He said, "Hold your division in readiness to move at a moment's notice. I'm going on down to Pittsburg Landing and find out what's going on."

"Right," Wallace shouted back as the *Tigress* restarted the steam engine. The ropes were quickly untied, a brass bell rang, and the boat resumed its laborious journey against the current.

They reached Pittsburg Landing just before nine. The firing had grown to a constant roar now. Grant stood on the crutches and made his way over to Ann Wallace. He said, "Misses Wallace, I'm gonna have to ask you to wait here on the boat. General Wallace will no doubt be at the front with his division by now, and it will be impossible for you to find him under these conditions. You'll be safe back here until we can find out what is going on."

Ann didn't make any attempt to argue. From the sound of things, the boat was as far as she wanted to go at the moment.

The boat pulled up to the landing, and a plank was run out. Private Trembly led Grant's horse across the plank and waited for the general. Grant hobbled across the plank on the crutches as members of his staff attempted to support him the best they could.

Trembly helped Grant into the saddle and then tied the crutches to the side of the horse. Grant turned the horse and rode up the muddy hill to the plateau above. His staff trailed along behind.

They rode south through masses of retreating men. There were a lot of walking wounded, but what worried Grant the most was the panic-stricken men who should have been at the front fighting.

Grant rode south, out the Corinth-Pittsburg Landing Road toward the sound of battle. A half mile out, he ran into General William Wallace, who had his division on line.

Wallace saw Grant approaching and saluted. Grant ignored the salute and asked, "What's the situation, Will?"

Wallace shook his head. "It's a general assault. I'm sure it's the entire Confederate army or it would have been over by now. I'm about to move my command forward to reinforce General Sherman. I think he has bore the brunt of the fighting so far. He sent word he was being forced back and wanted me to move up and join him."

"Right," Grant said and turned toward Rawlins. "Captain Rawlins, ride back to the landing and have Captain Baxter take the *Tigress* back downstream to Crump's Landing. Tell him to have Lew Wallace move his division here to reinforce the army."

Rawlins saluted and spun his horse for the rear. Grant turned back to Will Wallace and said, "You may continue, General Wallace. I'm gonna ride forward and see how Cump is faring."

CSA

Sergeant George Dixon stood in line just south of a field the locals called Spain Field. The twenty-four-year-old sergeant was a member of Company A, 21st Alabama Infantry Regiment. He'd been a steamboat engineer before the war and had lived in Mobile.

The man was proud of his tailor made uniform and wore expensive rings on his hands. He'd been a member of the Washington Light Militia unit in Mobile before the war, which became Company A. He shifted from one leg to the other as he waited impatiently for orders to advance.

Brigadier General Adley Hogan Gladden rode to the front of the line and dismounted. The heavyset man stared ahead across the field through the fog that hung close to the ground. There was no use because he couldn't make out anything across the way.

Dixon admired Gladden. The man was fifty-one years old, and his hair and short, cropped beard were beginning to gray. His hair was beginning to recede, and his eyes drooped at the corners. Dixon liked the way he carried himself. The way he held his head back made him look rather distinguished. Born in South Carolina, Gladden had moved to Louisiana and become a cotton broker before the war.

The thing that Dixon most respected about him was the fact that he was a hero of the Mexican War and a veteran of the Seminole War. His reputation for bravery in those two wars was what caused his men to respect him so much.

Dixon remembered the little speech Gladden had given the men before they advanced this morning. Gladden had said, "I would rather be forced to live in the Sahara Desert than surrender our nation to the damned Yankees."

While Gladden scanned the field to their front, Dixon pulled the twenty dollar gold piece from his pocket. He thought about the romantic moment when his fiancée, Queenie Bennett, had given him the piece for good luck. Dixon placed the coin back in his pocket and waited.

The men around him were grumbling because they'd eaten all their rations the day before. Some complained about the lack of sleep and how they would all catch cold from sleeping on the wet ground last night. The sun was just getting high enough in the sky to cast an occasional ray among the men.

A courier galloped past the line of men and stopped beside General Gladden. He gave a sloppy salute and said, "Sir, General Bragg sends his compliments and says for you to wait for General Chalmers's Brigade to arrive on your right flank before advancing any further."

To Gladden this was an insult. He wondered how Bragg could insinuate that he couldn't find the Federal troops on his own. He said, "Inform General Bragg that I have as keen a scent for Yankee's as General Chalmers."

The courier didn't know what to say to that statement but simply nodded, spun the horse, and raced toward the rear.

Gladden turned back to his regimental commanders and announced, "Prepare your men to move forward. I'm gonna ride ahead and see what's on the other side of this field. Don't wait for me; just come on up when everybody is ready."

He climbed on his horse as he heard the colonels behind him shouting orders to the brigade. He eased the horse ahead into the field, followed by a couple of his staff officers. Halfway across the field, he could see some Federal tents beyond the tree line ahead. He wondered where the Yankees were.

Gladden strained his eyes along the fencerow on the other side of the field. He could see shadows there. The Federal infantry was drawn up in line defending their camps. He was just about to pull on his horse's reins to turn back when cannons opened fire to his left front. There was no time for Gladden to react. A shell exploded overhead, and a piece of shrapnel ripped through his left arm at the shoulder. He was thrown from his horse by the blow, crashing to the ground with a thud. His staff could hear the wind being knocked out of him by the fall.

His staff officers quickly gathered around him. His left arm was attached to his shoulder by nothing more than a thin shred of skin. They quickly decided that the arm must be amputated on the spot before moving the severely-wounded man. Captain Smith took out a pocket knife and completed the removal of the arm.

The horrible task completed, they lifted him the best they could and began to carry him back toward the south. He groaned in agony when they moved him. They carried him back to Corinth to Beauregard's headquarters at the Fish Pond House, where he would die six days later.

Sergeant Dixon saw his commander being carried to the rear. One of the staff officers yelled to Colonel Daniel Adams, "You're in command now, sir. General Gladden is wounded."

Adams nodded. There was only one thing left to do and that was to advance across the field and push the Federals back toward the river.

The brigade entered the field and, with a yell, charged ahead. They could see very little through the fog, but that didn't prevent the Federals from opening fire. Just as they began to clear the fog, another volley was fired from the Union line.

George Dixon felt as though a mule had just kicked him in the right thigh. He crashed to the ground, and his rifle went sailing ahead of him. Grabbing his leg, he rolled around in agony. When he was finally able, he rolled over and looked down at the wound. A bullet had struck the twenty dollar gold coin, driving it into his leg along with the bullet. The coin had stopped the bullet from striking his femur.

It would be the only thing that saved his leg—and probably his life. Surgeons would be able to retrieve the coin and the bullet. Though Dixon would survive, he walked with a noticeable limp the rest of his life. The coin was warped from the impact of the bullet, but he continued to carry it the to the day of his death. He would have the coin engraved to say, *"Shiloh, April 6, 1862, My Life Preserver, G.E.D."*

Two years later, he would be given command of a Confederate fish boat called the *Hunley* and would have the honor of being the first man to sink an enemy warship with a submarine.

CSA

Johnston had ridden to the front as soon as he'd heard the battle begin. He had positioned himself where he could see what was happening, regardless of the bullets flying around him. His staff had trouble keeping up, as he seemed to appear everywhere about the field.

Colonel George Baylor stayed at his commander's side. Tennessee Governor Harris followed along as best he could, considering he was on a slow-paced mule. He looked comical in his white coat and top hat. Johnston couldn't help but be amazed at the gentleman riding a mule into battle.

They reached the captured camp of the Eighteenth Wisconsin Infantry. Johnston watched a ragged private run out of a tent with the regiment's battle flag and wave it over his head. He saw Johnston, seemed to recognize him, and brought the flag over.

He said, "Sir, I present this captured battle flag to you."

Johnston took the flag and passed it to Governor Harris. He said, "Very good; now go rejoin your command and capture another."

The man realized he was being told to get back in the ranks. He saluted and moved toward the front.

The commander noticed a lieutenant coming out of another tent with his arms loaded with stolen goods. Johnston frowned and rode that way. The man saw Johnston and ran to meet him. He said, "General, look what all I've found."

Johnston's face betrayed his feelings. He said, "None of that, sir. We are not here to plunder."

The lieutenant's expression changed instantly. He looked down, obviously hurt from the rebuke. Johnston had always been a likable man, and it wasn't in his nature to hurt someone's feelings this way. He quickly reached down and took a tin cup from the lieutenant's arms and said, "Let this be my share of the spoils for today. Now, lieutenant, move forward and rejoin your command."

The man smiled and dropped the plunder on the ground. He raced away toward the direction of the firing. He was amazed at how a man like Johnston could force a person to obey him simply to avoid being a disappointment.

Johnston motioned for his staff to follow, and then he spurred the horse toward the heavy firing up the road. They rode into a small clearing where there had been some severe fighting. There were both Confederate and Federal wounded strewn about the field. Johnston stopped the horse and stared across the field. He turned to Doctor Yandell, his surgeon, and said, "Doc, I want you to stay here and treat the wounded."

Doctor Yandell tried to protest. "But, General," he said, "I need to remain…"

"Doc," Johnston interrupted, "treat the blue and gray alike. Don't make a difference in allegiance. These men were our enemies, but they are fellow sufferers now."

Yandell tried to think of a way to convince Johnston that his job was to stay with the commander of the army in case he was to become one of those wounded. He saw the expression on Johnston's face and realized that further argument would be futile. As Yandell began to dismount, he watched Johnston ride on up the road toward the fight.

Johnston rode north. They entered a large field as they continued riding down the Confederate lines. A Federal battery about eight hundred yards to the north noticed the commander, trailed by his staff, and opened fire. Shells were soon bursting overhead. The staff officers began to duck and dodge about under the fire, but Johnston rode on as if nothing unusual were occurring. A shell soon exploded close enough to send shrapnel raining down among the group. One piece struck Johnston just behind the right hip, causing a minor wound. The man acted as though nothing had happened and continued his ride eastward.

A moment later, a bullet fired from long range struck Johnston in his right thigh. The bullet had been fired from such long range that it didn't contain enough velocity to break the skin.

Colonel Baylor reined up beside Johnston and asked, "Are you wounded, sir?"

"Nothing to worry about," Johnston smiled at his best staff officer. "I have nerve damage in my right leg from the duel twenty-five years ago. I'll have a couple of bruises, but the good news is I won't feel a bit of discomfort."

They turned east and rode to the right flank. Johnston soon encountered Chalmers's brigade and watched them push the Federals back. After they had pushed the enemy back through the forest, he turned to Major Munford and said, "That checkmates them."

Things were definitely going his way today. After all he had been through during the long winter, the drawbacks earlier this year and the damage his reputation had suffered, he was actually turning things around. Johnston was relieved that things were finally going his way.

USA

Grant found Sherman about a half mile north of his headquarters attempting to make another stand against the overwhelming wave of enemy soldiers. Sherman was mounted a few hundred yards behind his main line. He sat on his horse and studied the raging battle. He turned to Major Sanger, one of his staff officers, and said, "Tell the men to use every fallen tree, stump, or any cover they can find to buy time for reinforcements to come up."

"Yes, sir," Sanger saluted and rode away.

Sherman turned as Grant arrived and quickly saluted. They were an odd-looking pair this morning. Grant was dressed in a new clean major general's uniform. Sherman was in his old dirty uniform with bullet holes. Sherman looked rough. His red hair was cut short and stood in all directions. He wondered if Grant was upset with him because he had told Grant there was no possibility of a Confederate attack.

"I've had two horses killed beneath me this morning," Sherman said. "I'm doing all I possibly can to stall them."

Grant looked from Sherman to the long blue line beyond them. Sherman quickly held up his hand with the bloody handkerchief tied around it.

"I've been wounded," he said. "And look at all these bullet holes in my uniform."

Grant quickly put his subordinate's mind at ease. He said, "You're doing a great job, Cump. I've got a new supply of ammunition being brought forward for your men, and Lew Wallace is bringing his division from Crump's Landing. I just need you to hang on as long as possible."

"Right," Sherman felt relieved. "When attacked this morning, I thought I had more than enough men to hold them off. I've been pushed back past McClernand's camps; and to be honest with you, I'm concerned about the situation."

Grant nodded and asked, "Do you think it's Johnston's entire army?"

Sherman nodded. "They just kept coming—and they're still coming."

Grant asked, "How's the hand?"

"Inflamed." Sherman held up the hand with the bloody handkerchief again. "It's throbbing, and my fingers are growing numb. I wish I had that bottle of laudanum back in my tent."

Grant asked, "Can you continue?"

"You damned right I can," Sherman gave Grant a sneer. "Take more than a hand wound to keep me out of action."

"That's good," Grant reached over and patted his friend on the arm. "I'm leaving you in charge of the right flank. I'm going to the left and oversee things. If they turn our left flank, we'll be cut off from the landing and Buell's reinforcements."

Sherman nodded and said, "By the way, Colonel Peabody is dead."

Grant stared at Sherman but said nothing.

"He was hit four times this morning, but he remained in command." There was a pause in the firing, which forced Sherman to look back toward the front. He soon continued, "A bullet struck him in the upper lip. He was dead before he hit the ground. General Prentiss blames him for bringing on the battle, if you can believe that."

Grant didn't have time to worry about casualties. That was just a part of battle. He said, "I believe you have seen the worst of the enemy's attack here. I'm going to find Prentiss. Like I said, the right flank is yours."

"Right," Sherman gave another sloppy salute as Grant rode eastward.

Grant rode toward the east. He had to find Prentiss and let him know what was happening. It was imperative that Prentiss hold as long as possible in the center. The army couldn't afford to be cut in half at this point in the battle.

He thought about what General Smith had said yesterday when Grant told him he was concerned about an attack from Corinth. Smith was still lying ill in the upstairs bedroom of the Cherry Mansion from the skinned leg. Smith had said that he asked for nothing better than the Rebels coming out and attacking us. He'd said they could whip them all to hell and back. Smith had gotten his wish, but Grant was beginning to worry about whipping them. Things were definitely not going his way at the moment. He hoped Lew Wallace would hurry and arrive because he needed all the men he could get just now.

Grant rode past a group of Federal soldiers who appeared to be reforming their ranks. He overheard one of the men saying, "There's General Grant."

Another soldier quickly replied, "That's not Grant. That fellow don't look like he has enough sense to command a regiment, much less an army."

Several of Grant's staff laughed at the remark. Grant ignored the group and continued eastward. He hoped to find Prentiss somewhere in this mess. Like Johnston a few moments earlier, Grant inadvertently rode through the north end of a large field, and like his adversary, an enemy battery soon opened fire on his group of mounted officers. Unlike Johnston, however, Grant immediately put spurs to his horse and raced for cover in the forest a couple hundred yards across the field. Cannon balls and shrapnel rained about their heads.

Once they reached the trees, the shells stopped coming in, the Confederate gunners finding other targets. Grant stopped to see if everyone was alright. Lieutenant Colonel James McPherson's horse was panting like a dog on a hot August afternoon. Upon inspection, they found a projectile had passed completely through both of the animal's lungs. In less than a minute, the horse collapsed.

Rawlins asked, "Are you alright, sir?"

Grant looked down and noticed a dent in his scabbard. A piece of shrapnel had struck his scabbard and bent it outward away from his leg. It would be impossible for him to pull the saber out. He looked up and noticed that McPherson was taking one of his orderly's mounts. Private Putnam looked strange when McPherson took his horse and left him standing in the forest. They soon rode on eastward.

Grant soon found Prentiss in a position that came to be known as the Hornet's Nest. The man was under a heavy assault just as Grant arrived.

Prentiss was dismounted and standing behind his men in the sunken farm lane. He saw Grant and saluted. He said, "It's damned bad. I told Sherman I felt we were in danger here."

"Never mind that," Grant waved him off. "I need you to hold this position at all hazards. Lew Wallace is on his way up, and Buell is marching here from Savannah."

"Right," Prentiss looked around at the approaching line of gray infantry. He wondered how long he could hold.

"I'm riding to the east flank," Grant puffed on the cigar in his mouth. "Sherman is in charge of the west flank, and you've got the middle. I can't emphasize enough how important it is for you to hold the center."

Prentiss gave a sloppy salute and watched Grant ride off northward into the forest.

Grant realized things were getting extremely ugly. As they rode north, attempting to make a circle around the bow-shaped line, he turned to Rawlins and asked, "Where in the hell is Lew Wallace?"

Rawlins shook his head. He had no more information than Grant.

Grant said, "Send a courier to General Wallace and tell him it is urgent that he get his command here. Tell the courier not to spare horseflesh in getting that message to Wallace."

Rawlins had never seen Grant as worried as he appeared here today.

CSA

Major General Braxton Bragg was furious over the disorganization caused by Beauregard's plan. The three corps had each made one long line almost three miles wide. When Hardee's Corps, the first in line, had engaged the enemy, Bragg's Corps had come up and become mixed with Hardee's men. Polk's Corps had followed suit, and what resulted was one huge mess. There was no way a man could command his entire corps when it was stretched through these woods and thickets across almost three miles.

Bragg rode down his long line from left to right, and as he neared the center, he encountered Leonidas Polk. Approaching Polk, Bragg didn't bother to salute. He understood rank was a sore spot with Polk because technically Polk ranked him; but Bragg was the army's chief of staff, which gave him the right to give Polk orders. Bragg said, "General Polk, we must work out a command arrangement."

Polk nodded but said nothing. He wasn't sure what Bragg was talking about at the moment.

Bragg said, "We must find General Hardee and arrange something to correct the mess we're in. There's no way we can command our corps with each spread out almost three miles and intermingled with the other two. A mistake was made here lining us up one behind the other."

"I agree," Polk nodded in agreement. "What do you suggest?"

"I'm gonna work my way to the right," Bragg nodded his head past Polk. "You take the center and try and locate Hardee. Tell him to take the left."

"I will," Polk looked over Bragg's shoulder toward the sound of heavy firing. "God go with you, General Bragg."

Bragg ignored Polk's comment. He said, "Order all the men to move toward the heaviest firing. That is one of Napoleon's maxims."

"Right," Polk nodded and rode on past Bragg.

General Bragg didn't realize that by ordering each unit to move toward the sound of the heaviest fire that he was moving them toward the strongest Federal position. This violated anything a good commander would want to do. Great commanders always wanted to attack the enemy's weak points.

Braxton Bragg rode on eastward, trailed by his staff. He approached the area of the battlefield that would soon become known as the Hornet's Nest. He stared through the underbrush toward the Union position to the north. There was no way he could tell what strength the Federals had here, because the thicket was so dense that he couldn't even see the enemy. They were there for sure; he could sense them.

59

Bragg was about to turn his horse eastward when a bullet struck the animal between the eyes. Horse and rider crashed to the ground at once. Braxton Bragg managed to move clear of the beast as it hit the ground, barely missing it pinning him down.

He jumped to his feet and looked at the poor horse. Had its head not been raised, the bullet would have struck Bragg in the chest. He continued to stare at the animal. Captain Hypolite Oladowski asked, "Ish you hurt, Sheneral?"

"No," Bragg replied, "but that is the noblest creature I've ever seen. In dying, this great war hero saved my life."

Bragg quickly mounted an orderly's horse and rode back south in search of reinforcements. He passed through a small wheat field where a cabin stood just east of the field. To the south was a large open field that contained a brigade of Confederate infantry. Bragg rode there to find one of his brigade commanders, Colonel Randall Gibson. He couldn't believe these men were several hundred yards in rear of the main line standing idle.

He rode up to Gibson, who was dismounted and holding his horse. Bragg's one continuous bushy eyebrow dipped just above his nose. He didn't bother to dismount but yelled at the handsome colonel from Louisiana. "Colonel Gibson, what in hell are you doing way back here?"

The twenty-nine-year-old colonel was taken aback. Gibson replied, "I've been ordered to stay here and serve as a support for Cheatham's division."

Bragg didn't care that Gibson was best friends with Sidney Johnston's son. He didn't care that Johnston loved the young man like a son. He hated the fact that Gibson was considered one of the most promising men of the South. People often said that there was no limit to what this young Yale-educated lawyer could accomplish. He was often mentioned as a future governor, senator, or maybe even president someday.

The young man was always neatly dressed and acted distinguished. Women all thought he was extremely attractive. Bragg disliked him, if for no other reason than that. Bragg had never been called handsome by women.

"That's a load of bullshit, Colonel Gibson," Bragg shouted. "I'm ordering you to move to the front and assault the enemy. If there is one thing I abhor, it is cowardice in the face of the enemy."

Under normal circumstances, Gibson would have challenged Bragg to a duel to prove he was no coward, but this wasn't the proper time. He simply turned and shouted at his brigade. "Forward march!"

The line surged forward across the field, through the underbrush and into the small wheat field. Gibson called a halt and had his regimental commanders dress their lines before moving into the thicket against the Federal position.

Randall Gibson was about to give the order to advance, when one of General Hardee's aides named Young Vertner came riding down the line with a captured Federal flag wrapped around his waist. He was attempting to encourage the men with the display. As he reached the Fourth Louisiana Infantry Regiment, Gibson heard a man call out, "Here's your Yankee flag!"

Instantly, over a hundred men raised their rifles and opened fire on the poor man. Vertner and his horse crashed to the ground, both hit multiple times by the gunfire. Gibson shook his head in disbelief at what had just transpired.

At that very moment, the Ninth Tennessee Infantry appeared out of the underbrush in his brigade's rear. When they heard the firing, they assumed Gibson's men were Yankees and opened fire. Almost one hundred men fell to this friendly fire. Several officers rushed back to the Tennessee men and straightened things out before further harm could be inflicted.

Once everything settled down, Colonel Gibson gave the order for the brigade to advance. The line moved on across the wheat field, climbed over a fence, and entered the thick underbrush. The vegetation was so dense at that point that it was impossible for Gibson to keep his men in line. Still they pressed on through the tangled undergrowth.

Gibson followed his men, straining to see what lay ahead. Suddenly, the world seemed to explode in their very faces. The Federals were lying flat in the sunken road, and they opened fire when the Confederate line was within twenty paces of their position. Gibson could actually hear a moan from his men. Bragg had sent his men into an ambush. There was a Federal battery posted in the road, and he could actually hear the canister fire ripping through bodies. His men returned the Federal fire, but because they couldn't see the enemy in their front, their fire had little effect.

A bullet crashed into Gibson's horse, and the animal fell to the ground. Gibson sprang to his feet and moved up close behind his line. His men were firing at the muzzle flashes of the enemy rifles. Because of the underbrush and the Federal troops lying concealed in the sunken road, there was no enemy to be seen.

The Confederate line seemed to break at once. They'd advanced into this thicket with less than a thousand men. There were parts of three Federal divisions here. Gibson followed his men back out of the brush and into the wheat field where the assault had begun. He saw General Bragg riding among his men calling them cowards. He wondered how anyone could call a man a coward who had gone into that ambuscade.

Gibson turned around and called on one of his volunteer aides named Robert Pugh. He said, "Go to General Bragg and ask him if he can provide my brigade with some artillery support."

Pugh ran to where Bragg was chastising Gibson's men and within moments he came racing back. He said, "Colonel, Bragg denied your request for artillery support. He says you don't need artillery to take that position. He says these men need their commander to step up and lead them."

Gibson shook his head. He moved among his men and began reforming them. He heard one man refer to the position they had just attacked as a hornet's nest. Gibson would have to agree with the man. Once he had them on line again, he gave the command to advance back into the same area they had just failed to take.

Again, they marched across the wheat field, climbed the fence, and moved into the thick forest. When they approached the wounded and dead that marked the spot where they had been repulsed earlier, Gibson gave the command to charge. The line surged forward, and the gray line began screaming like banshees. The Federals opened fire from the sunken road again. The fire was more destructive than before. The artillery opened up with canister again. Gibson's men never had a chance. It was as if Bragg had sent them into a slaughter pen.

The young colonel was amazed when his men actually reached the Federal line. The men in blue were forced to stand, and the fighting became hand to hand. The artillery fell silent as Gibson's men shot all the horses and most of the gunners. He couldn't believe they had actually overrun the battery. It appeared the charge would succeed this time.

The Federal infantry on each side of the artillery crashed into Gibson's men and retook the guns. They slowly pushed the Confederate line back into the brush. Gibson's second line was about twenty yards back, and they soon began to fire. They didn't pay any attention to where their bullets went. He noticed his front line was being hit by enemy fire in front and friendly fire in back. Before he could correct the problem, the front line broke and raced to the rear, taking the second line with them.

Gibson wished there was something more he could do. He looked at his dead and wounded. They lay in heaps. A man could walk over the entire area without touching the ground if he wished. There were mangled bodies in front of the cannons from the canister fire, and he noticed one man had been cut in half. The scene sickened him. He could have never prepared himself for this. When the war began, he had believed it would be a romantic affair. All the romance was gone now.

As he began to follow his retreating men, he noticed the woods had caught fire. Most of the wounded couldn't escape, and he could hear his wounded screaming as the flames reached them.

Gibson stumbled into the wheat field, and there waiting for him was General Bragg. The man was furious now. He almost screamed at his unlucky colonel. "You have allowed your brigade to be repulsed by a few Federal sharpshooters. You're an embarrassment to the Confederate army."

Bragg spun his horse without waiting for Gibson to reply. He rode into the field and began attempting to reform the Louisiana brigade himself.

Gibson turned to Pugh and said, "When this fight is over, I'm gonna demand a court of inquiry."

"I'll testify on your behalf, Randall," Pugh reached out and patted Gibson on the shoulder.

"Colonel Gibson," a voice called from behind him. Gibson spun to see Colonel Hodge approaching. The man's face was red, and he appeared angry. "That fool Bragg is sacrificing our men for nothing. An idiot can tell this position can't be taken by frontal assault."

Gibson nodded in agreement. He asked, "What can we do about it? He's the commander."

Bragg grew frustrated with rallying Gibson's men. He turned to Captain Lockett of his staff, and pointing to the regimental banner, he said, "Take those colors there and lead those men back to the fight. The colors must not fall back again if it kills every man in this brigade."

Lockett thought about what Bragg was telling him. It was as if he had just received a sentence of death. Riding back into that thicket with a regimental banner, he would be an inviting target; but he knew better than to argue with Bragg.

He rode up to the Confederate color bearer and grabbed the flag. He said, "General Bragg says for me to take this flag because it cannot fall back again."

He had barely finished the sentence when a stray shot struck the color bearer in the head, killing him instantly.

Colonel Henry Allen of the Fourth Louisiana Infantry strode up to the staff officer on the horse. Blood coursed down the colonel's face and neck. He had been shouting an order when a Federal bullet hit him in the left cheek, passed through his mouth, and exited his right cheek. The man was obviously angry. He asked, "What are you doing with my colors, sir?"

"General Bragg ordered me to carry them in the next charge, sir," Lockett replied.

When Colonel Allen spoke, blood sprayed from the holes in his cheeks. He shouted, "Let me have them. You tell General Bragg if any man but my color bearer carries these colors, I am that man. You tell him this position cannot be taken from the front. He must work around the Federal flank. There are five thousand men in that thicket."

Lockett surrendered the flag to the wounded colonel and rode back to report to Bragg. The angry general seemed to calm down when told what Allen had said. He rode over to speak with Colonel Allen. He said, "Colonel, I believe the Federals think you command a bunch of cowards. They'll be foolish not to advance against us. Move your men back into the thicket and ambush them the way they ambushed you."

"General Bragg," Allen rubbed his aching cheeks, "a thousand men couldn't take that position, and now you're asking me to take what's left of my regiment back in there alone. How can two hundred men do what a thousand couldn't?"

Bragg scowled at the remark. He said, "Colonel Allen, I don't want excuses. Now do as you're told."

Allen spun back toward his men without bothering to salute. He had lost all respect for Braxton Bragg. Now he understood why some of Bragg's men had attempted to kill him during the Mexican War.

Bragg turned to Captain Lockett and said, "Ride to Colonel Gibson and tell him I expect him to reform his men and attack again. Tell him not to fall back if he loses every man in his command. I'm thoroughly tired of his cowardice."

Lockett delivered the order. Gibson never acknowledged he heard the man. He was busy reforming his men and soon had them advancing again. They crossed the fence and crashed back into the brush. They swept through the flames, and the smell of burning flesh almost caused Gibson to vomit. His men got within thirty paces of the sunken road and halted. They fired blindly toward the Federal position. The Federal troops returned fire from their protective cover. Gibson's men stood there for half an hour taking severe casualties against a foe they couldn't see in the heavy undergrowth. The enemy fire was heavier than before. It was obvious they had brought up more men. Gibson began to wonder if any of his brave men would survive the useless slaughter.

Men soon began to break for the rear. Colonel Hodge approached Gibson and said, "Sir, it would be madness to remain here any longer."

Gibson nodded. "Pass the word we are falling back. To hell with General Bragg."

They moved back into the wheat field, most not bothering to stay in line. Gibson came trudging out of the thicket behind them. He dreaded having to listen to Bragg's insults.

Captain Lockett rode over to Colonel Allen's regiment and began trying to reform them. Allen walked up to Lockett and said, "You tell Bragg that he has uselessly sacrificed good Louisiana men for nothing. My dead are lying in heaps back in that damned thicket. Ask him why he wouldn't allow us to have artillery support?"

"Right," Lockett replied. He felt as though he were caught in the middle. He spurred the horse back across the field where Bragg was waiting.

He told Bragg what the Louisiana colonel had said. Bragg shook his head. "This is all Gibson's fault. He is nothing but an arrogant coward. I want you to tell Colonel Gibson that I expect nothing more from him today except to at least have his mob hold their position in the wheat field. I'm going to the right and see what can be done."

CSA

The cantankerous General Daniel Ruggles rode along behind his men as they pushed the Federal army from one position to another. The Federals now occupied a sunken road across an open field that belonged to a family called Duncan. There was no way to advance across this field without being subjected to murderous fire from the Federals sheltered in the road.

Bragg commanded the corps that Ruggles's division belonged to, but things had changed in the confusion. Major General Hardee had taken command of the left wing, and now Ruggles found himself reporting to an officer he wasn't very familiar with.

Major Francis Shoup, Hardee's chief of artillery, surveyed the scene and brought several artillery batteries to the edge of Duncan Field. Colonel James Trudeau had escaped from being captured at Island Number Ten on the Mississippi River and arrived at Corinth just as the Confederate army was departing for Shiloh. Beauregard had given Trudeau the title of chief of artillery for the entire army. Trudeau arrived on the scene and watched Major Shoup placing the cannons. He watched the skinny officer with the long neck and large head order the cannons to shell the sunken road across the way. Trudeau immediately spun his horse and rode back to bring up all the artillery he could find.

He was soon busy placing guns, and within half an hour, he had a continuous line of sixty-two cannons firing at the Federals in the sunken road. General Ruggles rode up to the colonel and said, "Bravo. We'll blast them out in no time."

Daniel Ruggles rode back to the left and dismounted. A thought suddenly occurred to him. He would send one battery across the field to spray canister in the very faces of the Federals.

Ruggles walked over to Captain George Hubbard. Hubbard saluted. When Ruggles told him to advance, he stared at the general with the long gray beard that could be tucked into his belt if he wanted. His hair was almost white, and he combed it back over his receding hairline. The curls in back bounced as he talked.

"Sir, beggin' your pardon, but I only got two smoothbores," Hubbard hoped Ruggles would change his mind.

Ruggles reached up and dug in his large nose. He said, "That'll be plenty, Captain. Spray canister right in their faces."

Captain Hubbard wondered how a West Point trained officer who had seen action in the Mexican and Seminole Wars would send two cannons across a field against an enemy line that long. He understood why no one liked the man now. Hubbard asked, "Will you be sending infantry support with us?"

"Negative," Ruggles replied. "They'd be sitting ducks out in that field behind you."

Hubbard wanted to ask Ruggles what his men would be in the middle of that open field facing a line of Federal infantry almost half a mile long. He knew better than to argue with the old man. A funny thought dawned on him as he watched his men hitch the cannons for the forward movement. *Ruggles was born in Massachusetts. I wish the Federal Army had him instead of us, he thought.*

They soon moved out into the field to within a hundred yards of the sunken road. His battery immediately began taking fire from the infantry, and several cannons began to pound them from the east. Hubbard's men only managed to get off two rounds before they were forced to retire. He barely had enough men and horses left to get the guns back across the field to safety.

When he reached his original position, General Ruggles walked over and asked, "Pretty hot out there wasn't it?"

Hubbard shook his head. "I don't care to ever try that again."

Ruggles laughed and turned back to a large tree he was using for shade. Just beyond the tree, the Crescent Regiment of Louisiana stood waiting for orders. The men were the strangest outfit in the Confederate army. They wore bright red caps, baggy red trousers, and blue coats with gold braid that glistened in the sunlight.

The uniforms were only a small part of what made this infantry regiment so strange. Its soldiers consisted of Germans, Irish, Mexicans, Italians, and even a large number of Africans fighting alongside the white soldiers.

An artillery round came sailing in from someplace and struck one of the privates in the chin, cutting his head off at the shoulders. Ruggles noticed several men gagging at the sight.

Beyond the Crescent Regiment, Ruggles watched a Tennessee regiment approaching. Seeing the men in blue standing in their front, the commander ordered his men to open fire. Bullets ripped into the back of the men from Louisiana.

Colonel Marshall, commanding the Crescent Regiment, ordered his men to about face. At that moment, the Tennessee colonel realized he had made a mistake and began to yell for his men to cease fire. Colonel Marshall's face was red. He was furious at the carelessness of the Tennessee troops. He shouted, "Take aim, men. Fire!"

65

The Tennessee commander saw what was about to happen and began to race forward shouting, "Cease fire! We're friends!"

It was too late. The Louisiana troops opened fire on the Tennessee men. The colonel continued running through the fire. It was a miracle he wasn't hit. He ran up to Colonel Marshall and shouted, "Cease fire, you're firing on friends!"

"I know it, damn it," Marshall replied, "but I fire on anyone who fires on me!"

Ruggles spun his horse and rode to Colonel Trudeau's position. He said, "Ride to the rear and bring any cannons you can find up here. We can't assault that position with infantry, it's too strong. We'll have to blast the bastards out."

"Yes, sir," Trudeau saluted. He couldn't understand what the hell Ruggles thought he and Major Shoup had been doing for the last thirty minutes.

Within moments, Trudeau and Shoup opened the largest bombardment on the North American continent up until that time. The effect was tremendous. He watched as tree limbs were blown off the trees across the field. It was a wonder that anyone could survive that pounding. Explosions ripped the air as cannonballs ignited and rained shrapnel down on the defenders of the Hornet's Nest.

One hundred and four miles away in Florence, Alabama, citizens sat on their porches and listened to the sound of the guns. Almost three shots per second were fired from what would come to be known as Ruggles's Battery, and it lasted for almost two hours.

CSA

Sidney Johnston's hat had long since been gone. He'd ridden from one flank of the battlefield to the other, across fields and through woods. Somewhere along the way his hat had been taken off by a limb, and he never slowed long enough to retrieve it.

He'd also not bothered to pull his sword from the scabbard. He'd been directing the battle with the tin cup he'd taken off the lieutenant who he'd corrected for plundering.

Johnston soon arrived south of the peach orchard on the extreme right flank. He stared across the open field toward the Federal line in the orchard. He could see a cabin at the tree line behind the orchard.

Major Dudley Haydon, one of his staff officers, was just itching to see some action. He complained to Johnston, "Sir, you keep your staff under your wing like an old mother hen. Let me do something."

"There will be plenty of work for you soon," Johnston replied. He never bothered to take his eyes off the action. He could count six Federal cannons in front of the orchard and six more a hundred yards to its left.

A courier came galloping up and saluted Johnston. He said, "Sir, General Breckinridge begs to report. He says he is being hard pressed and needs support."

Johnston raised the tin cup as if he were offering a toast to the young man. "Tell General Breckinridge that help is on the way."

He watched the man salute again before spurring the horse away. Johnston turned to Major Haydon and said, "Here is your chance. Ride back and order General Bowen to move his brigade up to Breckinridge's support."

"Yes, sir," Haydon couldn't suppress the smile as he wheeled his horse and galloped toward the rear.

It wasn't but ten minutes before Johnston noticed Major Haydon and General Bowen moving up to the edge of the field. He rode over, returned John Bowen's salute, and said, "General Bowen, the enemy is hurting. Only a few more charges and the day is ours."

Johnston then rode past Bowen and to his men as they stood in line of battle waiting for the order to advance. Every man had his bayonet attached to his rifle. Johnston began to ride down the line. He tapped the bayonets with the tin cup.

"Men of Arkansas and Missouri," he said, "the enemy is being stubborn here today. I want you to show Generals Breckinridge and Bragg what you can do with these weapons and your bowie knives."

The men began to cheer their leader. As Johnston neared the center of the brigade, he stopped. Governor Harris was by his side, willing to go anywhere the brave man was willing to lead. General Breckinridge came galloping to the scene. He stopped, and in an excited voice, he said, "General, I have a Tennessee regiment that refuses to fight. I've been doing my utmost to rally them and lead them into battle."

Johnston looked at Governor Harris. He saw the look of disparagement on the man's face. Harris asked, "What regiment is it?"

Breckinridge looked at Harris and recognized he was the governor of Tennessee. He hadn't meant any offense to the man. Breckinridge was a southern gentleman and would never offend another gentleman. He lowered his head. "The Forty-Fifth. I can't get them to charge with the rest of my men, sir."

Johnston smiled at Breckinridge's misfortune. He said, "Then I will help you."

They followed Breckinridge down the line. Johnston looked at Harris and said, "The enemy is making a stubborn stand here. We'll have to give them the bayonet."

"Right," Harris nodded as he spurred the mule to keep pace.

As they rode past Rutledge's Tennessee battery, an artillery shell exploded overhead. Johnston saw men dodging about, some flattening out on the ground. He said, "Major Munford, have those boys correct their fire. They aren't even firing close to that Federal battery."

He watched Munford ride off toward the cannons. Johnston, Harris, and Breckinridge soon arrived at the position of the Forty-fifth Tennessee Infantry. This unit composed the center of Johnston's line of over five thousand men here. The three men placed themselves in front of the line and began to lead them forward. It would be the highest-ranked charge in American history. Harris was the governor of Tennessee, Major General Breckinridge was the ex-vice president of the United States, and Johnston was the highest ranking field general in the Confederate army. Johnston wheeled his horse toward the front and yelled, "I will lead you!"

It was the greatest moment in his career. The long line soon cleared the tree line and entered the field. They soon broke into a charge toward the Peach Orchard.

Johnston yelled to his men, "The cold steel will do the job! They are stubborn, but the bayonet will move them!"

Breckinridge was at his side, yelling, "Double quick—come on boys!"

Johnston stayed out front most of the way before dropping to the rear with Breckinridge and Harris. Four bullets had struck his horse, and his clothes were riddled with bullet holes. The sole of his boot had been ripped by a bullet and was hanging from his foot. As he slowed "Fire-Eater," he turned to Harris and said, "Governor, they came very near to killing me in that charge."

Harris looked concerned. He asked, "Are you wounded, sir?"

"Not at all," Johnston replied. "Well, almost not at all. I think a bullet grazed my shoulder, but it's just a scratch. I'm fine, Governor."

As his staff followed him toward the right of the line, he began to think about his pregnant wife and young children. He couldn't help but wonder what would become of them if he'd been killed leading that charge. It wasn't the smartest thing for an army commander to do. That was why he had subordinates. His job was to direct battles, not lead charges. But things were different now. His nation had lost two states, and drastic action had to be taken.

Johnston said, "Governor Harris, ride forward and tell Colonel Statham to keep his brigade moving."

"Yes, sir," Harris spurred the mule to the north.

Captain Wickham eased his horse up alongside his commander. He said, "I could have sworn I heard a bullet strike you, General. Sounded like someone thumping a watermelon. Captain O'Hara heard it also. Are you sure you're not wounded?"

"Struck my horse, Captain," Johnston replied. He continued to ride toward the right flank.

Captain O'Hara was riding behind and noticed blood dripping from Johnston's boot. He got Wickham's attention and pointed toward Johnston's leg. Wickham said, "General, I believe you're wounded. We'd better find a place where you're not so exposed to the enemy's fire."

"No, Hardee's fire is heavy," Johnston mumbled. It didn't occur to Wickham that the commander wasn't making much sense. "We must go where the fire is heaviest. Ride to General Hardee and tell him to press the enemy."

Wickham spun his horse and galloped away. As Johnston began to turn his horse, O'Hara noticed a bullet hole in the flank of Johnston's horse. He said, "General, your horse is wounded."

"Yes," Johnston agreed, "and so is his master."

Captain O'Hara helped guide Johnston's horse to a small rise on the east side of the Hamburg Road. Major Hawkins rode up a moment later, not noticing that Johnston was swaying in the saddle. The man was extremely agitated about something.

Hawkins said to O'Hara, "I saw Major Haydon trying to get part of the Forty-fifth Tennessee to charge. There were almost a hundred lying behind a fence. They were scared shitless. I told him to have the cowards shot dead on the spot."

Other than looking extremely pale, there was nothing about Johnston to indicate he was wounded. He'd been in front of his men when the bullet impacted the back of his right knee, slicing open the popliteal artery. The blood was filling his boot, which almost reached his knee. The duel he had fought before the Mexican War almost twenty-five years ago had tragic results. Because of the numbness in his leg due to the nerve damage from that wound, Johnston couldn't feel the gaping hole from the .577 Enfield bullet that struck him. Worse still was the fact that he had been accidentally hit by friendly fire.

A moment later, Isham Harris rode up and noticed Johnston slumping in the saddle. The man was extremely pale, and something was obviously wrong with him. Harris asked, "General, are you wounded?"

"Yes, I fear it is serious," Johnston replied. His body swayed and then fell. Luckily, Harris was near enough to keep him from crashing to the ground. He held him, suspended between Johnston's horse and Harris's mule, until Captain Wickham, who had just returned, could dismount and ease his commander to the ground.

Harris dismounted and said, "Captain, let's get him into that ravine and see if we can locate the wound."

The two men grabbed the unconscious man and carried him into the ravine about twenty-five feet away. Captain O'Hara led Johnston's horse behind them.

Colonel Baylor saw the group carrying his commander into the ravine and followed. He quickly dismounted as they laid the general beneath a tree.

"Wickham, what's the matter?" he asked.

"The general is wounded," Wickham replied. "Send someone back to find a surgeon."

The staff officers tore their commander's coat and shirt open searching for the wound. They searched his body, looking for anything, and that was when Wickham found blood on his pant leg. He and Harris pulled the boot off and found it filled with blood. The general was bleeding so bad that blood quickly made a small stream about six feet down the ravine and formed a small pool.

Colonel Baylor walked over beside Johnston and noticed that his eyes were wide open, but his face was as pale as a ghost. He couldn't help but think about the difference between the excited face of this morning and the lifeless one before him now.

Baylor's eyes quickly filled with tears. He bent over Johnston as the tears dripped off his cheeks and asked, "Sir, do you know me?"

One of the tears struck Johnston's face. The stricken general gave a slight quiver and then closed his eyes. Baylor turned to move away and realized all the staff officers had tears in their eyes as well.

William Preston soon arrived and couldn't believe his eyes. He sat on the ground against the tree and held Johnston's head in his lap. Preston began to sob. He lifted Johnston's head and began repeating over and over again. "Sidney, don't you know me?"

A faint smile spread over Johnston's face. The entire staff had arrived. Captain Haydon decided to pour whiskey down Johnston's throat in hopes of reviving the man. The strong liquid caused no reaction from the general. Most of it just ran out the side of his mouth. Haydon then bent over and placed his ear against Johnston's bare chest and listened for a heartbeat. He heard nothing.

As he slowly raised his head, Colonel Preston sounded as if he were in agony. He could barely be understood as he said, "My God, my God! Haydon, tell me he's not dead!"

Colonel Baylor reached into Johnston's coat pocket and removed the general's watch. It was exactly two-thirty. He noticed that Preston's tears were running through his thick mustache and off his clean-shaven chin onto his brother-in-law's face.

Preston said, "Gentlemen, you'll have to pardon me. You all know how much I loved him."

"We need to keep his death a secret from the troops. It would be too demoralizing for them to continue the battle," Baylor said.

Several staff officers gently lifted Johnston's body and placed him in an army blanket. They draped him across "Fire-Eater" and began to slowly lead him toward the rear.

Preston turned to Governor Harris and said, "Find General Beauregard. Inform him that Johnston was killed after making a victorious attack on the enemy's left flank. Tell him it's up to him to complete this victory and destroy the enemy."

The horse was so weak from wounds it could barely walk. Several soldiers asked about the corpse on the horse. Preston replied, "It's Colonel Jackson of Texas."

Harris found Beauregard at Shiloh Church. Beauregard saw the comical-looking man approach and wanted to laugh. It would be difficult to think the man was a governor the way he was dressed, along with the fact that he was riding a mule.

Governor Harris dismounted. He blurted out the news. "Sir, Johnston's dead. You're in command now. The battle's won, you must finish it."

Beauregard thought for a long moment. His doctors had ordered him to bed this morning; his pulse rate had been over a hundred. Now he was on the verge of exhaustion. The laryngitis from his throat surgery was especially bad today. He could barely speak. Now he was in command of an army in the midst of a major battle that he hadn't wanted to be fought at all.

Beauregard said, "Well, Governor, everything else seems to be going well, don't you think?"

Harris was taken aback. He expected a larger reaction from the man. He replied, "I suppose so."

Colonel Munford and Captain Wickliffe came galloping up and dismounted. Both men saluted.

Beauregard saw the tears on Wickliffe's face and said, "Gentlemen, you can't possibly know the extent of my regret at the death of General Johnston. I still believe we'll be successful here. I would like you men to escort the body back to Corinth."

The three men had just left when General Bragg arrived. The grouchy-looking man dismounted. He didn't look a bit happy. He walked up to Beauregard and said, "The entire right wing has stalled because of Johnston's death."

Beauregard shook his head. He wanted to ask Bragg why he wasn't over there doing what Johnston had been doing—forcing men into battle and pressing the victory. He began to speak, but Bragg interrupted. "Withers and Cheatham's men are too exhausted to continue."

"Let's keep the news of Johnston's death from the men. They don't need to know." Beauregard tried to clear his throat and winced from the pain. "We have an ammunition shortage on the left, but the center is pressing forward rather well. If they break in the middle, it's all over. Tell all your commanders to press forward, and let's finish the enemy off."

Bragg saluted and climbed back in the saddle. He spun the horse and rode away. He'd come back here half expecting Beauregard to withdraw the army now that Johnston was dead. He was a little shocked that the man wanted to continue. Both men had been arguing against this attack for two days now.

Soon Fire-Eater came by with his master's body and the rest of Johnston's staff. It was a somber scene. They continued on to Corinth.

Arriving in Corinth the next morning, Misses Inge welcomed the Confederate hero's body into her home again. She found the sandwich that she had prepared for the famous man half-eaten. The cake had been consumed. The thought of him eating her food would make her very proud the rest of her life, and she would often speak of it.

She helped to clean the general's body, wrapped him in a Confederate flag, and had him laid in state in her home for several hours. The man had exited the war and would remain one of the famous questions surrounding the Confederacy. President Davis believed Johnston would have eventually won the war for the South had he lived.

CSA

Lieutenant Colonel Nathan Bedford Forrest was just itching to get into the fight. His men felt the same way. General Breckinridge had sent him to Lick Creek this morning on the Confederate right flank to guard a damned ford. Forrest was growing angrier by the minute.

Private Charles Warren watched as Colonel Forrest began to pace beneath a large oak tree. Forrest was a striking man, just over six feet tall. He was lean but powerful for his size. Charles had been told that Forrest's father was a blacksmith, and he figured that's where Forrest got his strength. He was forty years old but had the energy of a man half his age.

The one thing that amazed Charles about Forrest was his piercing blue eyes. They seemed to change hues with Forrest's mood. Charles almost wondered what color Forrest's true eye color was supposed to be. At the moment, his eyes were dark blue. The man was angry.

Private Warren remembered the men talking about Forrest spending money out of his own pocket to pay for his troop's equipment. They'd said he had ridden into Kentucky with five teenage boys and smuggled the supplies out in coffee sacks. The man was a millionaire, though he'd earned his money by trading slaves.

Warren's battalion had only been placed under Forrest three weeks ago. It hadn't taken long for them to understand that Forrest was a true commander. Men had grumbled at first. There was no give and take with Forrest. Everything had to be done his way. When giving an order, he would tolerate no arguments or appeals. He also cared for his men, and that's what drew Charles to Forrest. He always checked on them, making sure there was nothing they needed. Charles Warren had made up his mind that he would follow Forrest no matter where he led him.

Charles noticed a slow-witted young man from another company approaching Forrest. He had already asked Forrest for a furlough twice this morning. The colonel had been patient with the poor man both times, yet he denied the request. Charles felt sorry for the young man. Charles thought about what his dad used to say about people like him—*"The man's bread wasn't quite done."*

Forrest was still pacing, eyes down, staring at the ground ahead, when the man cut him off in mid stride. Forrest glared at him. The man said, "Colonel, sir, uh, I need a furlough. Got to get back home and check on pa."

Forrest exploded. He threw his hands in the air and shouted, "I done told you twice already, goddamit—no!"

The man's shoulders sank as he slowly turned away. Forrest continued to watch him in disbelief. The colonel shook his head. He resumed his pace, mumbling to himself, "I've got no respect for a man who would abandon the colors in the face of the enemy."

Charles had already learned a lot from Forrest. He was with a group of men who had brought a captured Federal officer to Forrest's headquarters on the march into Tennessee. When Forrest came out of his tent, someone handed him the officer's sword. Forrest immediately pulled it from its scabbard. He noticed that only the first three inches of the blade had been sharpened.

Forrest had demanded a grindstone to sharpen the captured weapon. The exasperated Federal captain had informed Forrest that the weapon was more for show than for combat. Forrest had replied, "Damn such nonsense. War means fightin' and fightin' means killin'. Turn the grindstone."

Another thing that amazed Charles about Forrest was his personal escort. He had forty-seven of his slaves as his escort, and these men were as brave as any in the Confederate army. Forrest had told them that, whether the South won or lost, they would all be free.

Warren watched Forrest pacing. All the men were watching their commander's temper rise with each passing moment. Suddenly, Forrest spun and shouted, "Boys, do you hear that musketry and artillery?"

His men knew what was about to happen. Their commander had had enough. Everyone yelled in reply.

Forrest shouted, "It means our friends are falling by the hundreds while we're back here guarding a damned creek! I didn't ride all the way up here to guard no damned ford! We didn't enter the service for such work! May as well be guarding a damned latrine! We are needed on the field! I say we go and help our men! What do you say?"

Every man in the command replied with a shout. Forrest climbed on his horse and watched as his men began to mount. He yelled, "We're goin' up there, and we gonna bust hell wide open!"

They rode north and soon turned on the Hamburg-Purdy Road. There were long-range artillery shells bursting overhead. Forrest rode on, impervious to the shrapnel raining down around him. Just up the road he found General Frank Cheatham.

Forrest approached Cheatham, and not bothering to salute, he said, "I can't have my men back here in this artillery fire. I need to charge."

Cheatham looked at Forrest with an expression of indifference. He wondered why Forrest was telling him this.

Forrest asked, "Will you give me permission to charge?"

Cheatham shook his head. "I don't have the authority to give you permission to charge. You're not under my command. Besides, several charges have been bloodily repulsed from going across that field already."

Cheatham noticed Forrest's face growing redder by the minute. His blue eyes flashed. Cheatham quickly added, "I can't order you to charge, but you can charge under your own orders. The responsibility will rest on you."

"Then I'll charge under my own orders," Forrest grumbled. He spun in the saddle and shouted to his men. "Form ranks in column of fours. We will advance in that formation."

They followed him as he rode into the edge of a field. Across the way, there was an old cabin that stood behind a peach orchard. It would be a long ride across the field under fire, but they were mounted, and horses could cover the distance in a hurry.

A shell exploded overhead, and Forrest saw three horses go down, throwing their riders to the ground. He quickly ordered a halt. He had his men dismount and tighten their saddle girths. He said, "Now, boys, keep quiet. The Yankees are in that tree line yonder."

There was no use in trying to quiet his men. They were already giving the Rebel yell, and he hadn't given the order to advance yet. Forrest climbed back on his horse and watched as his men did the same. He stared across the way and figured it would be best to skirt the edge of the tree line as they crossed the field. He spurred his horse, his men following. They advanced across the field with few casualties. The artillery had already abandoned the field, and the Federal infantry was slowly pulling back.

As they approached the halfway point, Forrest turned to his bugler and shouted, "Sound the charge, Isham!"

The bugler didn't have time to get the instrument to his lips before Forrest was shouting for everyone to charge. The column of cavalry surged ahead toward the fleeing infantry.

His timing couldn't have been more perfect. As they approached the tree line, the Twenty-Third Missouri Infantry had just been given the order to retreat. His men crashed into the retreating mass of men. The enemy soldiers panicked and fled through the trees in terror. Forrest and his men were amid them, firing their pistols and slashing with their sabers. Forrest was in a fury. All of his life, he had been a man who loved the fray.

Forrest was yelling at his men, "Mix with 'em! Mix with 'em!"

Charles Warren came face to face with Forrest during the melee. He couldn't believe this was the same man he'd watched pacing in the rear. His expression had completely changed. His face was flush and reminded Charles of a painting he'd once seen of an Indian chief in battle. Forrest's eyes normally looked calm, but now they seemed to flash fire.

Warren watched Forrest strike down a fat man with his sword. The man was having trouble keeping up with the others, struggling to carry his rifle and his own weight.

The charge had gone perfectly until they reached the tree line. Forrest's horses hit the Black Jack thicket with a crash. Men were thrown over their horses' heads, while others were knocked from the saddle by tree branches. Vegetation had stopped what the Federals had failed to do with rifles. The charge was over.

Almost immediately, Forrest decided his cavalry wouldn't be worth much in the trees. Ha also realized that, if they remained there, they would be sitting ducks. It was just another lesson learned for the young commander, and he gave the command to fall back.

Charles Warren had learned a valuable lesson about his new commander. When in combat, the man seemed as if he could be as dangerous to his friends as to the enemy. He'd watched him swinging the saber overhead without regard to who may have been near him. He seemed to be possessed by Satan himself. He had also had another effect on Charles. By his example in this one fight alone, Charles made up his mind that he would follow the man even if he ordered him to charge the gates of hell itself.

USA

Grant had just departed the Hornet's Nest, where he had instructed Prentiss and Will Wallace to hold out as long as possible. He needed to buy time for Buell's troops to arrive. If the Confederate army broke his line now, he would be forced to make a stand with his back to the river.

Arriving back at the heights overlooking Pittsburg Landing, Grant turned to Colonel Webster, his chief of artillery, and said, "J.D., I want you to mask all the cannons you can find on these hills. This is where we'll make our last stand if the Rebs break through."

"Right," Webster replied and rode away.

At that moment, the courier Rawlins had sent to find Lew Wallace's lost division arrived. The man's horse looked as though it would fall over, and the rider looked just as bad.

The courier saluted Grant and said, "Sir, beg to report."

"Report," Grant said plainly.

"Sir, I found General Wallace," he said as he jerked a thumb over his shoulder toward the west. "He had marched his division right past the battlefield and was heading southwest toward Memphis, Tennessee."

Grant grimaced. "Doggone it; what for?"

"Said he wasn't sure where to find your flank." The young courier felt as though he was the one that messed up and was having to explain his own mistake. "Sir, I mean, he just got lost. He was afraid he would come marching in behind the enemy and get trapped."

"Is he gonna countermarch?" Grant asked.

"He's not making an about face, if that's what you mean," he shrugged. "When I left, he was ordering the front of his column to turn and march back past the rest like a giant snake changing directions."

"Lovely," Grant said mostly to himself.

Grant looked toward the river. He could imagine the Confederate army pushing his men into the water. It would be a disaster and possibly end the war for the Union.

He stared at the crowd of fugitives racing down the steep hill toward the landing. He estimated the number at about five thousand men. It sickened him to see so many able-bodied men hiding back here while their fellow soldiers were up there fighting and dying.

General Grant spurred his horse down the hill into the mass of cowards. He begged and pleaded with them to return to the fight. Nothing seemed to work. He attempted to shame them into going back. It was useless. The general turned his horse and rode back to the top of the hill where his staff and thirty-man cavalry escort were waiting.

He looked at the young lieutenant who commanded the squadron of cavalry and said, "I want you to send half your men to the left and half to the right. Draw sabers and ride these men down since they refuse to fight."

The lieutenant looked shocked. He wasn't sure if Grant was serious or not. After an awkward pause, the lieutenant saluted and ordered his men down the hill. Grant watched as the thirty cavalrymen rode through the mass of men with their sabers raised. Men began to scatter from the charging horses. They raced into the trees and even into the river. As soon as the two groups met in the middle, they turned and rode back to the top of the hill where Grant was watching.

The young lieutenant was smiling. He asked, "How was that, sir?"

Grant looked past the cavalryman at the mass of men returning from the woods and water. He said, "I guess it'll have to do."

He climbed off his horse and handed it to one of his aides. Across the river, he could see a group of horsemen with a signal officer. The man was busy waving his flag, sending signals across the river. Grant remembered a young West Pointer named Edward Porter Alexander who had helped to create the semaphore system. Grant remembered that Alexander was from Georgia. That boy was now serving with the enemy.

Grant strode out away from the trees to get a better look. He hoped to see General Nelson's troops arriving across the way. All he could see was a group of horsemen but no infantry.

Ulysses Grant had inadvertently stepped in front of the signal man on this side of the river. The man was waving his flag furiously. In front of him was a sloppily-dressed man in an old military coat with no insignia. He didn't have time for this idiot; he had messages to send.

The signalman shouted at Grant, "Get out of the way, you damned fool! Can't you see I'm signaling?"

General Grant politely stepped out of the man's way without a word.

USA

Brigadier General Benjamin Prentiss paced furiously in the Hornet's Nest. His men had turned back at least eleven separate Confederate charges here. He wasn't sure how long they could hold this position. He'd promised Grant he would hold to the last, but Grant had also promised him reinforcements soon. It was beginning to appear that neither of them would keep their promise.

Brigadier General Will Wallace rode through the trees and found Prentiss pacing. He saluted and said, "Did you send for me, General?"

"Yeah," Prentiss scowled. "I need to borrow another regiment."

"Another?" Will asked. The look of surprise appeared on his face. Prentiss had already borrowed the Eleventh Iowa to bolster his position.

"Yeah," Prentiss ranked Will Wallace and didn't want to have to ask. "They're trying to get around my unprotected left flank. I've already refused my line, but they're still coming."

Wallace shook his head. "I don't know, Ben. I mean I'm hard pressed on my right also. Sherman is supposed to be over there, but I'm not in contact with him. He may be gone for all I know."

"Look, Will," Prentiss stepped close to Wallace's horse, "if they get around my left, it won't matter anyhow."

"Right," Will Wallace lowered his head in thought. "I'll send you the Fourteenth Iowa."

"Just hold as long as you can. Lew Wallace should be here anytime." Prentiss patted Will Wallace on the leg.

Will saluted and rode back west. Prentiss continued his pacing. His division was pretty much used up. He didn't like the fact that he had recently been promoted to division command and now his men were being sacrificed to save his old antagonist Grant's ass. *If I were in command of this army like I should have been, we wouldn't have been surprised here, Prentiss thought.*

The orders had been clear. They were to do nothing to bring on a general engagement before Buell arrived. Prentiss hadn't even sent out pickets for fear of causing a fight. He'd made up his mind earlier that he wouldn't take responsibility for this mess. His brigade commander, Colonel Everett Peabody, had ordered out the patrol that began the battle this morning, and Prentiss was gonna make sure that's where the blame rested. It didn't matter that the man had been killed this morning; it would make laying the blame on him easier.

He hoped he could cover up the mistakes he had made this morning. When the Confederates had struck this morning, he'd been so surprised that for the first hour he couldn't force himself to make a rational decision.

Prentiss had seen action in the Mexican War and believed himself to be a military genius. They'd fought out in the open in Mexico, and he felt like they should do the same here. One of his brigades had taken up a good position in the trees near Spain Field this morning. Prentiss had ordered them out into the field to fight. It hadn't taken long for his troops to break from the onslaught.

His division had soon broken and raced for the rear. Prentiss had been swept right along with them. They had met Will Wallace's division moving up here at the Hornet's Nest, and that's the only thing that had stopped his men from racing all the way to the landing.

The sunken road and Hornet's Nest had proven so strong from continued attacks, that Prentiss decided then and there he would proclaim that he chose this naturally strong position.

He stopped pacing and looked at his men all huddled in the sunken road. He'd begun the morning with almost five thousand men, and now he was making his last stand with less than a thousand. The rest had either raced off to the landing, been captured, or were fighting with other units. Prentiss's ego wouldn't allow him to admit it, but he wouldn't be able to hold here if not for Will Wallace's fresh division on his right.

There was a burst of fire to Prentiss's right. He spun and looked toward the sound. It was so far to his right that it was actually fifty yards in his rear. He heard a voice yell his name and turned to see Captain William McMichael of Wallace's staff.

Prentiss screamed above the din. "Not now, Captain; I've got more pressing matters!"

McMichael was taken aback momentarily. He yelled, "Just thought you should know that Wallace's division has broken. We were turned on the right. I came here to tell you that you better make for the rear or you'll be surrounded!"

"Damn," Prentiss said to himself and watched McMichael race for the rear. He turned back to the sounds of firing in his rear. It was beginning to grow louder. There was no longer time to react. It was time to go. He quickly gave the order to his staff officers to get the men moving toward the rear.

He raced back down into the ravine behind the sunken road with his men. Briars and branches tore at his uniform. His hat was knocked off his head, but he didn't bother to retrieve it. The Confederate infantry was pouring a devastating fire into their backs. It was quickly growing apparent that they would be lucky to escape.

Prentiss stopped at the bottom of the ravine. Men were racing up the other side, while other men passed them coming back into the ravine. He walked up the rise and looked toward the rear. Confederate soldiers were pouring into the field from all directions. There was nowhere left to go.

Ben Prentiss heard screaming behind him. He turned to see a man on his hands and one leg crawling toward him. He was dragging his useless right leg.

The disgusted general lowered his head and wished he didn't have to give his next command. Bullets were flying past in all directions. It was useless, and there was nothing to do but order his men to stack arms. Holding out any longer would result in nothing but more casualties to his men.

Some of his men obeyed and began stacking arms and raising their hands. Others refused to allow the Confederates to take their weapons and began smashing the rifles against trees. The enemy soldiers were close by this point. Every time a man would smash his rifle, he would be shot down. Prentiss quickly raced around, attempting to stop the useless slaughter.

The Confederate soldiers ran down among the Federal troops. They were elated at the thought of capturing so many men. The heat had become unbearable, and the enemy soldiers were low on water. Prentiss noticed a puddle of muddy water with a dead Federal soldier lying in the edge. Confederate soldiers took their tin cups and scooped the foul liquid and drank it. They were so parched they didn't seem to notice the dead man lying there.

It wasn't long before an officer arrived and ordered Prentiss and his men to the rear. The Confederate army had captured over two thousand of Prentiss and Wallace's men.

USA

Will Wallace had just sent Captain McMichael of his staff to warn Benjamin Prentiss that his division was breaking, when his men finally gave way. The Confederates had moved around his flank and began to advance across his rear. Wallace wondered where Sherman had gone. The man was supposed to be protecting his right.

At least there was the Corinth-Pittsburg Road, which ran through his division. Most of his troops could escape up this road to Grant's last line at the river. The situation was hopeless, and all Wallace could think about was getting his men out. He gave the order and watched his men race through the trees and down the road. He rode across a small ravine with his aide and brother-in-law, Cyrus Dickey, at his side.

Wallace paused at the edge of the road to allow his men to run past as he studied the situation. Cyrus pointed toward the Confederate soldiers coming up the road not thirty yards away.

Will Wallace raised himself high in the saddle to study the situation, when the bullet struck him behind the left ear and exited his left eye. Cyrus watched his commander crash to the ground, face down onto the road. There was no doubt in the young lieutenant's mind that Wallace was dead, but he refused to leave his body behind.

He quickly rounded up an orderly and two privates, and the four of them began to carry him toward the rear. They'd almost gone a hundred yards before the enemy began to close on them.

"We've gotta leave him," the orderly said.

Cyrus shook his head. "I can't leave him. He's my sister's husband."

"He's dead anyway," the orderly replied as he dropped Wallace's leg and raced toward the rear.

Cyrus noticed some ammunition crates alongside the road. He ordered the two privates to help him prop his brother-in-law against the crates to prevent his body from being trampled. The three men then scattered into the woods.

Cyrus raced through the forest. His eyes were soon blinded by tears. He couldn't believe he had just abandoned his brother-in-law. He tried to convince himself that the orderly had been right. Will was dead, and there was no real purpose in continuing to carry his body to the rear. It felt as if Cyrus had lost his own brother. Will Wallace had been the most likable man he'd ever met.

He moved along the edge of the tree line and managed to skirt the field that was filled with so many Confederates and the Federal prisoners. It was important for him to get to the rear and let Grant know that Wallace was dead and his division scattered.

Cyrus reached the landing exhausted, sweating, and out of breath. He found Grant behind a long line of cannons just west of the river. Grant recognized Cyrus as a member of Wallace's staff. Cyrus tried to speak but couldn't catch his breath.

"Take your time," Grant insisted. He began puffing on a cigar as he patiently waited for what would surely be a report from Will Wallace.

"He's dead," Cyrus gasped. "Will's dead. His division is scattered to hell and back—the few that weren't captured. Pretty sure Prentiss is captured also."

"Dead," Grant repeated to himself. At that moment, Grant remembered Will's wife on his headquarters boat below. He stared at the tears running down Cyrus Dickey's filthy face. He said, "Do you know Will's wife?"

"Yes, sir," Cyrus mumbled. "She's my sister."

Grant lowered his head. The situation was very sad, but Grant didn't have time to deal with it at the moment. Prentiss and Wallace's divisions had broken, and Lew Wallace's division was still missing.

He said, "Young man, Ann is on my boat at the landing. It's the *Tigress*. I left her there this morning. I need you to go down there and tell her."

Cyrus nodded and then stumbled on past Grant toward the river.

Ann Dickey Wallace was a nervous wreck. Her husband, her father, two brothers, and two of her husband's brothers were in the army fighting somewhere on that bluff. When the wounded began arriving, she had busied herself in caring for them. If not for the wounded, she may have suffered a breakdown just like William Sherman had last winter.

Things had suddenly quieted down. There had been severe cannon fire for the past two hours, and now they had fallen silent. Hearing all those cannons made her wonder how anyone could survive. She wondered what the odds were for all of her family members to come out unharmed. There was still the occasional sound of rifle fire, but nothing like earlier. She hoped that meant the battle was over.

Men were stationed all around the boat to prevent the stragglers from boarding. She had seen men so frightened this morning that they had raced out into the river and drowned. They had become so panicked they had forgotten that they couldn't swim.

She was bent over a man who had been shot in the leg. The man was waiting for a surgeon to amputate. She gave him water and had just begun to wash his face when she saw a familiar face approaching.

Ann stood up and smiled. She said, "Cyrus Dickey, I'm so relieved to see you."

That was when the expression on his face struck her. He continued walking toward her, eyes filled with tears. He grabbed her and held her tight.

"Who is it?" Ann asked as she attempted to pull away from Cyrus's grip.

"I'm sorry," Cyrus pulled her back into his chest. "Will's been killed. I tried to bring his body back, but I was about to be captured. I was forced to abandon him and run through the trees to escape being captured."

She fought back the tears as she buried her face in her brother's chest. Ann kept thinking that maybe her brother was wrong. Maybe he just thought Will was dead. She made up her mind that she would hold out hope until she actually saw Will's body.

After a few moments, Ann turned and continued helping with the wounded. Staying busy was the only thing she could do to keep from crying.

CSA

Colonel Thomas Jordan sat on his horse and studied the Federal line on the hill across the ravine. His map told him this was Dill Branch and just beyond was the hill overlooking Pittsburg Landing. Jordan understood that if that hill could be taken, Grant would be forced into the River or the swamps to the north. Either way, the battle would be over.

He watched Brigadier General Chalmers's men fighting their way up the steep slope. Men were slipping because their brogans could get no traction. They grabbed at vines and roots, anything to pull themselves up the hill.

Jordan heard another explosion down in the river and watched a huge shell from the gunboats fly high overhead in an arc. Besides the noise, little damage was being done.

He turned back to watch Chalmers's men as they approached the top. He could barely see through the trees beyond them, but somewhere up there was Grant's last line. Jordan could almost feel them.

Chalmers's men burst into a charge and disappeared into the foliage. Suddenly, it sounded as if every gun in the Federal army opened fire. A good deal of it was rifle fire, but the cannons almost drowned out the sound. It hadn't lasted but a few seconds. Chalmers's men came crashing back out of the brush and slid down the slope. They weren't in full retreat but stopped far enough down the hill to prevent getting hit. *We're gonna need more men up there, Jordan thought.*

Jordan mounted his horse to go find more troops to support Chalmers's attack. He was about to put spurs to the horse when he saw Chalmers and his brigade coming off the hill. He met Chalmers as he crossed Dill Branch.

Chalmers recognized Jordan and nodded.

Jordan said, "General Chalmers, why are you quitting the field?"

Chalmers looked surprised at the question. He replied, "You should know. Beauregard ordered us to fall back."

"What?" Jordan asked. He couldn't believe his ears. Beauregard would never order the men back before the battle was completed.

"That's right," Chalmers said. "The order is for all commands to fall back and reorganize for the final assault tomorrow—if Grant is still here."

Jordan was bewildered. He was Beauregard's top staff officer, and here was a brigade commander that knew more about what was happening than he did. Chalmers watched Jordan shake his head and turn his horse southward.

There was nothing left to do but ride back to Shiloh Church and talk to Beauregard. Along the way, he noticed that all the commands were pulling back. Jordan looked toward the western sky. The sun was beginning to set. It wouldn't matter what Beauregard had done, the battle was over for today.

Arriving at Beauregard's headquarters, there was still enough light left for Jordan to recognize the army commander surrounded by his staff and General Braxton Bragg. There was another man standing in the group that Jordan didn't recognize, but he was definitely in a Federal uniform.

Beauregard saw Jordan dismounting and attempted to call him over. The words barely came out above a whisper, and his voice was so raspy that the words were barely comprehendible. "Colonel, I'd like you to meet someone."

Jordan noticed that Beauregard's voice was almost gone now. The man looked like he would collapse at any moment. He wondered why the commander hadn't retired long ago and let someone else direct the battle.

"Sir," Jordan gave Beauregard a stiff salute.

Beauregard turned to the man in Federal uniform and whispered, "This is Thomas Jordan, my chief of staff."

Prentiss nodded and then extended a hand. Jordan shook his hand stiffly. He wondered what this was all about. Prentiss said, "It would be a privilege meeting you under different circumstances."

Beauregard turned to Jordan and said, "This is Brigadier General Benjamin Prentiss, late commander of the Federal Sixth Division."

"A pleasure to make your acquaintance," Jordan replied and then turned to Beauregard. "Sir, did you order the men to halt?"

"That's right," Beauregard strained to speak. "Our men are disorganized, and we need to regroup."

"Sir, we almost took the landing," Jordan began to explain the situation. "Grant was about to be pressed into the river."

"It's fine," Beauregard whispered. "Prentiss and his division have been captured, and Wallace's Second Division is destroyed. In the morning we will make short work of Grant."

To the south, a courier approached on horseback and asked where he could find General Johnston. One of Beauregard's staff officers informed the man that Johnston was dead.

"Where can I find the present commander?" the man asked.

"You've found him," Jordan spoke up. "What you got?"

"Message from Corinth," the courier replied.

"I'll take it," Jordan stepped forward. Upon close inspection, he could tell the man had been riding hard. His uniform was disheveled, and his horse was soaked with sweat. The courier passed him the note.

Jordan opened the paper and attempted to read. It had grown too dark for him to make out the words. He called for a lantern.

A camp aide quickly lit the lantern and held it up for Jordan. Beauregard stood patiently and watched Jordan scan the message. Jordan said, "It's a message from Helm in North Alabama. He says Buell's entire army is advancing toward Decatur."

"Splendid," Beauregard tried to say. "I told you we had nothing to worry about."

"He's mistaken," Prentiss quickly spoke up. "He'll be here in the morning, and he won't be alone. Lew Wallace's division will have arrived from upstream also. Between Grant's men, Buell's men, and Wallace's division, you'll face seventy thousand men in the morning."

Beauregard smiled. He knew Prentiss was just trying to scare him. *The man knows Grant's in trouble, and he's trying to save the Federal army.* Beauregard wondered if the general thought he'd take him at his word and order a retreat tonight.

An orderly was busy building a fire for the officers. Beauregard took a camp stool between Bragg and Jordan. He turned to his chief of staff and said, "Send a message to Richmond. Tell General Cooper that General Johnston has been killed, but we have won a complete victory here today."

Jordan scribbled furiously and then called for a courier. Beauregard looked across the fire at Ben Prentiss. The man sat on a camp stool and stared into the fire. Beauregard said, "Thomas, I'm leaving General Prentiss in your charge tonight. I want him to be treated as well as I would want one of our captured officers treated."

"I'll see to it," Jordan replied.

"In the morning we'll send him back to Corinth with the other prisoners," Beauregard said. He glanced at General Bragg and turned back to Jordan. "We'll need to talk in private. Can you find a place for Mister Prentiss until we've finished?"

"Yes, sir," Jordan stood. He found an orderly and ordered him to take General Prentiss out of earshot and feed him. Jordan returned to the fire in time to see Generals Hardee and Breckinridge arriving. Both men dismounted and walked to the fire. Several staff officers politely gave up their seats to the two men.

Breckinridge, being the junior officer, decided to let Hardee speak first. General Hardee scratched at his gray goatee and said, "We just came by for orders, sir."

Beauregard was trying to sound upbeat, but his voice wouldn't cooperate. He whispered, "We were so disorganized that I decided to call a halt so we could rest the men and prepare to finish this thing tomorrow."

Bragg spoke up. "Our commands are all mixed together, and there's no way for us to command our own troops. The alignment forced us all into one big line."

"Doesn't matter," Beauregard whispered. "Grant's army is whipped. Just continue to do what you did today."

The four generals sat together quietly for a long moment. It was obvious to the others that Beauregard needed to rest and remain quiet to prevent ruining his voice. Hardee said, "If that's all, I'm gonna return to my men for the night."

"That's all," Beauregard whispered. There was nothing they could do now. It was completely dark.

Breckinridge gave a sloppy salute as he rose and followed Hardee back to their horses. Bragg was shaking his head. He said, "I'm not going back out there tonight. A man can't sleep with all the wounded howling. Is there a tent available here?"

"You can share mine," Beauregard smiled. "It was the property of one General William Sherman this morning, but he left too fast to take it with him."

Braxton Bragg, ever humorless, nodded and rose from the stool. His knees creaked. He mumbled, "I'm too damned old to be sleeping out on the ground anyhow."

Jordan watched him walk back toward the tents. He asked, "Just how old is he?"

"He's in his mid-forties," Beauregard whispered. "I'm forty-four, and I think he is a year older than I am."

"Damn," Jordan said louder than he meant to. "I thought he was in his sixties. He looks way older than you."

Jordan always loved to stroke Beauregard's ego, but this time he was serious. Bragg had a haggard look—hair almost gray and face wrinkled from continuous frowning.

There was a commotion on the road. Both men turned and saw the prisoners passing by in the night. The fire reflected off their faces as they trudged along the road. They were filthy, their faces smeared with black powder, some with blood. Most were so exhausted from the long day that they could barely manage to place one foot in front of the other. There were over two thousand of them, and it took quite some time for them to pass.

Beauregard stood from the stool and said, "I'm going to Sherman's tent and get some rest. The doctors have been ordering me to bed all day. I'll have Prentiss sent back over here."

Jordan nodded. He picked up a stick and began to poke at the fire. Across the fire, he saw a figure approaching from the road. Smoke blew into his eyes, and he rubbed them with his hands.

"Colonel Jordan," the man said as he took a seat. "How goes it?"

Jordan recognized the voice. It was Beauregard's newest aide-de-camp, Colonel Jacob Thompson. He replied, "Going alright, Jake, but I wish we could have finished it today. Where have you been?"

"General Beauregard sent me to inform General Polk that we were falling back to reorganize and rest the men," Thompson spat into the fire.

Jordan poked at the fire again. "How'd the bishop take that?"

"Hell, Thomas, you know Bishop Polk," Thompson half crouched and dragged his stool around the fire closer to Jordan. "He'd just as soon be passing a collection plate as fightin' a war."

Prentiss arrived and slumped onto a stool beside Jordan. Thompson cocked his head to the side and studied the Federal prisoner. He said, "Now, if I didn't know any better, I'd have to say that fellow looks like Ben Prentiss, the politician from Illinois."

Prentiss looked up. He squinted with his already small, beady eyes. "Sounds like Jacob Thompson, the politician from Mississippi."

"You'd be right," Thompson sprang from the stool. He reached out, and the two shook hands as if they were old friends. "I had no idea you was a soldier too."

"I'd have said the same thing about you," Prentiss laughed. "Actually, I did see action in the Mexican War."

Thompson grinned. "I saw all my action in the halls of congress until now."

Prentiss took the jab lightly. He had wanted to be a congressman for a long while but had lost the election miserably. He'd given Thompson a jab about not seeing action in the Mexican War. Thompson had been elected to congress while that war was being waged. He'd risen to be the Secretary of the Interior in President Buchanan's cabinet.

Jordan lowered his head and began to rub his eyes. He mumbled, "Just what I need—stuck between two politicians for the night."

Thompson slapped Jordan on the back. He was used to all the lawyer and politician jokes. He actually enjoyed them. They soon began to reminiscence about the old days. Prentiss had begun his career as a businessman, while Thompson had begun his as an attorney. Jordan actually found some of the stories quite humorous.

The subject soon changed to the present situation. Thompson asked, "Ben, I bet you fellows were surprised this morning."

"We were," Prentiss grew serious. "I told Grant and Sherman we were in trouble here. I wanted to entrench the men, but the two absolutely refused. I tried to warn 'em."

Thompson nodded and smiled a toothy grin. "We'll capture those two in the morning."

"You gentlemen have had your way today," Prentiss smiled back grimly. "Tomorrow it will be very different. You'll see. Buell will have arrived, and we'll turn the tables on you in the morning."

Thompson laughed out loud. The loud laugh caught Jordan by surprise, and he recoiled from the sound.

Prentiss asked, "Why did Beauregard call it off today?"

Thompson shook his head. Jordan said, "Mostly because he is unwell. He's been back here in the rear all day watching stragglers. He thought we were disorganized and needed rest. If he'd been well, he would have been at the front like he was at Manassas."

"It was a mistake. Buell will be here in the morning." Prentiss replied. He then stared into the fire.

"I believe you're wrong," Jordan said. "I have a message that he is advancing on Decatur, Alabama."

"It's a mistake," Prentiss replied in sincerity. It was obvious he wasn't joking around any longer. "He'll be here. You'll see."

Thompson began to smile again. He didn't believe a word Prentiss was saying. The man was just trying to scare them. He would be the one to see who would be in trouble tomorrow.

Jordan looked at Prentiss and said. "It's been a long day—a long week actually. I'm ready to turn in for the night."

"Right," Prentiss replied, "and I'm ready also."

Thompson smiled again. "I'm with you fellows. You know I'm not a spring chicken anymore."

Jordan remembered that Thompson was in his fifties. He looked ten years younger than Bragg. They rose from the stools and prowled around the area until they found some dismantled tents piled together. They made a bed of the heap. Jordan placed Prentiss between him and Thompson for security reasons. He had a difficult time going to sleep because the two politicians continued hacking on one another. They finally grew tired of the banter and fell silent. Thomas Jordan finally went to sleep.

At daylight, they were awakened by the sound of distant artillery fire. Prentiss sat straight up between the two and announced, "There is Buell, just like I told ya."

CSA

Before dark, Forrest had been up near Grant's last line. There was nothing behind the Federal army but a river and some swamps. One more push and it would have been over. He had watched General Chalmers's brigade move against that line alone and get cut up. It was obvious it would take more than a few disjointed brigades to break that line. At that point he sent a message to General Polk to say that a concentrated attack here would destroy the Federal army. The courier had returned with an order for Forrest to fall back and reform his men during the night. He wasn't very happy with that order.

He had ridden back to camp only to learn that his fifteen-year-old son, Willie, was missing. The boy and two of his friends about the same age had ridden out of camp together. Forrest had promised his wife that Willie would be safe with him. No one had seen the boy in over an hour. Forrest began to worry and soon mounted his horse to search for his wayward son. He already planned to whip the boy with a leather trace when he found him.

It had soon grown too dark to see anything, so Forrest rode back to the area covered by Indian mounds, where his men were bivouacked. He climbed the Indian mound overlooking the river. He would do a little scouting to try and take his mind off his missing boy.

He studied the damned Yankee boats moving back and forth across the river. That could mean several things: they could be ferrying the wounded across the river and out of harm's way; the Federal army could be retreating after the whipping they'd taken today; or it could mean Buell had arrived and they were bringing reinforcements across the river. Whatever it was, Forrest needed to know. He stood there watching the lights on the boats and the smoke rising against a darkening sky. He could hear the occasional ring of a bell and the sounds of steam exhausting.

Nearer to him were the two gunboats. Every fifteen minutes they would lob a couple of shells into the sky. Other than the noise of the exploding ordnance, their fire did very little damage.

He'd been studying the scene for about fifteen minutes when he heard a commotion behind him. Standing by a fire in the near distance were his son and his two buddies. There were fifteen other men gathered there dressed in blue uniforms. Forrest stomped down the mound and toward the fire.

"Pa," Willie smiled a toothy grin, "we captured fifteen Yankees hiding in the woods."

Forrest saw the look of accomplishment on his son's face. He no longer had the heart to discipline the boy. He'd left camp without permission, but in doing so he had helped his old man out. Forrest was struck with an ingenious idea. He looked at the three proud lads and said, "Good work, boys; very good work."

The three smiled with pride. Forrest turned to his staff officers and ordered, "Have these Yankees undress down to their drawers. I'll be right back."

The staff officers were taken aback. They looked at each other, not believing what they were hearing. As Forrest left the fire, the staff officers quickly had the prisoners undressing. If they had learned anything about Bedford Forrest, it was to not question orders.

Forrest returned with fifteen handpicked men of his command. He looked at the half-dressed Federal prisoners. He said, "We gonna borrow your clothes for a bit. You can put on these fellers' clothes or just stand by the fire. Don't matter to me."

One of the Federal prisoners giggled. Forrest eyeballed the man. He asked, "Somethin' funny?"

"The way you talk is all," the man replied in a heavy northern accent. It was obvious the man wasn't quite right by the way he acted. "The way you said borrow. I thought you said bar."

"Yeah, well..." Forrest stepped toward the man. He could do several things here. He had slapped men for far less an insult but decided he didn't have time at the moment. "I may not talk like you fellers with all the learnin', but I'm not the one standing half-naked in front of a fire as a prisoner either."

The man's smile disappeared. Forrest told his men to put the prisoners' uniforms on. The fifteen troopers quickly complied. Forrest stepped in front of the group and said, "Lieutenant Sheridan, you're in command of this little outfit."

He watched Sheridan nod and was about to continue, when he recognized one of his handpicked men. He asked, "Do you have any idea why I picked you?"

"No, sir," Charles Warren replied in surprise that Forrest even knew him.

"Cause you was right with me during the fight this afternoon, and I didn't see no fear in your eyes at all," Forrest said and then continued delivering his orders. "I want you men to infiltrate the Federal lines in these uniforms. Find out anything you can—especially if those are Buell's troops coming over on them damned boats. Don't talk to none of them Yankee sons-of-bitches neither. They may catch your voice like this smart one over here. Just stand around the fires with 'em and pick up on their talk. Take your time, but bring me back some information."

"Right, sir," Lieutenant Sheridan replied and turned to the others. "You heard him. Let's go."

He watched them disappear into the night. Forrest returned to the Indian mound and studied the boats again. He was anything but patient. He wanted to know what was happening, and he wanted to know now.

Lieutenant J.P. Strange of his staff made his way up the mound and sat next to Forrest. He stared at the boats for a moment and then said, "The Yankee prisoners are protesting against such harsh treatment."

"Harsh treatment?" Forrest asked. "What harsh treatment?"

"They say it's against the rules of warfare to force them to undress," Strange smiled. He couldn't wait to hear Forrest's reaction to this.

"Rules of war," Forrest repeated. "Let me get this straight. I can kill 'em in battle, but it offends them for me to take their clothes."

"That's pretty much it," Strange agreed.

"Damned," Forrest shook his head. "I'm glad I ain't went to no West Point."

Forrest and Strange sat on the mound watching the boats and making small talk. Sheridan's group had been gone for over an hour when Strange glanced around and noticed them approaching the fire. He said, "Sheridan's back."

Forrest jumped to his feet and raced toward the fire. He stumbled off the mound and almost fell. The man never slowed down. He reached the fire, and as Sheridan was beginning to salute, Forrest asked, "What have you got?"

Sheridan cleared his throat. "It's Buell's men alright."

"You sure?" Forrest asked again. He needed to be certain if he was gonna go up the Confederate chain of command with this information.

"I'm positive," Sheridan replied. "We've all stood around the fire with his men. They're all clean and neat—nothing like Grant's men who've been fighting all day. Only thing is, only a small part of their army has gotten across. Grant's army is in disarray. We've stood by their fires also. They're beaten. Buell's men are confident that tomorrow they'll beat us."

"Damned," Forrest muttered to himself. Of the three scenarios he'd had in his mind, this was the worst possible one. He stood there in thought a long moment. He said, "Sheridan, just keep them Yankee clothes on. I may send you out again."

He turned to Lieutenant Strange and said, "Come on, J.P.; let's go wake up some generals."

The two men mounted their horses. Forrest looked back by the fire where the Yankee prisoners sat in their underwear. A few yards away was another fire surrounded by members of his staff, Willie, and his friends.

Forrest said, "Willie, you and your buddies better be here when I get back."

"Yes, sir," Willie nodded.

Forrest wanted to make sure Willie got the message. "If you're not, I'm gonna beat all three of ya'll with a plow line."

Forrest and Strange rode back up the winding trail to the top of the hill. Here they emerged from the forest and entered a large field. A half mile beyond was where Prentiss and his men had surrendered. There were troops camped here. Forrest made his way among them and was directed to their commander's tent. He ordered one of the staff officers there to wake their commander.

Forrest and Strange waited patiently. General Chalmers stepped from the captured Yankee tent and wiped his eyes. His face was barely visible in the light of the candle lantern hanging from the tent pole. Chalmers asked, "What's the problem?"

"Do you know where Johnston is camped?" Forrest ignored Chalmers's question.

"I have no idea," Chalmers stopped rubbing his eyes and looked up at Forrest. The man was only a silhouette in the darkness. "The army is scattered to hell and back. Is that you Forrest?"

"That's me," Forrest replied. He had been working with Chalmers all afternoon on the right. "Buell's army is here, and we've got to hit them tonight before they all get across the river."

"Buell?" Chalmers asked.

"That's right; I've had scouts in their damned lines," Forrest realized he needed an officer higher than a brigade commander to report this information to, but if Chalmers believed him, the man might try to do something himself. "We had better finish them tonight or withdraw. We wait until tomorrow and we'll be whipped like hell before ten."

Chalmers personally didn't like this man. Forrest was a slave dealer. He'd earned his money in a disgusting way. The man wasn't polished. *Hell, he wasn't even a gentleman for that matter. The only reason he'd been made colonel was because he had paid out of his own pocket to outfit his regiment. This man won't ever make a soldier, Chalmers thought. He probably doesn't even know what he's talking about.*

"I don't have the authority to order an attack," Chalmers decided to pass Forrest off on someone else. "You'll have to go higher than me. I command one brigade, which at the moment is less than eight hundred men."

"Come on, J.P.," Forrest said as he spun the horse toward the west. There was no use in trying to get help from Chalmers. He obviously wasn't interested.

They rode on westward as another barrage of shells from the gunboats began to arc overhead. Forrest rode past a Sibley tent that contained four Confederate soldiers who were playing cards. It amazed him that anyone had the energy to play cards this late. Most had long since been asleep, except the few who were prowling the battlefield searching for wounded comrades.

One of the shells failed to explode overhead and struck the tent. Cards flew through the air, along with the men themselves. The lantern on the table crashed to the ground, catching part of the tent on fire. All four men were dead—killed by a random shell. Forrest ignored the carnage and continued his search.

They found Breckinridge's headquarters near the spot where Prentiss had surrendered. He was awake, sitting by a fire sipping from a flask. Forrest had heard rumors about Breckinridge and his bourbon. Breckinridge saw Forrest and rose from the stump. He didn't recognize him but noticed the stars on his collar.

"What can I do for you, Colonel?" Breckinridge asked.

Forrest noticed the way Breckinridge sounded. He was sipping bourbon from a glass, but he wasn't drunk. The man had been the Vice-President of the United States. He was smart enough not to become intoxicated while commanding his troops.

"We've got a problem," Forrest leaned forward in the saddle. "Buell is crossing the river with his army as we speak. You've got to give the order for an attack right now."

Breckinridge looked stunned. He said, "I just left Beauregard not two hours ago, and he has information that Buell is headed toward Decatur."

"His information is wrong," Forrest began to grow frustrated. He wondered why these people refused to believe him. "Look, I've had scouts in their lines tonight. They're Buell's troops alright. My men have stood by the enemy campfires and listened to enough conversations to know it's true."

Breckinridge lowered his head. He believed Forrest, but then again what could he do? He said, "You'll have to find Hardee or Beauregard. I'm the junior corps commander; I only command the Reserve Corps, which is hardly bigger than most divisions."

"Where can I find Hardee?" Forrest asked.

"I have no idea," Breckinridge shrugged. He genuinely wished he could help. He'd been doing his job tonight and was trying to find someone to help. He added, "You've done the Confederate service justice tonight, Colonel."

"Not yet I haven't," Forrest replied and reined his horse to the west.

He and Strange rode through the night, searching for Hardee or Beauregard. No one seemed to know where they could be. It was like searching for a needle in a haystack. Near midnight, the sky began to cover with clouds. The night became darker. Lightning began to flash from the western sky. *And the good news just keeps a coming, Forrest thought.*

It was just before one when they found General Hardee's headquarters. The storm was almost on top of them when Forrest and Strange dismounted from the horses to stretch their legs.

One of Hardee's staff officers was still awake and asked what the two men wanted.

Forrest had long ago lost patience with these damned staff officers that think they're above him. He said, "I need to see General Hardee now."

"What for?" the man asked. It was obvious that he wouldn't be bullied by some colonel.

"I have information about the Federal army," Forrest hated that he had to explain himself to this educated idiot. "Important information—and I'm losing my patience with you."

The staff officer said, "The general has had a long day and needs his rest. There's really no need to wake him. Grant is whipped. In the morning there will be nothing left to do but take his surrender."

Forrest stepped forward. His nose was just inches from the staff officers. He wasn't about to waste any more time with this young man. He yelled, "Let me tell you something, you little snot-nosed son-of-a-bitch. If you don't go in there right now and get Hardee up, I'm gonna kick your ass so hard you'll be brushing the boot polish off your teeth in the morning!"

Forrest and Strange watched the young officer disappear into the tent. Hardee soon stumbled from the tent with a candle lantern in his hand. He squinted at Forrest out of narrow eyes.

The man had extremely narrow eyes that reminded Forrest of an old Oriental man he'd met once. As exhausted as Hardee was tonight, it amazed Forrest that he could even see out of those narrow slits.

Hardee asked, "What's the problem?"

"I need to find General Johnston," Forrest replied, ignoring the question.

"Johnston is dead," Hardee announced matter-of-factly. "Beauregard commands the army now."

Forrest was shocked for a moment but recovered quickly. *It don't matter who is in command, he thought. I need to find someone with the balls to make a decision.* He said, "Buell's army is crossing the river as we speak. We've got to finish this thing tonight."

"A night attack?" Hardee asked. He paused in thought. "I can't order that."

"In the morning we'll be whipped like hell," Forrest spoke loudly in an attempt to shake Hardee into acting. He asked, "Who in hell can take some initiative around here?"

"General Beauregard," Hardee rubbed his gray goatee. "Like I said, Colonel, he's in command now. He ordered the army to halt and rest. I'm following orders."

"Damn," Forrest said out loud. He was growing more frustrated by the minute. These men refused to take any responsibility. There was nothing left to do but to locate Beauregard. Forrest didn't bother to salute. He spun and climbed back into the saddle.

They rode southward, checking each field for Beauregard. They had no idea where anyone was located. Strange was exhausted. The day had been long and trying, yet Forrest was willing to continue the search in an attempt to win a victory here.

Forrest noticed Lieutenant Strange yawning. He said, "Here is the deal, J.P.—if Beauregard ain't in this next field, we're goin' back and see what I can get Hardee to do."

"Right," Strange said as he fought the urge to yawn again.

They had been riding around in the darkness since nine. It was almost two in the morning. The first rain drops were beginning to fall. Forrest was through hunting commanders. He decided to return to his command, but on the way, he would stop by General Hardee's tent one more time.

Upon their arrival, the young staff officer put up no protest about waking his commander. Hardee stumbled from the tent again. He didn't bother to light a lantern this time.

Hardee asked, "What can I do for you?"

"Can't find Beauregard," Forrest replied. "I need someone to order an assault on the Federal lines now."

"You'll have to keep looking," Hardee replied. "I'm not about to be court-martialed for insubordination. My orders are to await first light. Keep a vigilante picket line tonight. We'll take care of Grant tomorrow."

Forrest considered arguing with Hardee but thought better of it. There was no need at this point. The biggest part of Buell's army had probably gotten across the river while he was riding around in the dark looking for someone with a backbone. Instead, he simply turned his horse and headed back to his command.

He and Lieutenant Strange rode past the wounded. Lightning flashes lit their faces. Worse still were the faces of the dead. He was especially affected by the face of one particular man. He'd obviously died in severe pain. It was difficult even for a hard man like Forrest to deal with.

He arrived back at camp at two. The storm was in full fury. The fires had long since been doused by the rain. He obtained a lantern and managed to find his way to his group of scouts. Most had nodded off, while others were complaining about the weather.

Lieutenant Sheridan was asleep. Forrest held the lantern near his face and shook him awake. Sheridan sprang up in a start, almost colliding with Forrest. He asked, "What you need, Colonel?"

Forrest said, "Awaken your men. I need ya'll to go back into the Federal lines and find out how much of Buell's army has arrived."

"Right," Sheridan rubbed the rain from his eyes and tried to focus. "Are we gonna hit them?"

"Nope," Forrest replied, "but in the morning, they'll hit us."

Forrest sat on the Indian mound watching the boats moving back and forth across the river. Lieutenant Strange had fallen asleep by his side. Forrest couldn't sleep. He was thoroughly frustrated with the Confederate high command at the moment.

It was just past three in the morning when Lieutenant Sheridan climbed the mound. The man looked as if he were about to drop. Forrest felt sorry for him. This time he waited patiently for him to report.

"Same as before," Sheridan said as he collapsed on the ground beside Forrest. "Buell's army is crossing. Couldn't find out how many, but I'd say at least half. Sorry I couldn't find out more."

"It's fine," Forrest patted Sheridan on the shoulder. "Hell, it wouldn't matter if it was the second coming; them West Point bastards wouldn't act."

Sheridan leaned back against a tree in the rain. Rain drops splashed on his face. He mumbled, "Got to tell ya, that one feller you chose is good."

"Which one?" Forrest asked.

"That Private Charles Warren," Sheridan replied. He was exhausted and on the verge of passing out. "He saved my ass up there. I almost fell asleep among the enemy."

In a moment, Sheridan was snoring. Forrest placed a blanket over his lieutenant's face so he could sleep through the rain. There was nothing left for him to do but blow out the candle.

USA

Ulysses Grant leaned against a large oak tree near the steep hill that overlooked Pittsburg Landing. The day had been exhausting, but he had made up his mind that tomorrow would be different. He thought back to a statement his father had made to him a few months ago. He'd said, "*You're a general now. It's a good job; don't mess it up.*"

So far in Grant's life, he had managed to mess up everything he'd ever done. His father had gotten him an appointment to the Military Academy. He'd graduated and saw a little action in the Mexican War. It was the peace times that were difficult for him. As long as he stayed busy, he could avoid the temptation of the bottle. The bottle had cost Grant a lot in life. He'd been forced to leave the military and make a life as a civilian, but that hadn't worked either. The low point of his life was when he was forced to peddle firewood on a street corner.

Grant heard footsteps and turned to see one of his favorite staff officers approaching. It was Lieutenant Colonel James McPherson. The man had begun the war as an engineering officer on the staff of Grant's boss, Henry Halleck. Halleck had sent him to Grant to keep an eye on this officer who had a habit of drinking too much. Under other circumstances, Grant would have despised the man, but he'd learned that McPherson actually liked him and would follow him anywhere.

McPherson squatted beside Grant and said, "Sir, Lew Wallace is on the field."

Grant asked, "What time is it?"

"It's after midnight," McPherson replied. "He's been here since just after dark, but he had no idea where in hell he actually was."

Grant thought a long moment. He thought about the Confederate surprise attack and the fact that he had been caught totally unaware. He thought about what his father had told him about messing up a good thing. His life hadn't been very kind up until the war began, but now things were different. He'd become a hero, and now he'd been surprised because he didn't have his army prepared for an assault. If things went bad in the morning, there was a way for him to escape responsibility. Every officer in the army would have to agree that Lew Wallace should have been on the field sometime after lunch. It was after midnight, and the man was just now reporting that his division was on line.

Grant began to formulate the casualties in his head. There had been almost nine thousand men lost during the day's fighting. If Wallace would have arrived in a timely fashion, he could have turned the table on the Confederates.

Grant looked at the figure squatting next to him in the dark and said, "Let's go find the..."

Grant paused. He'd never been the type of man to curse, so he searched for the right words. Finally, he said, "...man."

They mounted their horses and rode west out the Pittsburg Landing Road. Men of Buell and Grant's army were gathered around campfires trying to stay warm through the night. Most of Grant's men were exhausted and asleep.

McPherson cleared his throat and said, "Sir, I just wanted to mention to you that we don't have enough medical supplies on hand to treat all the wounded. We weren't expecting a fight here. Besides, what medical supplies we had on hand were in the camps that were overrun by the Rebels this morning."

"Tell the surgeons to just do the best they can," Grant said. He pulled a cigar from his coat pocket and began fumbling in another pocket for a match.

"Sir," McPherson paused. He was searching for a way to say what was on his mind without upsetting his commander. "Hogs have been seen eating the dead already. The wounded men have no shelter. Most of the army is destroyed. I mean, Will Wallace and Prentiss's divisions are destroyed, and the rest are scattered everywhere. Some of your staff officers want me to ask you when you plan on giving the order to retreat."

"Retreat?" Grant repeated. The man was genuinely shocked. He'd never even given thought to ordering a retreat. He turned to McPherson and said, "I will not retreat. In the morning I plan on attacking and whipping the Confederate army."

McPherson lowered his head. He wondered if Grant was refusing to see the obvious. *The man doesn't want to lose his job and truly believes he can still win this battle.* He said, "Sir, quite a few men have broken into the sutlers' stores and stolen whiskey. The men are intoxicated and acting lawless. Some have even attacked their commanding officers. I meant no disrespect when I mentioned retreating."

"I want the names of those men that have assaulted their officers and those who have gotten drunk on duty," Grant's voice became firm. "We will not retreat. If they could have taken this position, they would have done so today. Tomorrow, we will turn the tide of battle and destroy the enemy."

"Right," McPherson nodded. He was glad to hear Grant sounding so confident. The entire world had seemed to be coming to an end this morning. "All of Buell's army won't be on the field by dawn, but we should have a couple fresh divisions. And as I said, Lew Wallace's division has also arrived."

Another barrage of fire from the gunboats echoed across the field. They'd been firing off and on all night long. Grant asked, "What are they firing at?"

"Buell ordered them to fire every fifteen minutes throughout the night to prevent the Rebels from getting sleep," McPherson replied.

Not a bad idea, Grant thought.

They rode on past the soldiers looking for Lew Wallace's headquarters. Grant began to formulate the plan in his mind. He'd told Wallace to march to the field around nine yesterday morning. The man had taken a full day to march around fifteen miles. In Grant's mind, he should have been here by one at the latest.

Grant and McPherson rode through the night looking for Wallace. They found his men, but no sign of the wayward general. It didn't take long for Grant to grow frustrated with the search. He tugged on the reins of his horse and turned to McPherson. "Hell, let's just ride back. It's not my job to find Wallace; it's his job to find me."

On the ride back, McPherson noticed members of Sherman's staff gathered around a fire. They both dismounted near the group. The staff officers pointed toward a large maple tree. Grant noticed the red-haired general leaned back against the tree. He was asleep. Grant hobbled over to his friend. His ankle was still swollen and extremely painful when he placed weight on his foot.

"Hello, Cump," Grant said as he sat down on the cold ground next to his friend.

"Sam," Sherman looked up. "We've had the devil's own day today."

"Yep," Grant nodded. "Whip them tomorrow though."

"That's what I wanted to hear," Sherman replied. "They won't expect a thing."

"They'll think we've retreated. It'll be a shock when they find us advancing on them," Grant puffed on the cigar.

Sherman grew serious. He eyed Grant out of wrinkled eyes and asked, "Are you coordinating with Buell?"

"No," Grant replied. "It's obvious the man isn't gonna work with us."

Sherman nodded. It bothered him that Buell was uncooperative. He said, "He came here earlier and asked me to draw him a map of the field. The man believes your army is destroyed and that he will have to do all the fighting. He says he'll have about eighteen thousand men on the field by daylight and that he's planning on advancing while we reorganize our command."

"Well, he's wrong," Grant said. "We're going forward with him."

"I think the man truly thinks he's arrived to save the day," Sherman let it go with a sigh. He said, "No telling what he's telling all those reporters he keeps with him. We'll probably be reading in the northern papers about how Buell saved our army from destruction."

Grant reached over, patted his friend on the knee, and said, "Be ready to advance at first light."

Grant limped over to the fire and warmed his hands for a long moment. He and McPherson then mounted their horses and rode on back toward the landing.

They returned to the large oak tree Grant had been using for a bed earlier. Captain Rawlins was pacing back and forth beneath the tree when they arrived. He looked up and saw the shadow of two officers walking toward him. He asked, "Is that you, Grant?"

"Yep," Grant replied. He didn't understand Rawlins, but he appreciated him. He'd been the victim of an alcoholic and abusive father as a child and hated liquor. He saw it as his duty to watch Grant and make sure he didn't relapse into his old habits.

"Where have you been?" Rawlins asked.

Grant began to wonder who was in command here. Rawlins, a lieutenant colonel, was scolding Grant, the major general, for being absent without permission. Grant said, "I've been searching for Lew Wallace."

Rawlins paused in thought. He said, "Well, while you were out looking for him, he sent a member of his staff to inform you that he has his entire division on line and prepared to advance at first light. He says he will try and get some sleep under a large tree."

"Very well," Grant replied. He limped over to the large oak he'd been resting beneath before and sat down. Rawlins followed him and sat uncomfortably close. He kept leaning close to Grant's face. Grant rubbed his temples. He wasn't in the mood for Rawlins's annoyances at the moment.

Grant said, "Rawlins, I'm not drunk, and I haven't drank a drop of anything except water all day long."

Rawlins seemed to relax. He eased back away from Grant. McPherson took a seat on the other side of his commander.

Grant's ankle was beginning to throb from the strain he'd placed on it today. There was no way he was gonna get any sleep in this shape. A shot of whiskey would have been nice, but then he would have to deal with Rawlins. He thought about asking one of the surgeons for some laudanum, but wanted to save that for his wounded men.

Grant struggled to his feet and began to limp toward the landing.

"Where are you going?" Rawlins asked.

Grant shook his head. The man was truly beginning to grate on his nerves. He said, "Just to see if Buell's men are still crossing in good order."

He limped on to the edge of the overlook. There was no doubt that Buell's men were still crossing. He could hear the bells and steam from the boats. Men were constantly struggling up the steep hill just a few yards to the south of Grant's temporary headquarters. Actually, what Grant needed most just now was a moment to himself. He needed to work things out in his mind.

Looking down on the landing, he watched the men filing off the boats. Back and forth the boats went, busy all night ferrying more men over. In a way, Grant wished Buell hadn't arrived. He could have ordered his army forward in the morning and whipped the Rebels alone. Now he will have to share the victory with Buell and also listen to reports of how Buell saved his army.

Grant began to think about Halleck. The man was extremely cautious and despised everything about Grant's way of fighting. He wondered if he would still be a general after this battle ended. It seemed that Halleck was just looking for a way to fire him.

Lightning flashed behind him. Grant spun and looked toward the west. A storm was rapidly approaching. *Just what I need, he thought, a damned storm*.

By the time he'd limped back to his tree, the first drops of rain began to fall. Within fifteen minutes, he was resting beneath the tree in a deluge. Water ran down the tree and into his collar. This wasn't the type of headquarters for a commanding general, yet here he sat out in the elements. He'd never seen it rain so hard in his life. The lightning was so bright it hurt his eyes.

Grant remembered the cabin just a few feet up the hill. It was a small, one-room cabin from what Grant could remember. He decided to limp up the hill. As he got close to the building, he could see a light on inside. Something was being thrown from the one window and piled outside almost to the window sill. When he got to the door, he realized that the pile was arms and legs from his wounded soldiers. Surgeons were inside amputating and treating the wounded as best they could.

Stepping inside, Grant found a table covered with blood. Orderlies were bringing the wounded in and placing them on the table. When the surgeons were finished with their grizzly task, the orderlies would take them back out into the rain. It made Grant wonder if any of his men would survive.

The cabin had no floor, and the general found a corner out of the way that was covered with hay. There was an old chair sitting there. He sat down and draped his arm over the back of the chair. Using his arm as a pillow, he attempted to get a few hours of sleep. He nodded off a few times, but the screams of his men enduring amputations without anesthetic would wake him. The sounds of the poor men were more than he could bear. He hobbled out the door, his swollen ankle throbbing, and made his way down to the overlook again.

Buell's men were still unloading there. Men were falling every moment as they struggled up the mud-covered hill in their slick brogans. It was raining too hard for Grant to hear them, but he was certain they were cursing down there.

Off to his right, Grant noticed a fire. It was difficult to believe it was still burning in all this rain, but the men who'd built the fire had made it so large that it continued to burn. Flames leapt fifteen feet into the air. Gathered around this one surviving fire were almost five hundred soldiers. Grant shook his head and limped back to his tree.

It was after three when the rain stopped. The poor commander had only managed to nod off a few times. He had just managed to really fall asleep when he was woken by a courier. Grant had always been the type that could function on very little sleep. Another advantage the man had was the ability to instantly come awake. He asked, "What do you have?"

The courier said, "General Buell wanted me to inform you that he is advancing his men into the darkness. He wanted to make sure that you knew they were out front and for you to make sure your men don't fire into their backs while they're battling the enemy."

Grant shook his head. Buell was in such a hurry to get the jump on Grant that he couldn't even wait for daylight. Grant asked, "How long have they been gone? How far out are they?"

"Not long, sir," the man shrugged his shoulders. "Probably not over four hundred yards at the most. They're moving pretty slow. Hell, a man can't see his hand in front of his face out there."

"Thank you," Grant dismissed the man. He stood on the swollen ankle and called for his horse. While he waited, he gave orders for his staff to find all his division commanders and inform them that it was time to advance.

Grant and his staff were soon mounted and began riding west. Artillery fire began from the southwest. They rode almost a mile to the right flank where they encountered Lew Wallace. It was growing daylight, but fog hovered low on the fields to the south. Confederate artillery was firing from across the field in the trees.

Wallace saw Grant approaching and saluted. Wallace said, "I'm calling up my artillery to try and pound those Confederate cannons out of there before ordering my men forward."

"Nonsense," Grant replied. He jerked a thumb over his shoulder toward the enemy guns. "Send your men in at once."

Wallace nodded in agreement. He didn't like to send his men into battle against artillery fire, but Grant didn't seem to be the type to worry about his men. He quickly turned and gave the order. The second day's battle had begun.

Part III

"Fear is a reaction. Courage is a decision."

Sir Winston Churchill

April 7

USA

Grant's men quickly caught up with Buell's troops. Bull Nelson was moving his troops forward with extreme caution. He would advance a hundred yards and then pause to realign his men. Grant was growing angry with the two men. Nelson didn't seem to understand that the Confederates had attacked through this wilderness yesterday without pausing every ten minutes. Buell and Nelson wanted their men to be in perfect alignment when they encountered the southerners.

The first enemy troops they met were Bedford Forrest's cavalry pickets. These men fired only a few shots before falling back. They'd wasted almost two hours just moving forward a half mile. There they reached the triangular shaped field where Prentiss's division was forced to surrender late yesterday afternoon. Dead and wounded men lay strewn across the ground. It was difficult to march past the poor wounded soldiers. They begged piteously to be carried to the rear and not be left on the field any longer. Buell hated to abandon them, but his job was to retake the field and push the Confederates back to Corinth.

Buell had to steer his horse around a group of dead and wounded. There was a man lying there with his leg shattered below the knee. He looked at the heavyset general on horseback and pleaded, "Oh God, have mercy! Sir, please just shoot me. I want to die!"

Buell turned his head from the sight and continued forward. They still hadn't met any serious resistance. The Federal commander began to suspect that the Confederates had abandoned the field. They'd probably learned of his arrival and retreated during the night.

As they approached a small field, Buell could see a pond beside the road in the trees on the other side. As he watched his men begin to move across the field, the tree line on the other side erupted with rifle fire. The enemy was still here after all. Buell watched his men fall back into the trees and begin a long-range fire with the Confederate infantry. The northern advance had stalled.

Buell sat back in the trees and watched this fire fight. He refused to send his men across the field because he wasn't sure how many Confederate troops were in the trees across the way. Nelson soon rode up and saluted. He said, "Where in the hell is Grant?"

Buell shook his head. He had no idea what his hot-tempered subordinate was talking about. It amazed him that a man as large as Nelson could ride a horse. The man had a head the size of a stump, and his long, wavy hair made it look even larger.

Nelson shouted, "The son-of-a-bitch was on my right, and now he's gone!"

Buell wasn't sure how to take his high-strung commander. He asked, "Have you sent anyone out looking for him?"

"Yeah," Nelson pulled off his large hat and slapped it against his thigh. "I sent out several staff officers over the past hour, and no one can find the drunken son-of-a-bitch. How are we supposed to save his army from defeat when none of them are willing to fight to save themselves?"

"I'll send back and see what's going on," Buell waved Nelson off. "Just do the best you can. We're all stalled at the moment. At least hold your position as long as you can, and if you get flanked, be sure and let me know so I can fall back with you."

"Right," Nelson thundered. He spun his horse and rode away.

Buell turned to his chief of staff and said, "Colonel Fry, send a courier to the rear and find Brigadier General Tom Crittenden. Tell him to move however much of his division he has on the field up on Nelson's right flank. Tell him to hurry."

"Right," Fry shouted and rode back to find a courier.

Buell turned back to the front. The fire fight between his troops and the Rebels had been going for over an hour now. Something needed to be done. No one was gaining an advantage in all of this. Both lines were concealed in the trees, and there were hardly any casualties being inflicted. Other than the waste of ammunition and noise, nothing was being accomplished.

It was after seven when a courier arrived to inform him that Crittenden was on the right flank. The courier informed Buell that McCook's division was close behind.

Buell turned to Colonel Fry and said, "James, that gives me about fifteen thousand men on the field."

"With Grant's men, we should have plenty," Fry replied.

"Yes, plenty, but I don't put much faith in Grant's men after the way they behaved yesterday," Buell spurred his horse forward to see how things were going in his front.

Across the field, he could see the Confederate infantry swarming back past the pond, through the trees, and into the open field beyond. They were falling back. It was time to press his advantage.

CSA

Brigadier General James Chalmers watched his men fall back, separating as they passed the pond with bodies around the edges. There was a faint tinge of gray along the edge of the water. A mule lay about ten feet out from the bank of the water, nothing showing but his shoulders and back. His men had put up a gallant fight for the past hour and a half before running low on ammunition. He'd sent to the rear for more, but no one had been able to locate a supply train yet. Chalmers had reluctantly ordered his men to retreat. His one weak brigade couldn't hold off fifteen thousand men forever without either ammunition or support.

He rode along as his men raced past the peach orchard and across the large field toward the tree line in the distance. He told his staff to reform the brigade at the edge of the trees and then he rode ahead in search of reinforcements. A couple hundred yards beyond the trees, Chalmers encountered Brigadier General Jones Withers. He asked the man for help, and the Alabama brigadier was only too glad to advance.

Chalmers rode along with Withers to make sure he would arrive at the correct position. They soon arrived at the Hamburg-Purdy Road. Major General Braxton Bragg was waiting there with his staff.

Bragg rode over to the two general officers and asked, "Where are you two going?"

Withers saluted. He stroked his thick mustache and replied, "General Chalmers wants me to move forward and relieve his men. They're running low on ammunition, sir."

Bragg was already shaking his head before the man finished his sentence. "Hold your men in readiness here with Chalmers. I am thoroughly convinced that you are advancing into a trap. Those are Buell's men, and they are just hoping you'll come out and fight them in the open."

"Right," Withers nodded and looked at Chalmers. General Chalmers's head was lowered. He wasn't about to argue with a major general. If Bragg had information about the Federals, then Chalmers was sure the man was correct.

"Just hold here and await developments," Bragg replied before spurring his horse toward the rear.

Chalmers didn't have time to argue his case anyway. He put spurs to his horse and rode across the field to meet his hard-pressed brigade.

Back at Shiloh Church, Colonel Jordan didn't need Federal General Prentiss to tell him what was happening at the front. Instead of the surrender Beauregard had been predicting last night, Buell had indeed arrived. It didn't take a genius to understand that the firing was slowly moving south.

Jordan had walked to Beauregard's tent at daylight and found his commander and Bragg in deep discussion. Bragg had just begun replying to a question posed by Beauregard when Jordan had stepped into the tent. Bragg paused, glanced at Jordan, and then continued, "General, my men are exhausted, disorganized, and totally demoralized. If that's Buell's army…"

Bragg left the rest unsaid. Beauregard quickly finished the sentence for his subordinate. "If that's Buell's army, I will be forced to retreat. My men are in no condition to fight fresh troops."

"Besides," Bragg mumbled, "my men have used up most of their ammunition. I mean, we brought plenty, but my officers haven't bothered to re-supply their men because they all expected Grant to surrender about daylight this morning."

Bragg paused a moment and then added, "Or at least retreat if nothing else."

Jordan heard a courier outside ask where Beauregard was located. He heard men showing him the large tent. Jordan opened the tent flap to let the man inside.

"General Beauregard?" the courier asked as he entered the tent and looked from Jordan to Beauregard, then to Bragg.

Beauregard nodded his head and asked, "What do you need?"

"Colonel Trabue sent me back here for orders," the young man replied. He shifted from one foot to another, betraying his nervousness about standing before a full general. He continued, "He commands a brigade in Breckinridge's Reserve Corps. We've been searching for a ranking officer to give us orders since midnight. Colonel Trabue has no idea what the situation is at this point."

Beauregard exhaled. His throat ached, and now he had to give orders to brigade commanders. He wondered what the use was in having division and corps commanders if he was going to have to bypass those men to give orders to brigades.

Beauregard said, "Tell Colonel Trabue to follow Napoleon's maxim. Advance to the sound of heaviest firing. That's where he will find the enemy, and that's the position in which he will be most needed."

"Right," the courier saluted and quickly exited the tent.

Beauregard watched the man leave and then turned to Jordan. "Tom, I need you to ride to the front and find out who we are fighting. I need to know if Buell has arrived or if this is some scheme by General Grant to scare us into giving up the fight."

"Yes, sir," Jordan replied and then turned to leave.

He rode back to the front and stared across the field to where the peach orchard and cabin stood. Jordan took out his field glasses and studied the tree line. The Federal troops were in there waiting. He needed to know if those were fresh troops as quickly as possible.

Chalmers's brigade was waiting a few hundred yards in his rear. They had some Federal prisoners back there. Jordan rode over and introduced himself to one of them.

The man gave a sloppy salute and said, "What can I do for you, Colonel?"

Jordan was impressed that the man understood his rank in a Confederate uniform. Federal officers had their insignia on small shoulder boards. Confederate officers had large insignia on their collars. There wasn't much of a way for a Confederate officer to hide his insignia. It was supposed to be a sign of bravery. A Federal colonel would have an eagle on his shoulder boards, whereas a Confederate colonel like Jordan would have three gold stars on his collar.

Jordan answered the man's question with another question. "Which outfit do you belong to?"

"First Kentucky," the man replied proudly. "Bruce's brigade, Nelson's division, Army of the Ohio."

That told Jordan all he needed to know. Buell commanded the Army of the Ohio, and that meant the exhausted Confederate army was facing fresh troops. Jordan spun the horse and rode hard back to Beauregard's headquarters at Shiloh Church.

He found Beauregard standing outside of Sherman's tent in deep discussion with another officer. Jordan rode up and jerked on the horse's reins so hard the animal almost reared. He leapt from the horse and jerked a thumb over his shoulder. "Buell's army is what we're facing. We have prisoners that confirm it. We're up against fresh troops. Not just fresh troops but an entire fresh army."

Beauregard's face betrayed his shock. It was the worst scenario he could think of at the moment. He lowered his head in thought a moment and then asked, "Is he pressing us?"

The question caught Jordan by surprise. He'd been so sure Beauregard would order an immediate retreat that he hadn't noticed the obvious. He replied, "Come to think of it, no. They're just sitting about a half mile away in the tree line waiting."

"That's a mistake," Beauregard replied. He studied the situation a long moment. *We caught them by surprise yesterday, he thought, but they caught us by surprise today.* Beauregard continued, "Buell is cautious. The man is giving us time to reform our ranks."

"I hadn't thought of that," Jordan mumbled. He scratched at his short, cropped beard. "I mean, I studied their position, and it's strong; but they're not advancing."

"Maybe he hasn't gotten his entire army on the field yet," Beauregard said. "Perhaps he's waiting for the rest to arrive."

"Perhaps," Jordan suddenly remembered a conversation he'd had with General Chalmers. "I spoke with James Chalmers at the front. He says Buell moved forward and engaged him, but when he fell back, the Federals failed to pursue. He said they've been in that tree line for over an hour doing absolutely nothing."

"Doesn't make sense," Beauregard said to himself. "He's either bluffing or buying time."

"Want me to ride back and keep a watch on the situation, General?" Jordan asked.

"Yes I do," Beauregard replied. "But I'm going with you. I can't command from back here."

Beauregard and Jordan mounted their horses, and with a few staff officers, they moved back toward the front. This would be the first time Beauregard had visited the battlefield. He'd remained in the rear yesterday while Johnston had commanded on the field. He could just as easily command from the rear today, but things had changed. It was time for him to be seen by his men in the face of fresh Federal reinforcements.

They found General Hardee studying the field that contained the peach orchard and cabin. Hardee saw Beauregard and saluted. He pointed across the field and said, "Damnedest thing I've ever seen. They just moved a brigade out into the middle of that orchard. They've halted with no infantry support on either flank. It makes no sense."

"Nothing is making sense today," Beauregard said. He studied the unsupported Federal brigade across the field. There was a Confederate artillery battery over on the flank of the lone brigade. They were pouring a destructive fire into the enemy ranks. The fire was hitting them in enfilade, which meant they were firing down the enemy line. If a shell missed the target, it would continue down the line until it hit someone. The ground trembled with each cannon shot. He continued watching the destructive fire hitting the line of men. They stood it for about ten minutes before they'd had enough. He watched them break and race back into the trees, despite their officers attempting to stop them.

It was time to act. Beauregard turned to Hardee and said, "Organize an attack with General Breckinridge. Hit them while they are disorganized."

Hardee nodded and spun his horse. He rode to his right to find a good group of men. *This is ironic, he thought. Yesterday we endured heavy losses taking the same field we're about to attack again.*

He rode down the line to his extreme right flank and found Colonel John Martin, commander of the Second Confederate Infantry. Martin saluted. Hardee asked, "Which regiment are you commanding?"

"Sir, I've got Bowen's brigade. The man went down with a severe wound yesterday," Martin replied.

Hardee thought about Bowen's Brigade. The men were mostly from Missouri and had impressed him with their bravery yesterday. He pointed across the field and said, "I want you to assault that tree line yonder."

"We'll follow any order you give, sir," Martin lowered his head, "but we're not near the strength we were yesterday."

"I'll help you lead them," Hardee reached out and patted Martin on the shoulder. "I don't want you to do this alone. I'll be sending more men to flank them while you engage them from their front."

"Right," Martin nodded.

The two officers soon had the brigade moving out into the field. Hardee was conspicuous on his large black horse. The men were impressed and began to yell as they advanced. Hardee realized these men were going to make the assault. They were shouting over and over, "Bull Run! Bull Run!"

He told Martin to continue the attack while he rode back and brought up more men. He spun the horse and rode toward the rear. Behind him, he could hear Martin's brigade give the Rebel yell as they charged. Federal artillery began to fire at the advancing Missourians, and Hardee glanced over his shoulder in time to see the brigade disappear into the trees beyond the cabin.

USA

Buell was on the Hamburg-Savannah Road when the attack began. He could see Confederate troops rushing into the trees after his men. In this thick forest, he couldn't tell for sure how many men were hitting him. He spun the horse and rode hard to Colonel William Hazen's position. The man commanded a brigade that Buell was holding back as a reserve force for just such a moment as now.

He found the dark-haired, neatly-dressed officer mounted near his men. The man held a rattan switch he'd acquired somewhere. Instead of leading his men with his sword, he used the Oriental switch to direct them. Buell quickly gave Hazen orders to advance and strike the enemy force in his front.

Hazen saluted and ordered his men to attention. Officers rushed to their assigned positions. His men betrayed their nervousness. They'd never seen combat before. Today they would "see the elephant," which is how soldiers referred to being in combat.

William Hazen stared at his men through piercing eyes, above a knifelike nose. His energy seemed to convince his men that he would be there with them, no matter what they faced. The way he carried himself seemed dignified, and any man present would have thought Hazen was far older than his thirty-one years, especially with his thick mustache and goatee.

Once his men were aligned, Hazen rode to the center of his brigade and pointed toward the front with the rattan switch. He shouted, "Forward march! We've got to push the traitors from the trees!"

The line surged forward. Hazen had been a regular army officer before the war, and he'd always instructed his men to behave like soldiers. Before they'd even met the enemy, he noticed one Kentucky regiment beginning to falter. Their officers were screaming at them to push forward, but it was no use. Soon the entire line melted away and raced for the rear. *That's the only thing about new troops, Hazen thought, you never know if they'll face fire or not.*

He spun his horse and rode amid the fleeing infantry. He swung the rattan at them, but this only seemed to increase their speed toward the landing in the rear. Hazen's staff was attempting to help him but to no avail. He shouted, "Let the cowards go! We'll press on with the rest!"

He returned to his men and rode with them through the thick forest. They were practically on top of the enemy without having seen them. The Confederates' gray uniforms seemed to blend into the thick forest. His brigade lunged forward, and the fighting became hand-to-hand.

It didn't take long for the outnumbered Confederates to break and fall back past the trees and into the open field. It was one regiment facing both Hazen and Bruce's brigades. As the Confederates retreated past the tree line, Hazen watched them trying to reform on the other side of the peach orchard.

He looked to his right and noticed a wounded Confederate captain limping through the trees in an attempt to escape with his retreating men. Several of Hazen's men had gathered around the poor man. He saw one man raise his rifle and charge forward with his bayonet. Hazen spurred the horse forward and knocked the man away just in time to save the Confederate officer's life.

Hazen stopped the horse and dismounted. He turned to see the Confederate captain, blood running down his pant leg from a bullet wound, drawing his sword. He took the blade, laid it flat in both hands and extended the weapon toward his savior. The young officer said, "Your prisoner, sir."

"Keep it," Hazen replied. "You're too brave to surrender your sword."

"Thank you," the man nodded.

Hazen gave a graceful bow, turned to one of his privates, and said, "Escort this brave man to the rear."

He saluted and stepped up next to the captain. Hazen turned to his men. They were scattered through the trees. He gave the order for his officers to reform the brigade so they could push the Rebels on across the field.

Within minutes, he had them moving out of the tree line. He watched the men part ranks, pass the cabin, and reform on the other side. All those hours of drill had paid off. They looked like veterans. It was a proud moment for William Hazen.

As soon as they reformed beyond the cabin, Confederate artillery opened fire from across the field. There were three guns firing just over a hundred yards away. Hazen scanned the area but could find no infantry support. He quickly decided to charge the three cannons with his brigade.

He had his brigade moving forward at the double-quick before the Confederate artillerymen had time to react. They soon realized they wouldn't have time to bring their guns off before the Federals overran their position. At fifty yards, Hazen gave the order for his men to charge. They raced forward and swarmed around the abandoned cannons.

His men were jubilant. In their first battle, they'd captured a Confederate artillery battery. Hazen realized there was no time to celebrate. He had to reform his men. There was no way the Confederates would take this without retaliating.

At that moment, Hazen saw a sight that truly scared him. A couple hundred yards south of the position was a split-rail fence with a road on the other side. There was Confederate infantry massed behind the fence. His men had taken severe losses to get as far as they had. He wasn't sure he could put up much resistance if hit by such a strong force. To charge that line would be pure suicide. He just hoped they didn't advance. His men were in no shape to face that many enemy infantry.

He was still reforming his men when he saw the Confederate infantry scaling the split-rail fence. He heard the sound of rifle fire in his rear. Bullets struck several of his men. He spun and saw friendly troops emerging from the trees behind the cabin. They were firing on his men, thinking they were enemy soldiers. An artillery fire burst overhead. He spun to his left to see another Confederate artillery battery shelling his men from a small knoll. The cannon balls came in from the flank in enfilade. He saw men being knocked around and limbs flying through the air. Things had gotten extremely ugly for Hazen and his men.

Hazen's brigade stood this fire from flank and rear far longer than he expected. They could see enemy infantry advancing. When they broke, Hazen didn't try to stop them. He couldn't blame them. They couldn't fight the Confederate army alone out here with friendly troops firing at them from behind. He simply followed them back toward the trees beyond the cabin. Just before reaching the tree line, he turned to watch the advancing Confederate infantry swarm around the guns he'd just captured and abandoned.

In the trees, he attempted to reform his men. It didn't take long for William Hazen to realize there was no use. They'd fought hard here this morning. They'd accomplished more than most men could have. His men were now scattered to hell and back. When he'd reformed what few men he and his staff could, he counted less than four hundred men. The rest were racing for the rear or hiding in the forest. His day was over.

CSA

General Hardee had been all over the field this morning. The normally calm officer was extremely excited. The gray and black hair on top of his head stood straight up, surrounded by his huge widow's peak. The man had spent two days on the battlefield, recklessly exposing himself to enemy fire. A bullet had struck his horse in the shoulder, but the animal continued on without the slightest limp. There were two rips in Hardee's coat from close calls by enemy bullets.

Things had looked good for the Confederate army yesterday. Today, however, things had changed drastically. The entire army was disorganized, and now it appeared they were facing fresh troops. It had been a shock to learn that Buell's men, who were supposed to be approaching Huntsville, Alabama, were here at Shiloh, Tennessee.

If the army had taught Hardee anything, he understood that now was the time for extreme measures. He'd spent the past hour studying the Federal line. They hadn't even attempted to cover the fact that their extreme left rested on the Hamburg-Savannah Road. That was a serious mistake for the Yankee army.

Hardee decided that he needed to make a counterattack against that exposed flank. It was in the air, and a strong force sweeping around that flank and into the enemy rear could save the day. The problem was finding a strong force. He'd been searching everywhere, and the largest number he could organize was a four-hundred-man Texas brigade under Colonel John Moore.

The short Texan saw Hardee approaching and saluted. The colonel with the scraggly beard and graying mustache waited for the lieutenant general to give him his orders.

General Hardee pointed toward Martin's brigade, which was swarming around the recaptured artillery pieces beyond the fence. Moore had never seen his commander this excited. Hardee said, "Take your brigade and wheel around that exposed Federal flank. I know you're weak, but do all you can to roll them up. I'll be finding you some help. Whatever you do, don't fire into the friendly troops."

Hardee was about to leave Moore and his brigade, but he wanted to make sure they knew where they were going before he left. Moore was attempting to form his men, but they acted as though they were getting ready for morning parade. Not one man seemed to be in a hurry. General Hardee had seen enough. He jerked his hat off and threw it to the ground. He shouted, "Form at once! I need celerity!"

He rode down the line shouting. He saw some of Moore's subordinates patiently waiting and shouted at them, "Get your men on line! You sons-of- bitches are losing the battle for us! Do your jobs!"

Colonel Moore was shouting also. Once they came on line, Hardee rode to the front beside Moore and gave the command for the line to advance. He rode beside Moore as they entered the field. Once he was confident that Moore was heading in the right direction, he again instructed the man not to fire into friendly troops. He then spun his horse to the rear to bring up reinforcements.

It would have been better for Hardee to have turned the enemy flank with a minimum force of two thousand men, but things had become dire. He was forced to gamble with Moore's small brigade.

He turned west along the Hamburg-Purdy Road and began to scan the area for any available troops. He glanced back over his right shoulder in time to see Moore's small brigade pass the Federal flank and continue toward the tree line beyond. There were enemy troops in those trees. Moore hadn't bothered to open fire but continued moving toward his enemy. *What the hell is going on, Hardee wondered.*

He halted the horse and watched the coming disaster unfold. Moore had led his brigade to within fifty yards of the tree line, when the enemy opened a devastating fire. The Texans instantly broke and raced back across the field. Hardee decided that finding reinforcements would have to wait. He spurred his horse into the field to meet his retreating men. He turned to his staff and shouted, "Stop these damned cowards!"

He and his staff rode among the panic-stricken men, begging them to stop, but to no avail. They followed the frightened men into the trees. There General Hardee found a lieutenant hiding behind a tree.

William Hardee spurred his horse that way and said, "You damned Texans are the biggest bunch of cowards I've ever encountered."

"I don't care what you call us," the young officer replied.

Hardee spun his horse and raced toward the rear. There was no need to attempt to form the Texans any longer. They'd done all they were going to do today. A few hundred yards down the road Hardee encountered James Chalmers and what was left of his brigade. They'd seen heavy action yesterday and barely had enough men to be called a regiment.

Chalmers saluted. His curls bounced beneath his kepi. If Hardee hadn't known better, he would have thought the man was still half asleep. Chalmers was in Bragg's command, but Hardee had learned a few things about him in the short time he'd known him. He was a lawyer, not a soldier. He thought of himself as an aristocrat, and his droopy eyelids always made him appear as though he was about to nod off.

"I need your men," Hardee shouted. He'd almost said he needed Chalmers's *brigade*, but it couldn't quite be called that.

Chalmers was shaking his head. "I just got them reformed a few moments ago. They've seen heavy fighting for the past two days. I'm not sure how much help they'll be to ya."

"We must try," Hardee tried to sound calm. "Look, I need all the help I can get just now. They have fresh troops, and we're gonna lose this battle if we don't all at least try and do something."

Chalmers spun his horse and shouted at his men. "General Hardee needs every one of us to advance one more time. He expects you men to do your duty. *I* expect you men to do your duty. I know you're tired. I also know what a fine bunch of men you are and what you're capable of. Now, I'm not about to let General Hardee down. Who is with me?"

The men replied with a cheer. Chalmers turned to Hardee and said, "Show us the way."

Hardee soon had them moving out of the tree line and into the open field. This time he made sure that Chalmers knew there were enemy soldiers in the trees across the field. He was about to go back in search of more men when he saw a sight that shocked him. A line of Federal infantry was advancing from the trees to meet Chalmers's brigade. The force was almost twice as large as Chalmers's force. They both advanced to near midfield, where both opened fire from a range of about fifty yards.

Chalmers's boys were holding their ground and giving as good as they got. Hardee was quite impressed with the Mississippi lawyer. The assault began to unravel soon enough. The fresh Federal troops soon gained the upper hand. When the Confederate line broke, it broke as one.

William Hardee shook his head. It had been that kind of day. No matter what he tried, it seemed he was checkmated at every turn. *If I only had two thousand fresh troops, he thought.*

Chalmers had lost about half of the men he'd carried into the field. As his men raced for the tree line, Chalmers turned his horse and rode to Hardee's position.

James Chalmers saluted and shook his head. "Sorry, sir; half my guns were fouled by the rain last night and won't even fire. There's just not much more my men can do today. You need to replace my brigade with some fresh troops."

"Who am I going to replace your brigade with?" Hardee asked. "If I had fresh troops, I wouldn't have asked you to make that assault."

Chalmers shrugged. There was nothing else he could say. Hardee finally relaxed. He said, "It's alright, James; I appreciate the effort. Go reform your men."

Hardee heard a shout behind him, "General!"

He turned and saw Brigadier General Jones Withers approaching on horseback. The man with the thick mustache and knifelike nose rode up and saluted. Hardee remembered the Alabama soldier from West Point.

"Sir," Withers said, trying to catch his breath, "I have Maney's Tennessee brigade and a few other scattered regiments formed and ready for battle."

"Very good, General," Hardee breathed a sigh of relief. He pointed toward the large Federal force still waiting in the middle of the field. "I want you to advance and drive those men from the field."

"Very well," Withers saluted again and rode back through the trees.

In a few moments, Hardee watched Withers and the dark-haired Colonel George Maney riding at the front of the line of men. The unit was larger than Hardee had expected. They almost numbered as many as what waited in the line across the field. When they approached to within a hundred yards, the Federal line opened fire. Most shots sailed too high. Withers still held his men in check. They passed on to within fifty yards, and Withers gave the order to charge.

The gray line surged forward, screaming like banshees. The Federals hadn't had time to reload, and the sound of the Rebel yell was more than they could stand. They broke long before contact was made and raced back through the peach orchard and into the trees.

There was a small battery of Federal cannons firing off to their left, but they had so many men out of action they could barely get off a round every minute or so. Hardee decided now was the moment he'd been attempting to pull off all morning. He spurred the horse to where Chalmers was busy reforming his men once again.

Chalmers saw Hardee approaching but didn't look very excited. He was afraid he knew what the man was about to ask of him.

Hardee jerked the horse's reins so hard it almost reared into the air. He said, "General Chalmers, I need you to rejoin the attack and help Withers. He's got them on the run."

Chalmers stroked at his goatee as he stared at Hardee out of his droopy eyes. He thought a long moment without replying. Hardee noticed Chalmers's men staring sullenly at the ground, acting as though they had heard nothing.

Suddenly, Chalmers spurred his horse forward and snatched the battle flag of the Ninth Mississippi Infantry from the color bearer. He rode back and forth in front of his men, waving the flag wildly overhead. He yelled, "Please help me to repel the Yankee invaders! Our families are counting on us!"

Again his men sprung to their feet with a shout. Hardee was genuinely impressed with these men and their leader. He spun in the saddle and noticed Withers's men being pushed back from the trees by fresh troops. Things were getting ugly.

Chalmers had his brigade moving forward across the field again. Just in front of the peach orchard, they came on line beside of Withers's men. Together they slowed the rearward movement but still couldn't stop the powerful Federal force. They gave ground ever so grudgingly. Hardee prayed they wouldn't break. There wasn't a single soldier left he could call on for help. As he sat on horseback and watched his last troops being slowly pushed in his direction, William Hardee realized for the first time that the battle was lost.

There was nothing left to do but report his situation to Beauregard.

USA

The private noticed an officer lying against a stack of crates beside the road. He noticed the man's left eye had been destroyed by a bullet. *What a way to die, he thought.*

For some reason, the private couldn't take his eyes off the horrid sight. The man looked pathetic, and this was the soldier's first time to see such carnage. He had never imagined anything close to the slaughter he'd seen here today.

The young man blinked his eyes and looked at the poor officer again. He could have sworn he'd seen the man's hand move. The man couldn't possibly still be alive. Not with a wound that severe. The private stared hard at the officer, and that's when he noticed it again. The man's right hand twitched.

The private elbowed the guy standing next to him and demanded, "Come on, Perry; help me."

Perry's eyes shot up as he watched his good friend Thomas Fogwell race out of the ranks toward a wounded man lying beside the road. He glanced back in time to see a lieutenant bearing down on his friend.

The lieutenant shouted, "Private Fogwell, where in hell do you think you're off to?"

Private Fogwell bent over the injured officer and motioned the lieutenant over. "Look at this. This is a general officer—got a star on his shoulder straps."

"So it is," the lieutenant said harshly. "Who gave this private officer permission to leave the ranks?"

"You don't understand, sir," Thomas Fogwell shook his head. "This man is still alive. Someone left a general out here on the field in this condition all night. Look, his clothes are soaking wet from last night's rain. You better let us carry him to the rear. What they gonna think if he dies cause you wouldn't let a couple of privates fall out and carry him back?"

"All right," the lieutenant gave up with a sigh. "You take one man and carry him back. If they want to know who helped save this man, don't forget that I'm the one that allowed you to leave the ranks."

109

"Right, sir," Tom smiled. He turned back to the line of men and shouted, "Perry Paine, you gonna help me get this man back to a field hospital?"

Perry Paine practically leapt out of line to assist his good buddy. The man may have just saved both their lives by getting them off this horrible field. He had never been afraid of going into battle. He had actually looked forward to "seeing the elephant." However, that had all changed once he saw the sickening sights of yesterday's battle.

Someone had thrown an old wool blanket over the wounded man sometime during the night. They laid the blanket out and gently placed the general on top. That was when they noticed the man had been hit behind the left ear, the bullet exiting his left eye. The large caliber of an Enfield bullet made a mess of the officer's head.

Perry looked at Tom and asked, "You think he'll be alright?"

"Hell if I know," Tom reached down to grab his end of the blanket next to the blood-soaked head. "I know it got us off this field, and that's enough for me."

"Right," Perry nodded as he reached down and helped lift the man. They were soon headed for the rear. They carried him through what would become known as Hell's Hollow and out into the surrender triangle of yesterday.

They encountered a group of mounted officers riding across the field. The man leading the entourage reined up and inspected the man in the blanket. He seemed to recognize who they were carrying. He scratched at his beard and studied the two privates. Finally, he removed his slouch hat and rubbed his coat sleeve across his sweaty forehead. He asked, "Where'd you find him?"

"Back there a ways," Tom replied as he nodded over his shoulder. "Do you know who he is?"

The officer nodded slightly. "He's one of my division commanders."

The mounted officer turned to his staff and said, "It's Will Wallace."

Tom watched the sloppily-dressed officer and wondered who he could be. The man claimed to be over a division commander. He looked at the man, noticed one eye seemed to be lower than the other, and asked, "Where is a field hospital?"

The mounted officer started to say something, but one of his staff officers interrupted. He said, "General Grant, I thought Wallace was dead."

Tom's eyes grew wide when he heard the mounted officer's name. Here he stood, talking to the hero of Fort Donelson. He couldn't believe his eyes. This small man looked nothing like a general, much less a war hero.

Grant turned back to the two men carrying Will Wallace and said, "Take him back to the landing. Put him on board the *Tigress*. His wife is waiting there."

Tom started to salute, forgot he was carrying a wounded general, and almost dropped the blanket corner. He said, "Yes, sir."

As the two men began to move away with their precious cargo, Grant turned to one of his staff officers and said, "Captain Lagow, I want you to ride back to the landing ahead of these men. Brace Wallace's wife for what's coming. She thinks he's dead. Have them take him back up to Savannah to my headquarters."

"Right," Captain Lagow spurred the horse toward the landing.

On board the *Tigress* he found Ann Wallace tending to the wounded men. He removed his hat as he approached her and said, "Ma'am, we've found General Wallace still alive. He's been severely wounded, but General Grant is sending him back here now."

He watched as Ann's face lit up at the thought. He wanted to tell her that things were not as good as she thought but just couldn't bring himself to let her down again. He nodded and said, "Excuse me; I'm to inform the captain to be prepared to leave at once for Savannah when the general is brought on board."

"Thank you," Ann smiled. She watched him walk toward the pilot house. It seemed like an eternity for the two men to arrive with her injured husband. She stood near the bow, waiting. Her expression betrayed nothing, but deep down she was a mess. Yesterday, she had arrived in Savannah elated at the thought of seeing her husband. By yesterday afternoon, she had been told he had been killed. Now she's being told he's alive but wounded.

Soon, two men came down the muddy slope carrying a man in a blue wool army blanket. They paused until they figured out which boat to bring him to and then carefully made their way up the plank.

When they reached the deck, Ann rushed toward them and asked, "Is that Will Wallace?"

"Yes ma'am," Tom replied. He watched the woman look over into the blanket at the severe wound. Her expression went from elation to horror.

"Will?" she entreated the wounded man. "Can you hear me?"

By this point, Tom and Perry's backs were aching from the long trip here. Tom asked, "Where do we need to place him ma'am?"

Ann Wallace looked around the deck. Every inch of space seemed to be covered with wounded soldiers. It seemed ironic for her at the moment. Perhaps some of these wounded men belonged to Will's command. Surely they would respect him enough to give up their place for their commander. A thought hit her.

"Take him to the pilot house," she said. She hated to seem overbearing, but her husband was a general after all. They would place him in the pilot house where she would tend to him during the return trip downriver.

They carried him up the stairs as Ann Wallace led the way. They entered the pilot house and placed him against the back wall out of the way. Ann knelt beside her poor husband, took his hand, and said, "Will, it's me…your wife. Please answer me, Will."

The general never opened his eye but simply squeezed her hand. Ann's face lit up again. She looked up at the two privates and said, "He is conscious enough that he knows me. I know he knows me."

"Yes ma'am," Tom nodded in agreement.

Ann looked at the two men a long moment. She said, "I can't thank you enough for what you've done for me."

"It was nothing ma'am," Tom's eyes looked away. He asked, "Is there anything else we can do for you, ma'am?"

"Send a surgeon up here immediately," Ann said. She was pleading more than commanding. She turned to the pilot and gave an order. "I believe you have your orders from General Grant. Take us to Savannah."

Will Wallace seemed to recognize his young wife's voice. He attempted to speak to her, but the words came out unintelligible. Ann quickly patted his hand and said, "Remain quiet now, Will. Save your strength. I need you to save your strength for me."

The ride downriver seemed to take forever, although they were moving with the current. Ann couldn't wait to get Will in a clean bed where he could begin to heal.

They reached the Cherry Home, and several men carried Will Wallace off the gangplank and up the terraces to the house. Misses Cherry stood in the back yard staring at Grant's headquarters boat. She'd heard the whistle blow as the boat approached shore and came out to see what was happening. She was a southern lady, but she'd also been listening to the severe firing upriver for two days now and wondered what was happening. She watched a woman and several men make their way up the steps toward her home. The men were carrying someone in a blanket.

Ann Wallace reached the house before the men who were laboring with the loaded blanket. She looked at Misses Cherry with tears in her eyes and said, "General Grant has sent me here. My husband has been severely wounded, and he has ordered him brought to your home."

Misses Cherry immediately felt sympathy for this young lady. She couldn't imagine what life would be like if she were to be in this young lady's shoes. She replied, "Bring him inside. I have a bed for him. You're welcome to stay here as long as you need."

"Thank you," Ann said. She followed the woman into the house.

Misses Cherry took her to a room on the lower floor and quickly pulled the bed back. She said, "Put him in here. I'll have my servants bring some water so you can wash his wounds. General Smith is in bed upstairs."

"Thank you," Ann repeated.

Will Wallace lapsed in and out of consciousness for the next three nights. When awake, he seemed to know his wife, squeezing her hand and attempting to talk to her.

Two nights later, Will Wallace pressed his wife's face into his chest and said, "We meet in heaven."

Those were his last words. She would have his body loaded back on board a boat and carried back to Ottawa, Illinois, where he rests today. General Charles F. Smith, lying upstairs with an infected leg, would succumb to his injury just fifteen days after Wallace.

CSA

Beauregard's mood had made a complete turnaround from the elation he had felt upon awakening this morning. Over the course of the morning, it had grown apparent that he wouldn't be accepting Grant's surrender. He wouldn't be gathering up stragglers from the retreat of his army during the night. At worst, he had expected to find Grant completely gone, leaving him an abandoned field and making him the great hero of this war once again. He'd truly believed that Grant's army would be halfway to Kentucky by daylight if they weren't preparing to surrender for lack of boats.

The day had turned out far worse. Buell had arrived, united forces with Grant, and they were now pushing his army off the field. Not only did he find that to be disconcerting, but also the fact that he would be labeled the goat of the battle. Johnston had been in command yesterday when they were winning. The fact that they were losing after Grant had taken command would not be lost on the southern population.

It felt strange. He hadn't wanted to fight here to begin with. He'd begged Johnston to fall back before they were committed, yet now it was his army. The man who'd insisted on attacking was at this very moment headed toward Corinth in a wagon, his body covered by an old army blanket.

It was time for him to take action, regardless of his state of health. He turned to Captain Waddell of his staff, and in a raspy voice, he said, "Locate General Polk and have him brought here."

The man jumped on his horse and rode away. Beauregard walked over to the table where Colonel Jordan was working. He leaned over and patted the man on the shoulder. He bent low and said, "Tom, I want you to send a message to Corinth. I want every available soldier sent here at once. Tell them it doesn't matter if they're armed or not. We've captured plenty of weapons. Once you've taken care of that, we'll ride to the front."

Beauregard and his staff mounted and rode northward toward the sound of the firing. He rode toward the left flank and noticed a large group of disorganized men. Captain Lockett, engineer officer on the staff of General Bragg, was attempting to get these men to go back into the fight. They were paying very little attention to a mere captain they didn't know. Beauregard spurred his horse that way.

Captain Lockett recognized General Beauregard, and he instantly snapped to attention and saluted. Beauregard bowed his head toward the pale-faced man with the thick, drooping mustache. Lockett began to explain, "Sir, I was just attempting to get these men…"

"Men…" Beauregard interrupted as he turned toward the large group. He quickly estimated there were about a hundred and fifty men gathered in the immediate area. Upon recognizing Beauregard, they all began to gather around. "…we are on the verge of winning a grand victory here. I need your help. I need you men to go back into the fight and become heroes for our cause. Just think of the way you'll be treated when you return to your homes as victors."

"We ain't got no officer," one man shouted.

"Yes you do," Beauregard replied without hesitation. "This is Captain Lockett. I'm making him your temporary colonel. You will be known as the Beauregard Regiment today. Someday, you will have the honor of telling your grandchildren that you fought at Shiloh in my regiment. Can I count on you?"

The men raised a cheer. Beauregard turned to Captain Lockett and smiled. "It's your regiment, Colonel."

Lockett rubbed his large nose and shook his head. His bright, hazel eyes practically shined in the morning light. That was what impressed people about General Beauregard. The man understood how to motivate men to fight.

Beauregard spun the horse and rode toward the east. It was time to inspect the condition of his army and allow his men to see him at the front. He paused behind the brigade of Sterling Wood and watched them hold their ground against a strong Federal force.

Colonel Jordan pulled his horse up alongside Beauregard and leaned close enough to be heard. "Sir, I have a report that many units are running out of ammunition. It's the price we pay for having so many different caliber weapons in the army."

"It can't be helped at the moment," Beauregard replied. "Have the regiments with no ammunition send men among the captured enemy camps in search of rifles and bullets."

"Right," Jordan was nodding, "but the men are practically exhausted. Some haven't had anything to eat since yesterday."

Beauregard ignored the statement. He nudged the horse forward and rode down his line. Upon reaching the right flank, he did some quick estimates in his head. He figured that of the forty thousand men he had brought on the field yesterday, probably no more than twenty thousand remained on line. Of course, he hadn't lost that many as casualties. Probably more than sixty percent had simply left the ranks, some out of fear and others because they thought the battle was over yesterday. It embarrassed him that this army hadn't been properly drilled and disciplined before his arrival.

Beauregard asked Jordan, "How many men did Prentiss say we would be facing with the arrival of Buell?"

"He wasn't sure exactly," Jordan replied. "He did say that Grant had forty thousand on the field yesterday. Wallace is en route from Crump's Landing with another five thousand fresh troops, and Buell would arrive with twenty to thirty thousand during the night. I figure we face from sixty to possibly seventy thousand men at the moment. More of Buell's army is probably arriving as we speak."

Things had quieted down considerably on the right now. Beauregard decided he would return to the hard-pressed left and help hold the enemy back. He returned to find the left wing grudgingly giving ground. They seemed to contest every inch as if their lives were depending on it.

Deep down, the man knew he'd been defeated. He refused to betray the feeling. If he appeared concerned, his men would lose faith and falter. The line on this flank had been pushed back to within a half mile of Shiloh Church. Beauregard found the Nineteenth Louisiana Infantry marching toward the right flank. He spurred his horse out in front of the regiment. He smiled as if nothing were wrong and waited until he had every man's attention. He removed his hat and strained his voice to be heard. "Men, the day is ours. You're facing a whipped army. They have brought up fresh men, but now they too have done all they can. Remember to fire low and fire deliberate."

The men raised their hats and cheered the short, dark Creole. Beauregard saw Colonel Pond, now in command of the Louisiana brigade. He spurred his horse forward. Beauregard knew Preston Pond well enough to know the man was frustrated.

Pond saw Beauregard and gave a sloppy salute. If he hadn't known any better, he would have thought Pond was sad. The man had a high forehead, with sad eyes that drooped at the corners. He said, "Preston, there is a lull in the fighting on the right. Where are you headed with this splendid brigade of yours?"

"Damned if I know," Pond erupted. He rubbed his well-trimmed beard. "I've been ordered by Polk to support the right flank."

Beauregard shook his head. "Preston, you're needed on the far left. The situation there is becoming dire. I have reports that Wallace's fresh division is attempting to flank us there and cut off our retreat route."

Pond was shaking his head also. He spoke through clenched teeth. "I was facing Wallace's division at daylight. He was beginning to advance, and we were about to engage him, when General Ruggles ordered me to move over to the left and guard Owl Creek. Moved me right off the battlefield and out of the fight to guard a damned creek. What in hell for…I'll never know."

Beauregard waited patiently for Pond to finish his tirade. Time was wasting, but he needed to hear this. It was obvious this army was in desperate need of replacing some of these commanders. Had it been up to Beauregard, Daniel Ruggles wouldn't have even been given a commission.

Preston Pond continued his rant. "Anyway, I had just gotten my men moved over there through these thick-ass woods, when he sends word for me to march to the right to support General Hardee. We moved all the way across the battlefield, and I was in the process of deploying them to assist Hardee, when I receive word from General Polk for me to return to the left flank. We marched back across the field toward the left flank, and I just received word to return them back east to support the center. I've been marching my men all morning long and have not been engaged. I only succeeded in wearing my men out for no damned reason. Now you're telling me to go back to the west where I started this morning."

Beauregard watched the frustrated man let it all go with a sigh. Pond thought that he may have insulted Beauregard and quickly added, "This has been a fiasco."

He'd gotten the frustration off his chest and now seemed resigned to do whatever he was instructed.

Beauregard said, "Preston, I understand. You command a good brigade of Louisiana boys. I'm in command now. You will tell anyone else who tries to move your men that you have orders from the commanding general to hold your position until relieved by me."

"Yes, sir," Pond straightened up. He spun in the saddle and quickly began shouting orders for the brigade to begin yet another retrograde movement.

Beauregard rode past Pond's men and continued back toward the left flank. He could tell things were beginning to unravel. There was no way his men could continue to hold off against sixty thousand men, half of whom were fresh.

Beauregard called Jordan up beside him. He didn't have to worry about the others hearing him with his voice practically gone. He said, "Tom, I want you to discreetly have the captured rifles and ammunition loaded onto wagons and sent toward Corinth. I'm not sure how long we can hold the field, and those arms are valuable to us."

The general rode on past his left flank and scouted the position of Wallace's division. They were indeed stretched beyond his line, and if Lew Wallace had been an aggressive commander, they could have already enveloped his flank and forced him to retreat.

He rode back toward the rear in search of some troops. At this point, any troops would do. He soon came across Wharton's Texas Ranger Cavalry. They were patiently awaiting some sort of assignment. Cavalry was mostly used for reconnaissance work, but Beauregard was desperate. He found the regiment's youthful commander dismounted beneath a large oak tree. Beauregard rode up and watched the man come to attention.

Beauregard was pretty sure that Wharton was at least thirty years old, but the clean-shaven face and large ears made him look as though he weren't even old enough to be in the army. Beauregard said, "Colonel Wharton, I want you to take your regiment, sweep around the Federal flank here, and strike him in the rear."

Wharton's face betrayed the fact that he was taken aback. Beauregard was asking him to take his four-hundred-man cavalry regiment and attack an infantry division of possibly five thousand men. It sounded like a suicide mission, but orders were orders. He practically leapt into the saddle and said, "I will do my best, sir."

Beauregard watched the regiment file off to the west. He moved back to the front to watch for any weakening of the Federal line, which would indicate they were being attacked in their rear. If Wharton succeeded in making them move troops toward the rear, Beauregard planned on ordering his infantry forward and exploiting the confusion in the enemy ranks. He waited almost half an hour without seeing anything. Then he noticed a rider approaching from his left. It was Colonel Wharton riding a different horse than he'd departed on. His uniform was filthy and disheveled.

He reined up and saluted. "General, I did as you instructed. It could have worked, but we hit them at a most inopportune time. Wallace was shifting a brigade from his left toward the right just as we attacked. Because they were moving perpendicular to the main line, it means we hit a brigade of infantry with a frontal assault. We didn't have a chance. My horse was killed, throwing me to the ground and banging up my shoulder. I had to grab the horse of a man who'd been killed just to escape. I've lost a good many men and horses, but we've retired about a hundred yards off their flank to the west."

"It's alright," Beauregard reached out and patted the young colonel on the shoulder. He instantly drew his hand back when he noticed the young man wince in pain. Beauregard added, "I'm going to give the order soon for the entire army to fall back."

Wharton nodded and added. "From where I was, sir, I can tell you they got a lot of men—and they're fresh too."

"Thank you," Beauregard resisted the urge to pat the man's shoulder again. "When we begin to fall back, use your regiment to help serve as rearguard for our withdrawal."

"Right," Wharton saluted with his good arm and rode back toward his men.

Beauregard rode back to where his staff was waiting. He rasped out his instructions for Jordan. "Tom, I need you to ride to the center, find Bragg, and see how things are going there."

Jordan spun the horse and galloped toward the east. He searched down the line until he found Braxton Bragg riding toward a group of officers resting beneath a large maple tree. Jordan followed him and arrived about the same time as Bragg.

The man lying on the ground was Brigadier General Pat Cleburne, the Irishman who'd made Arkansas his home. He'd arrived here yesterday morning with over twenty-five hundred men. Jordan inspected the men resting in line of battle about fifty yards behind Cleburne and his staff. There were less than eight hundred men in his command now.

Cleburne saw Bragg, got to his feet, and saluted. Bragg ignored the salute. It was difficult to judge the man's mood. He had one thick eyebrow that dipped just above his nose, and he wore an expression on his face that Jordan had nicknamed 'the eternal scowl.'

Bragg commanded, "General, I want you to advance your brigade and attack Sherman's division that's located a couple hundred yards in the forest in your front."

Cleburne stepped closer to Bragg. Sunlight struck his head through an opening in the leaves overhead, making his red hair brighten up. He looked back at what was left of his once proud brigade and then stared hard into Bragg's eyes. He said, "Sir, I've crept forward into that forest. It's really just a thicket. I scouted Sherman's division the best I could. He has at least three thousand men in there. He outnumbers me at least four to one. I have no support on either flank…"

"That was not a suggestion. It was an order. Now, you'll move your brigade forward as directed or be arrested for insubordination," Bragg interrupted. He hated volunteer soldiers. *This man has had no military training whatsoever except a small stint as a private in the British Army, Bragg thought. Yet, here he stands attempting to act as though he knows more than a West Point trained officer who became a hero in the Mexican War.*

Jordan's interest was piqued. He wanted to see how this thing was gonna play out. He watched the Irishman move his brigade forward into the trees. They moved forward cautiously. The thick undergrowth here meant they wouldn't find the enemy until they were upon him.

They were gone almost five minutes, when Jordan heard the Federal line open fire. He heard Cleburne's men return fire, though not nearly as loud as what the large host of Federal infantry produced. There were a couple more volleys, and then everything was quiet. He heard a commotion in the trees and out popped the first few men. Then the entire brigade erupted from the trees and raced past Bragg and Jordan. Cleburne came out of the thicket but made no attempt to stop the flight of his men.

He rode straight to Braxton Bragg and reported, "I couldn't see twenty-five yards of my line in that mess. I don't know how bad things are, but I lost a lot of good men in there."

Cleburne rode on past Bragg to try and regroup his brigade—if it could still be called that. The man was furious at Bragg and didn't try to hide it. He never even bothered to salute. Cleburne had learned more yesterday about warfare than Bragg had learned during the entire Mexican War. And the lesson was that a direct frontal assault against a superior force is nothing but suicide. It just won't work.

Bragg rode away, followed by his staff and Colonel Jordan. Jordan could have asked Bragg what he thought and returned to Beauregard, but he wanted to see for himself how things were going. Bragg found Cheatham a hundred yards east of Cleburne's men.

Cheatham saluted. He had a carefree expression on his face, which made Jordan think the man didn't have a worry in the world. He asked, "General Bragg, how goes it?"

Bragg pointed over his shoulder in the direction Cleburne had just attacked and said, "Frank, I want you to take your brigade and assault that position yonder."

"Right," Cheatham nodded. He didn't care about strategy or tactics. The man was a fighter. He just wanted to be pointed in the right direction and do his job.

Bragg turned to Lieutenant Ellis, one of his staff officers. "Have that arrogant Colonel Gibson move his Louisianans up and have them go in with Cheatham."

The lieutenant wheeled his horse and rode away. Bragg turned to Lieutenant Urquhart, who had been an aide to Louisiana Governor Thomas Moore. Urquhart had volunteered his services to Bragg when the war began. Bragg said, "Lieutenant, have Patton Anderson move his brigade up and support Cheatham's other flank. He'll push them back. I helped him train those boys. They're the best troops we got here."

Jordan waited with Bragg while the three small brigades moved off into the trees. They hit Sherman's division with a crash and seemed to be making headway. There just weren't enough of them to push him back. The fighting lasted almost thirty minutes before the brigades began to slowly fall back.

Jordan reined up beside Bragg and asked, "Sir, General Beauregard wants a report on the condition of your men."

"Completely exhausted," Bragg mumbled. He watched his men moving back away from the fight, and with Jordan here, it embarrassed him. He lowered his head and said, "The enemy has been reinforced. They're stronger than what we faced yesterday, and even worse, they are fresh. My men are at the point of collapse. Without a fresh supply of ammunition, fresh troops, and some rest for my men…"

Jordan noticed that Bragg left the rest unsaid. Jordan thanked Bragg and spurred the horse back toward Water Oaks Pond where he'd left Beauregard almost an hour ago.

He arrived at the glade and rode to the knee-deep body of water that was referred to as a pond. He surveyed the Confederate lines across the field still fighting. Beauregard was nowhere to be seen. He thought about going in search of the man, but there was no way of knowing where he'd gone. He decided to wait. His commander had said he would be here, and he would return soon.

Beauregard was off to the west. He'd received a report from Colonel Pond that his men were on the verge of breaking. Beauregard found one of Pond's regiments attempting to regroup behind the main battle line. He spurred his horse over to the Eighteenth Louisiana Infantry. He knew this unit and its commander.

Colonel Jean Jacques Alfred Alexander Mouton stepped forward and saluted. He liked Beauregard, and Beauregard liked him in return. They had quite a lot in common.

Beauregard asked, "How are you, Alfred?"

"I've had better days," Mouton replied. "My men have done about all they can do here. I'm trying to get them back in the fight, but they don't seem to hear anything I'm saying."

Beauregard rode forward and grabbed the regimental flag and held it high above his head. He said, "I don't have to tell you gentlemen where this flag staff came from. I captured it at Fort Sumter and sent it to your colonel to be used by Louisianans in battle. I know it's been a difficult two days. I know you're tired, but I also know you hail from my state, and I know you can still fight."

The men began to cheer him. He then spun his horse, and as loud as possible with his damaged voice, he said, "Charge them; charge them, my braves!"

He surged ahead toward the enemy lines across the way. The line followed. There was no resisting this fiery little Creole. As they continued onward, a private ran up beside Beauregard's horse and yelled, "General, you shouldn't be so reckless. You could be hit!"

"Never mind me, good fellow. You do your duty, and I'll do mine," Beauregard shot back.

The private refused to give up the argument. "It's my duty to die, not yours."

Beauregard smiled as he passed the flag down to the private. He slowed the horse and allowed the line of men to pass. He rode back a ways and waited for the results. He didn't have to wait long, when he saw Colonel Pond approaching.

Pond reined up and saluted. "Sir, I have one regiment completely cut up. Colonel Mouton was just wounded in the head leading the Eighteenth back in."

Beauregard held up a hand. He thought about his friend Alfred Mouton. The man was a West Point graduate like Beauregard, but there was more to it than that. He was of French lineage just like Beauregard, and he'd only learned to speak English after reaching adulthood. Though he was younger and had seen no combat the way Beauregard had, the man was showing signs of being a promising young commander. Beauregard asked, "How bad is it?"

"My brigade's in bad shape..." Pond replied before being interrupted by the general.

"Not the brigade. How bad is Mouton's wound?" Beauregard clarified things.

"Oh," Pond shook his head as if clearing the confusion from his mind. "He was hit in the left cheek. May have damaged his left eye a little, but I think he'll be fine."

"Do the best you can, Preston. I'll bring up more troops," Beauregard spun the horse and rode back toward Shiloh Church to the south.

As he rode back, Lieutenant Helm of his staff eased his horse up beside Beauregard. He spoke to Beauregard as if he were in command here. "General, you shouldn't expose yourself to enemy fire. We lost a commander yesterday. If you go down, this army will be without a head."

"The word at this point is *follow*, not *go*," Beauregard replied.

119

The man had been operating on adrenaline since the battle began, but now he felt as though he'd used it all. He suddenly felt weak. He remembered what the doctors had told him about staying in bed and how dangerous it could be to his health if he continued to push himself. *But, what choice do I have, he wondered.*

He found two undersized Tennessee regiments reforming near the chapel. He rode over and grabbed the first unit's battle flag. The flag was large, almost six by nine feet. It was heavy, and he was extremely weak at the moment. He attempted to hold it high in the air but just didn't have the strength at the moment. Beauregard was forced to pass the flag back to the color bearer.

"Will you men follow me back into the battle?" he asked.

The men replied with a cheer. Beauregard turned to Lieutenant Helm and asked him to lead them back to support Pond's brigade. He felt as though he would fall from the horse. Helm led the two regiments up the road toward the fighting. The men looked as exhausted as Beauregard felt. He looked at each powder-blackened face as they passed by. A feeling of depression swept over him. He wanted to tell these poor boys to just forget the battle.

There was no time for weakness, and he needed to get back to the front. He spun the horse and rode toward Water Oaks Pond, where Jordan should be waiting with a report.

Before he reached the glade, he noticed a line of troops wearing white coats. At first glance he suspected they were Federals, but they were standing in line with his troops and firing toward the north. The coats weren't just white; they were clean for the most part. These men hadn't fought here yesterday, not in clean white coats.

Beauregard turned to Lieutenant Steel and said, "See those troops there?"

Steel watched Beauregard point toward a line of men dressed in white coats. "Yes, sir."

"I hear Van Dorn's troops wear all colors of uniforms. If that's Van Dorn up from Arkansas, then we have fifteen thousand fresh men on the field." Beauregard fought back the urge to feel relieved. The same thing had happened at Manassas last summer. Fresh troops had arrived from the Shenandoah Valley just in time to save the army. He said, "Lieutenant, ride over and find out who those troops belong to."

He watched Steel spur the horse. If those were Van Dorn's men, the battle could have just been reversed once more. He watched Steel as he talked to the officer in command of the regiment. The man was shaking his head as if explaining something. Soon Steel spurred the horse back to where Beauregard was waiting. The expression on his face told Beauregard those weren't Van Dorn's men.

Steel reported, "Sir, it's the Orleans Guard Battalion. Their coats are blue. They took so much friendly fire yesterday that they've turned their coats inside out. The men have been referring to their coats as their death shrouds."

Without a word, Beauregard spurred his horse toward Water Oaks Pond. He needed to find Jordan and see how the rest of his army was holding up.

He saw Jordan ahead near the pond, but before he could get there, he was intercepted by a courier. The man said, "Sir, General Wood begs to report."

"Report," Beauregard said.

"He says he is the extreme left now," the man wiped his sweaty forehead with a handkerchief and then continued. "He says he is hard pressed and doesn't think he can hold much longer."

Beauregard looked across the glade and noticed the Federal artillery had gotten the range of his line there. Shells burst overhead. Most of his men were on the ground, but every once in a while, one would leap to his feet and race toward the rear.

His line was receiving pressure on the left and center. He knew that a concentrated effort by the Federal army would destroy his army. There was a good possibility he wouldn't even get them off the field.

Jordan had recognized the group of officers just twenty-five yards behind him. As he rode toward them, he noticed Tennessee Governor Harris off to the side on his mule, motioning Jordan that way.

Beauregard was busy talking to a courier, so Jordan reined up beside the comical-looking governor on the sorry-looking mule.

Harris removed his top hat and wiped at his sweaty, bald head with his hand. He asked, "Tom, do you not think the day is going against us?"

Jordan nodded in agreement but said nothing.

Harris placed the hat back on his head and asked, "Don't you think the army is in danger of being destroyed if we remain on the field much longer?"

"It doesn't look good. I believe a retreat should be made soon," Jordan replied. "I'll speak with the general."

He nudged his horse up close to Beauregard and patiently waited. Beauregard sent the courier away and turned, noticing Jordan for the first time.

After a long, awkward pause, Jordan said, "General, don't you think our army is in the shape of a wet sugar cube? It looks like a cube, but with any tiny bump, it will dissolve into nothing. Wouldn't it be wise to get away with what we have?"

Beauregard's voice was barely comprehensible. He replied, "I intend to withdraw in a few moments."

Jordan nodded and waited. Beauregard continued to stare across the glade toward his lines.

After another long, awkward pause, he said, "Send messages to the corps commanders. Tell them I want an orderly withdrawal. Once you have sent them orders, I want you to find as many broken and scattered units as you can. I want you to post them somewhere to the south to serve as a rearguard for the retreating army. I'm so weak I can hardly stay in the saddle. Use your own judgment, Tom, but place them somewhere easy to defend."

"I have just the place, sir," Jordan smiled. "That forested hill just south of the chapel."

Beauregard watched Jordan send the orders out and then ride away to find a rearguard. He spurred forward to the edge of the pond. Surveying the field, he began to shake his head. There were dead and wounded everywhere. Some of the bodies had been mangled, which told him how fierce the fighting had been. To his right were sixty horses that were all killed yesterday. They belonged to a Union artillery battery that the Sixteenth Alabama Infantry had overrun. They'd shot the horses so the artillerymen couldn't save their guns. That had been an excellent move on that commander's part.

121

During the lulls in the firing, Beauregard could hear the pleading of the wounded. It frustrated him. He found the entire battle embarrassing. It had all been fought for naught. It was a useless battle, and he would take the blame. There was no doubt in his mind about that. If Sidney Johnston had only listened yesterday, they could have fallen back to Corinth and waited for the Federals to hit entrenchments. He could have saved a lot of lives.

Somewhere along the way, Beauregard had forgotten that attacking Grant's army here was originally his idea. He had forgotten that his chief of staff had written up the confusing battle plans, while he had given the marching orders that caused the army to arrive two days late. His orders had been so confusing that the Confederates had begun the campaign at a severe disadvantage. Placing corps in front of each other had managed to jumble them together to the point that no corps commander could control his own men.

He turned the horse to the south and rode along beside his retreating men. They were so exhausted that they struggled to place one foot in front of another. They had accomplished all any mortal man could have. The failure hadn't been their fault, but Beauregard refused to believe that any of this was his fault either.

USA

William Tecumseh Sherman had been moving his division forward with extreme caution. Ulysses Grant had assured him twice that the battle would be won today, but Sherman had been on the receiving end of that devastating Confederate attack yesterday, and he understood the damage they were capable of inflicting. Besides, his division was in the center, and there was no way to push the Confederates back without heavy fighting out on the flanks. So he chose not to feed his men into a meat grinder.

They'd soon reached Jones Field, and Sherman ordered a halt. Lew Wallace was advancing slowly on his right, McDowell was on his left, and Buell was somewhere beyond him. Artillery fire rained down among his men from the far side of the field. He gave the order for them to lie down and not expose themselves.

Sherman's men had been through enough yesterday. He decided it would be a useless waste of life to send them across this open field into artillery and musket fire. There was nothing to do now but wait for his friends to flank them out of the position. No doubt, if Grant were here, he would order them across. But Sherman refused to attempt such a move.

He held this position until the ever-cautious Wallace finally advanced and threatened the enemy flank. He watched the Confederates begin to fall back through the trees. His division could now advance and take this field without high casualties.

Again, Sherman gave the order to advance but only at the half-step. He wanted to make sure he wasn't advancing into a trap. There was heavy fire to both sides of his division. The intensity seemed to rival what he'd heard yesterday. The Confederates were slowly giving ground, but Sherman understood they would not go quietly.

Just inside the trees, he allowed his men to rest. After a good half hour, the sounds of battle subsided on both sides of him. A courier approached Sherman from the front. He saluted Sherman and asked, "Where can I find General McClernand?"

Sherman pointed toward his left and said, "He's over that way somewhere. What do you know of the enemy in my front?"

"There is no enemy in your front," the man replied. He grinned broadly, a large gap appearing where his front tooth used to be. "They've pulled back off the field. We've won, sir."

Sherman breathed a sigh of relief. It was over. Grant had been right all along, but it had been a close call. *It could have meant the end of both our careers, Sherman thought...still might.*

One of Sherman's staff officers pointed toward the rear, and Sherman spun. A group of riders were galloping toward him. The lead rider had a cigar clenched between his teeth, smoke billowing out around his face. It was Grant, followed by most of his staff.

Grant had remained in the rear all morning, allowing his subordinates to direct the battle. He made sure there was a steady supply of ammunition and reinforcements from Buell's army sent to the front. The man's left ankle was aching, and he couldn't bare the pain of any weight placed on it. He'd had to ask his staff to assist him in mounting his horse.

Grant rode up and asked, "How goes it, Cump?"

"I have a report that the enemy has retreated, but I can't be sure. Everything has been quiet here for the past thirty minutes," Sherman replied.

"I've heard the same from Lew Wallace," Grant took another puff on the cigar. He took out his pocket watch and noted the time. "It's almost five. Listen; I would love to pursue them and finish this thing, but it's late and the men are exhausted. Let's let them rest this time. Besides, if I move forward, Halleck will have my hide."

"Right," Sherman nodded. He was thankful that his friend wasn't his normally-aggressive self at the moment. It puzzled him a little though. He wondered if maybe Grant may have lost a little of his confidence over the past two days. The man had never endured an assault of such force before. Sherman asked, "What's Buell gonna do?"

"Haven't heard a word from him since he arrived yesterday," Grant puffed on the cigar, pulled it from his mouth, and blew smoke toward the sky. "But, knowing him, he's going nowhere. He'll want to stay here and refit, reorganize, and replace the lost troops for a couple months."

Sherman knew Grant was right about Buell. He had been acting overly cautious since the war began. But Sherman had to admit that the man had marched hard to the field and helped save Grant. Sherman also knew that Grant would never admit that Buell had saved him. Following Fort Donelson, Sherman had noticed Grant's ego growing. Of course, that was the nature of the game, and Sherman's had been growing also. That sat well with Sherman because he would never admit that fact either. Grant was his friend; Buell was cold and aloof. The man didn't want friends.

Sherman thought about Halleck. That man won't let Grant forget he was surprised here. He'd tried to cashier Grant after he'd taken Donelson. This may be just enough reason for him to actually succeed in getting rid of his rash subordinate. The ever-cautious Halleck would have had the army entrenched. He will call this a fiasco, and partly he will be right.

Grant said, "Rest your men. In the morning, take a brigade and follow them far enough to ensure they aren't contemplating coming back."

Sherman couldn't help but think about the words Grant had said two days before the battle. He had said that all he wanted was for the Confederate army to come out and hit him here in the open. Well, they had obliged him, and now Grant was glad to see they were gone.

Sherman suddenly felt tired. "If it's alright with you, Sam, I'm gonna return to my tent, if I still have one, and get a few moments of rest."

"You've earned it," Grant began to turn the horse. "I'll return to Savannah tonight and notify Halleck of our success here. You did a good job, Cump. If Halleck will allow us, we'll be through Mississippi to the Gulf in three months."

Sherman saluted and rode away, his staff trailing behind. He'd been called insane early in the war for suggesting it would take two-hundred thousand men to conquer the Mississippi River. *I'll never admit it in public again, Sherman thought, but I still believe it'll take that many.*

He crossed the battlefield past the dead and dying. There were plenty of walking wounded with that look in their eyes—the look that said they had already seen too much war. When he rode past places where it had been particularly severe, Sherman noticed trees ravaged by bullets.

Back near the church, he found his tent. Two horses that belonged to members of his staff lay outside, shot down yesterday. His tent had eight bullet holes through it. There wasn't a tent in the field without bullet holes.

There were wounded soldiers of both armies lying around the church begging for help. He dismounted and walked into his tent. The Confederates had stolen his cot. There were scraps of paper on the ground, and he squatted to pick them up. He found signatures of Confederate generals Beauregard, Breckinridge, and Bragg. The irony made him smile. They'd used his tent as their headquarters. At least one of them probably spent the night here last night. He'd considered all three men personal friends before the war began.

Sherman found himself a roll of blankets and threw most of them on the ground. He kept the rest as cover. It soon began to rain, and the leaky tent became miserable. He finally shifted his blankets to a spot that wasn't getting soaked and wrestled with sleep until after midnight.

Daylight came, and the rains disappeared. He lay in the warm blankets dreading getting up. His head ached, and he longed for his missing bottle of laudanum. Voices could be heard outside, and he realized his staff was building a fire. He struggled from the blankets and made his way to the fire's warmth.

"Rained like hell last night, General," Captain McCoy commented.

"Means the Lord is cleansing the earth of man's sins," Sherman replied as he moved close to the fire. "How are the men?"

"Exhausted," Captain Hammond replied from across the fire. The man was Sherman's chief of staff. Sherman had ordered him to the rear two days ago when the battle began because he'd been in feeble health. Hammond had refused.

He was still present after the difficult past two days. Sherman noticed he looked like a corpse standing there. His expression told Sherman how badly he truly felt.

Sherman said, "Captain Hammond, I want you to report to a surgeon. You'll be no good to me if you fall over dead."

Hammond started to say something, but he noticed the tone of Sherman's voice. He mumbled, "Yes, sir."

Sherman smiled. "And while you're back there, get me a bottle of laudanum. My head is killing me."

The general turned to Captain McCoy and said, "Throw together a makeshift brigade for us of the more rested and fit troops. Have them cook breakfast and prepare to move out after we eat."

"Right," Captain McCoy looked surprised. He couldn't believe they were actually going after the Confederate army this soon.

Sherman ate his breakfast and then climbed on his horse. He rode among his men and noticed how slowly they cooked and ate their food. Once they were through, the men stumbled into line lethargically. It was if they were afraid to pursue Beauregard's army. They'd also been forced to sleep in line of battle last night out in the open air and rain. Two days of fighting with very little rest and then a night without even the benefit of fires was taking its toll on them. The men were sore, cold, wet, and aching.

Down the line, one soldier fired his rifle to see if it would still shoot after last night's heavy rain. The discharge seemed especially loud today on this peaceful morning. It amazed Sherman to see part of his line race toward the landing, while others dove on the ground. One shot and they'd panicked. They had assumed they were being attacked again, and they'd had enough. All of them were wide-eyed, as if in some sort of shock.

It took until ten before he was able to get them under way. They moved south, trudging. It could no longer be called marching. Sherman was also nervous, but he hid it well. Advancing down these narrow country roads was dangerous. It would be a perfect place for Beauregard to set up an ambush.

He'd sent some of Colonel Dickey's Illinois cavalry out front to reconnoiter. A cavalryman rode back at noon to report. The lanky boy had trouble keeping his horse still. He said, "General, we've found them. About a half mile ahead, there's this big old open field they call Fallen Timbers. There are Confederate cavalry on the other side just waiting on us."

"Right," Sherman nodded. "Just hold where you are. The infantry will push them back."

The man spun the horse and galloped back to the front. They marched onward and arrived at an open, muddy field. There lay heaps of felled timber all around the field. Someone had recently cleared this field for farming.

Sherman quickly counted the Rebel cavalry in the trees on the other side. He needed to know if they were a rearguard covering Beauregard's retreat or if they were protecting the Confederate army while they prepared for another assault on the landing.

He soon estimated that he faced about three hundred Confederate cavalrymen. Sherman had an entire brigade of infantry at his disposal. Sure, it was under strength, but it was just damned cavalry. He outnumbered them at least two to one, if not more. He gave orders for the Seventy-Seventh Ohio Infantry to advance as skirmishers. His main line would advance fifty yards behind. He doubted that cavalry would stand to face the skirmish line, much less his infantry.

Once the skirmish line was well ahead, Sherman gave the order for the main line to move forward. He shouted, "Clear those damned Rebel sons-of-bitches from the trees!"

Sherman heard a commotion to his left as he entered the open field. His two left wing regiments had become jumbled together. Officers were shouting in an attempt to straighten the mess out. He heard threats and curses by the sergeants. That was when he noticed something from his front. The Confederate cavalry had noticed the confusion also. They decided to strike while everything was in turmoil. *Very smart commander, Sherman thought, but he is still attacking infantry.*

The Confederates dashed their horses among the skirmishers of the Seventy-Seventh Ohio and delivered close-range fire from their sawed-off shotguns. The entire regiment seemed to melt and race back toward the main line. Sherman was in a state of shock. He was so surprised by the enemy's attack and the retreat of his men that he never gave his men the order to open fire.

His attention became riveted on the leader of those reckless Confederate troopers. He was a tall man, at least six foot high, with dark hair and a fierce expression. The man wore a thick mustache and goatee. To Sherman he looked like the devil himself.

The Confederate cavalry soon realized they were on a suicide mission and turned back, but their wild leader came on through the retreating skirmish line directly toward Sherman. He held a pistol in his hand, which he fired at Sherman's retreating men as he rode past them.

Sherman was armed with nothing but a saber, yet he didn't bother to draw the weapon. The man was closing too fast. There was no time to react. William Tecumseh Sherman wouldn't remember it for some time, but he just sat there with his mouth gaped open, wide-eyed with disbelief. Of all the shocking things he'd seen over the past two days, this topped them all. His life—his career—was about to end on this very spot. There was nothing he could do at this point. It was funny how the thoughts raced through his mind in such a short time. He'd survived two of the bloodiest days of any war, and yet he was about to be killed by a damned cavalryman with no more common sense than to attack a line of infantry by himself.

Just as the Confederate colonel reached Sherman, he pointed the pistol at the red-haired Ohioan and pulled the trigger. Sherman heard the hammer slam home. He expected to feel the blow from a pistol ball entering his chest. Surprisingly, he heard and felt nothing. The colonel had used up all his rounds on the skirmish line.

If the man only had one round left, Sherman understood that he would have been shot. A pistol ball to the chest at this range would probably have been a fatal wound, yet fate seemed to save him. It wasn't over yet though. Who knew what the wild-eyed colonel would attempt next.

The fearless leader, unaware that he was alone behind the Federal line, spun in the saddle and noticed his men were retiring from the field. Sherman's men were shouting, "Kill that man!" and "Somebody shoot him!"

The wild-eyed, fearless leader was Confederate Colonel Nathan Bedford Forrest. He was lucky that he had a quick mind. Amid the shouts of the Federal soldiers calling for his life, he reached down from the saddle and grabbed a Union infantryman by the collar. At the same moment, another Federal aimed his rifle and fired. The bullet struck him in the back at an upward angle, lifting Forrest a good four inches from the saddle. The bullet stopped against a vertebra in his lower back. Still, Forrest held on to the man's collar.

There was no pain; Forrest was operating on sheer adrenalin now. With one arm, he raised the surprised infantryman completely off the ground and slung him on the back of his horse. The man wasn't sitting on the horse; he was dangling from the horse. The only thing keeping him suspended there was the man's hand on his collar. Forrest spurred his horse back toward the Confederate line. Together with his human shield, he raced back past Sherman and across the muddy field. No more shots were fired at him for fear of hitting the Federal soldier hanging from the back of his horse.

When Forrest was beyond range of the Federal rifles, he turned the hapless man loose at full gallop. The man seemed to bounce in the mud and tumbled end over end twice. Forrest never stopped or even bothered to look back.

Captain Dayton pulled his horse up beside Sherman. The young man was shaking his head. Sherman noticed that last night's rain had his hair all matted and clung to his skull. Dayton said, "That has to be the craziest son-of-a-bitch in the world."

"Yep," Sherman nodded in agreement. He could feel his nerves beginning to settle from the traumatic experience. "That's not even what bothers me."

Dayton cocked his head and stared at Sherman. He asked, "What could possibly be worse than a man like that?"

Sherman couldn't help but grin at Dayton. He said, "They probably got a million more just like him."

Dayton jerked his head back and thought a moment. "If they do, it's gonna be a long war."

"Order the men back to camp," Sherman said as he turned his horse toward Shiloh Church. "We've seen enough of the enemy. Personally, I'm happy to see them leave. The men have earned a rest. We can finish this some other day."

The general nudged his horse back toward his old camp site. Dayton had been right—it was shaping up to be a long and unforgiving war.

Epilog

The Battle of Shiloh was the first major battle of the Civil War. In contrast, the battles fought before pale in comparison. The two opposing armies facing each other at the Battle of Manassas only managed to get 36,000 men engaged, which resulted in 4,878 casualties. The two opposing armies at the Battle of Wilson's Creek managed to engage 17,550 men, which resulted in 2,549 casualties. Shiloh proved to be far different. The Federal army engaged 66,812 men and suffered 13,047 casualties. The Confederate army had 44,699 men engaged and suffered 10,699 casualties. There were many more battles following Shiloh, several with far more casualties, but Shiloh shocked the citizens of both sides. No one had expected so many casualties. Many of the leaders on both sides believed the war would be short and bloodless.

The severe loss of men at Shiloh, coupled with the loss of Albert Sidney Johnston, caused famous Louisiana novelist George Washington Cable to write, "The South never smiled again after Shiloh."

Afterward

Pierre Gustave Toutant Beauregard

He had begun the war as the "Hero of Fort Sumter." After winning the Battle of Manassas, southern papers began to refer to him as the "Hero of the Confederacy." Following the Battle of Shiloh, he became the "goat." Beauregard brought his army back to Corinth, where he endured a siege against both Grant and Buell's armies. Evacuating the town in order to save his army, he took an unapproved leave of absence because of his throat. Davis immediately relieved him. He held no more important commands for the remainder of the war.

Following the war, he and Jefferson Davis spent the rest of their lives vilifying each other. Davis blamed Beauregard, and rightly so, for the horrific alignment of the corps during the battle.

Beauregard blamed Davis for not allowing him to command an important army. He truly believed he was as good a commander as his hero Napoleon, but because of Jefferson Davis's jealousy, he'd never been able to prove his worth.

He died in New Orleans in 1893 at the age of 74. He rests there today in the Tomb of the Army of Tennessee in Metairie Cemetery.

Braxton Bragg

Braxton Bragg reported to Jefferson Davis that the Confederate victory was complete when Beauregard called off the attack on the first day at Shiloh. This resulted in Beauregard being removed when he took an unauthorized absence, and Bragg was then placed in command.

Bragg never became a leader like Sidney Johnston or Beauregard. His harsh discipline kept his men from loving him. His subordinates turned against him, and in the end, the army suffered a loss of morale. He commanded the army for a year and a half and then resigned following a series of defeats. For the rest of the war, he served as Jefferson Davis's military advisor.

Bragg was walking down a street in Galveston, Texas, with a friend in 1876, when he suddenly fell over dead. He was 59 years old. He rests today in Magnolia Cemetery in Mobile, Alabama.

Patrick Ronayne Cleburne

The red-haired Irishman, with little military training except a stint in the British army, rose to major general in command of a division. Largely due to his efforts, a small Federal army was destroyed at Richmond, Kentucky. He fought well at Perryville, Murfreesboro, and Chickamauga. Twice he saved Bragg's army and was voted the thanks of the Confederate Congress, which is equivalent to the present-day Medal of Honor. He went on to become known as the "Stonewall Jackson of the West."

Cleburne was well on his way to commanding a corps, if not an army, when he suggested slaves be given their freedom in return for becoming Confederate soldiers. Many believe this is the reason he was continually passed over by inferior men for a well-deserved promotion.

He served well throughout the Atlanta Campaign and the battles around Atlanta. He then marched northward with General Hood into Middle Tennessee in late

1864. He was killed at the Battle of Franklin. Initially buried in Columbia, Tennessee, he would later be re-interred in the town he called home. He rests there today in Maple Hill Cemetery in Helena, Arkansas.

Nathan Bedford Forrest

The fierce cavalryman who almost ended Sherman's life at Fallen Timbers had received a serious wound in the back. A surgeon removed the bullet a week later without the use of anesthesia. He recovered quickly and returned to action. He was eventually promoted to lieutenant general, and despite only having a sixth-grade education, he became the most feared cavalryman the war produced.

As an independent commander, the man had no equal; yet he failed to cooperate with his superiors. He despised West Point trained officers. He almost came to blows with Bragg and cursed Hood late in the war. Jefferson Davis admitted later in life, that his greatest mistake was in not recognizing Forrest's genius earlier in the war when it could have made a difference.

Earning the nickname "Wizard of the Saddle," Forrest claimed to have killed thirty enemy soldiers with his own hand. He had twenty-nine horses shot out from under him during the course of the war and claimed afterwards that he was "one up on 'em."

Surprisingly, he survived the war and died of diabetes in Memphis, Tennessee, in 1877 at the age of 56. He rests there today beneath his monument in Forrest Park.

Albert Sidney Johnston

Johnston's fate was the most surprising of all. He went from being criticized for his generalship while alive to becoming a hero and martyr following his death. Ranked higher than Robert E. Lee, he would be the highest ranked officer killed in combat on either side.

His body was carried to New Orleans and buried. In 1866, the Texas

130

Legislature passed a resolution seeking to have his body brought home. The next year, he was buried in the Texas State Cemetery in Austin, Texas.

Today, he is still remembered as one of the greatest commanders the war produced, and many enjoy speculating what would have happened had he survived the Battle of Shiloh.

Don Carlos Buell

He always believed that he had saved Grant's army, yet few would listen to him. Lincoln relieved him from command in October for failing to pursue Bragg following the Battle of Perryville, Kentucky. The man was extremely slow and obstinate. He remained in the military, awaiting another assignment, until May, 1864, when he grew frustrated and resigned.

Later, Grant offered him an assignment to serve under Sherman, but Buell refused because he had ranked Sherman earlier in the war. Because of his pride, he saw no more action. Don Carlos Buell died in 1898 at the age of 80. He rests today in Bellefontaine Cemetery in St. Louis, Missouri.

Ulysses Simpson Grant

Grant was severely criticized for not entrenching his army at Shiloh. General Halleck left his headquarters and assumed command of the army, forcing Grant to serve as second-in-command without a true assignment. The northern public nicknamed him "the butcher" because of the high casualty lists his army received in battle.

After Corinth fell, Lincoln ordered Halleck to Washington to serve as commander of all military forces. Grant again took control of the western army. He went on to take Vicksburg, Chattanooga, and then spent the last year of the war wearing down General Lee's army in Virginia.

He became famous when Lee surrendered, and he became president of the United States after the war. Unfortunately, his career as a politician wasn't as successful as his military career. He squandered his money with little regard, and despite being an ex-president, he was almost broke when he died.

Ulysses Grant died in 1885 of throat cancer at the age of 63. He rests today in New York City's Riverside Park.

William Tecumseh Sherman

Sherman eventually rose to command the army after Grant was sent east to deal with Lee. He became known for his "scorched earth" strategy in Georgia and South Carolina. Many in the South still despise the man today because of his war on civilians. He accepted the surrender of the very army that attacked him at Shiloh in late April, 1865.

He was eventually promoted to lieutenant general and became commanding general of the United States Army when his friend Grant became president. Following the Civil War, he claimed that he abhorred war and wanted all wars brought to an end. Ironically, as the commander of the United States Army, he called for extermination of the Native American race, including women and children.

Sherman died in New York City in 1891 at the age of 71. He rests today in Calvary Cemetery in St. Louis, Missouri.

Benjamin Mayberry Prentiss

Benjamin Prentiss was eventually exchanged and returned to the army. He was perceived as a hero in the North for having saved Grant at Shiloh. Grant refused to praise Prentiss, saying the man should have pulled back rather than allowing his division to be surrounded and captured. Because of Grant's influence, Prentiss was sent to Arkansas, where he led his troops to victory at the Battle of Helena.

He saw no more action during the war. He grew frustrated and resigned from the army in 1864. Prentiss felt like he was shelved after proving his military worth at both Shiloh and Helena. He spent the rest of his life holding to his finest moment—the defense of the Hornet's Nest at Shiloh. He is hardly remembered today outside of serious students of the war.

He died in 1901 at the age of 81. He rests today in Miriam Cemetery in Bethany, Missouri.

Tim Kent

Tim has been interested in the Civil War since the age of six. He has been writing for six years and published his first book five years ago. He has just released his second book "Never Smile Again" that covers the Battle of Shiloh. His second book "Die Like Men" covers the Battle of Franklin and is currently available at Books A Million and on Amazon.com. Tim is currently working on his fourth book about Antietam.

Tim enjoys re-enacting and is a first sergeant with the 26th Alabama infantry. He has re-enacted several battles including, Bryce's Crossroads, The Battle of Franklin, Bentonville, Twin Rivers, Resaca, The Battle for Decatur, Winfield and numerous Camps of Instruction. Besides re-enacting Tim enjoys making period clothing for himself and his family, collecting Civil War relics and books and most of all Confederate General autographs.

Tim is also the Lieutenant Commander of his local Sons of Confederate Veterans Camp 898. He has spoken at camp meetings and is a board member of Historical Truth 101. Tim has a personal library of over 400 books on the Civil War. He also uses the internet, other authors and historians and his local library as resources as well.

Tim has assisted other authors in researching material for their books and was involved with Wide Awake Films at Perryville. He has also acted as a guide for numerous family and friends on battlefield tours.

Tim spent 20 years working for Norfolk Southern Railway as an engineer riding the rails of the old Memphis & Charleston Railway, the backbone of the Confederacy.

Also Written by Tim Kent

Die Like Men

In November, 1864 the Civil War is almost over. The Army of Tennessee under its gallant commander John Bell Hood has a chance to reverse the Confederacy's sinking fortunes. With veteran troops, he plans to strike into Tennessee where he will capture Nashville and invade the northern states. General Sherman has taken the best troops with him on his famous 'March to the Sea. George Thomas, the Federal commander is forced to defend Tennessee with scattered forces and green troops.

The Confederate's move into Tennessee almost forty-thousand strong. The Federal's are in a race to concentrate enough men to save Nashville. Die Like Men will take the reader through the invasion from Florence, Alabama to Nashville and provide insight into the colorful personalities of the leading participants. This is a must read for any fan of the American Civil War.

ISBN# 978-1-934610-62-6

Bluewater Publications is a multi-faceted publishing company capable of meeting all of your reading and publishing needs. Our two-fold aim is to:

1) Provide the market with educationally enlightening and inspiring research and reading materials.

2) Make the opportunity of being published available to any author and or researcher who desires to be published.

We are passionate about preserving history; whether through the re-publishing of an out-of-print classic, or by publishing the research of historians and genealogists. Bluewater Publications is the Peoples' Choice Publisher.

For company information or information about how you can be published through Bluewater Publications, please visit:

www.BluewaterPublications.com

Also check Amazon.com to purchase any of the books that we publish.

Confidently Preserving Our Past,

Bluewater Publications.com

www.ingramcontent.com/pod-product-compliance
Lightning Source LLC
Chambersburg PA
CBHW051513260626
47162CB00008B/2956